TOP GUN TIGER

PROTECTION, INC. #7

ZOE CHANT

AUTHOR'S NOTE

The first three chapters of *Top Gun Tiger* take place at the same time as *Protection, Inc. # 1, Bodyguard Bear.*

All the books in the series are standalone romances. Each focuses on a new couple, with no cliffhangers. But as *Top Gun Tiger* is the last book in a seven-book series, it involves a lot of recurring plot elements and characters from earlier books. If you haven't read the other books in the series, I recommend that you start at the beginning with *Bodyguard Bear.*

CHAPTER 1

*I*f there was one thing Destiny Ford loved more than dancing, it was working. Not any kind of work, of course. Just the fun kind. The exciting kind. She'd liked being a military police officer in the Army, but she *loved* being a bodyguard at Protection, Inc. More action, less paperwork.

So when she hit the dance floor of her favorite club in her favorite dancing dress, she kept a tiny buzzer clipped into her bra, and was only slightly annoyed when it began to vibrate. When she ran to pick up her phone and see who was calling, even that little bit of annoyance disappeared. Her boss Hal wouldn't call her on her night off just to chat. Something was up. Something dangerous. Maybe the police hadn't swept up *all* the gangsters who'd tried to kill Hal and his mate, Ellie…

"Sorry to bother you," came Hal's deep voice. "But would you mind picking someone up at the airport?"

"Sure. Hang on a sec. Music's pretty loud in here."

Her dancing shoes clicked across the polished floor as she hurried toward the door, then made a duller clack as she stepped on to the asphalt outside. She looked for a place where they could talk privately. There was a dark alley beside the club. With her keen shifter vision, she saw that it was empty.

The sight of it reminded Destiny that Hal's mate Ellie, a paramedic, had witnessed a murder in a dark alley and gotten shot at when the gangsters had spotted her. She'd barely escaped with her life. But that had been how she'd met Hal—she'd needed a bodyguard. So it had all worked out for the best.

If Ellie hadn't taken a wrong turn, she'd never have witnessed the murder. Would she then have never met Hal? Or would their paths have crossed in some other way, maybe much later, as destiny drew them together?

Destiny.

She blew out a dismissive breath. She liked her name—it was pretty!—but she'd never been much of a believer in the concept. As far as she was concerned, people created their own destinies.

But whether lives were shaped by fate or chance or self-will, it was amazing how quickly and unexpectedly they could change. If Destiny stepped into that alley, might that be the seemingly small and random decision that would send her life down an unexpected new path?

Smiling at her own unlikely fantasy, she ducked into the alley and spoke quietly into the phone. "Is the pickup a new client? Who do they need protecting from?"

Hal gave a rumbling chuckle. "He does the protecting. He's Special Forces—a Recon Marine. It's Ellie's twin brother, Ethan. He just got back from Afghanistan, and he decided to surprise her with a visit. Good thing he called her cell phone before he showed up at her apartment."

"Oops," said Destiny. Hal and Ellie were in his little cabin up north, hours away from town. They'd taken refuge there after the gangsters had blown up Hal's car, then stayed for an impromptu honeymoon. "Does he know about... What *does* he know about?"

"Ellie filled him in on the basics," Hal replied. "He knows she witnessed a murder, I was her bodyguard, the gangsters went after us, Protection, Inc. got evidence to put them away, they're all behind bars awaiting trial, and Ellie and I are together. And I told him we're not in Santa Martina right now, so I'd send one of my team to pick him up."

"I'm alone, Hal. It's safe to talk. So, does he know about shifters?"

"No. We thought it would be better to explain that in person."

"In that case, I won't show up as a tiger," Destiny said, grinning. "Shall I drive him to the cabin?"

"If you don't mind," said Hal apologetically. "It's a bit of a haul."

"Nah, I like driving. Gimme the address."

The truth was, Destiny was curious to see Hal's cabin in the woods. It would be a glimpse into a side of him that she hadn't known before. Though they'd been friends and teammates for years, in many ways Hal was as closed-off and secretive as... well, as everyone at Protection, Inc. but her and Rafa, and even Rafa had a thing or two he refused to talk about. How had a friendly, outgoing girl like her ever gotten involved with that bunch of mysterious loners?

"How'd I get tapped to be the cabbie?" she asked, inwardly placing her bet. "Least likely to object to driving for three hours in the middle of the night? First to pick up the phone?"

There was a shuffling noise, and Ellie's clear voice came over the phone. "It was my call, Destiny. Ethan's just come back from six months in combat, and I dropped a whole lot of surprises on him all at once. I want him to have a nice, normal, pleasant ride to the cabin with a nice, normal, pleasant person." Hastily, she added, "Not that the other agents aren't nice! Or normal! Or—"

"But you don't want your brother's first contact with Protection, Inc. to be the Dragon Prince, the Ice Queen, the Invisible Man, F-Bomb Nick, or Rico Suave," Destiny said with a snicker. "Don't worry, Ellie. You know me, I'm the girl next door. Pretty as a picture, sweet as pie. Absolutely normal."

Normal, she thought as she hung up and got into her car. *Yeah. I'm good at faking that.*

She considered swinging by her home to change—it wasn't exactly *normal* to pick someone up from the airport in a sequined minidress and silver dancing shoes—but the club was much closer to the airport than her apartment was, and it was almost 2:00 AM. Destiny had never been in Special Forces, as none of them had been open to women when she'd enlisted. But she had vivid memories of coming back to America after a long deployment, simultaneously exhausted and wired, and how endless all the waiting around the airport had felt when she just wanted to find a bed and sleep.

No. She wouldn't keep Ethan waiting a second longer than he absolutely had to. And if he took one look at her and thought he must still be in Afghanistan, having a dream so sweet that he'd just about cry when he woke up and found himself sleeping on the ground and surrounded by a bunch of sweaty, grimy, very male Marines, well, a little looking never did anyone any harm.

And hey, he was a Recon Marine, which meant he had to be in fantastic shape. She might do a little looking herself. And who knows? If they hit it off, they might do more than just look...

Down, girl, Destiny ordered herself. *You haven't even met him yet. You might hate each other. And won't that be fun, stuck in a car together for hours with a jerk.*

She didn't even know why she'd drifted into thoughts of romance with some random guy. Destiny supposed it was by association: he was the brother of the woman her boss was in love with, therefore she thought of love. And there was absolutely no question that Hal and Ellie were deeply, devotedly, permanently in love. They had to be: they were mates.

Destiny had known about mates, of course, but she'd never expected to find one herself. Up until a couple weeks ago, none of her teammates had mates, which had reinforced her impression that it was more of an ideal than a common reality. Then Hal had walked into the office with Ellie on his arm, his rugged features transformed with happiness like nothing she'd ever seen on him before. Like nothing she'd ever seen, period.

Could I have that? Destiny had wondered, awed. *Is there someone out there who'll look at me like they're looking at each other, like I'm the most precious thing in the whole wide world?*

As she braked for a red light, she thought of how Hal had walked into a police station to meet a stranger, and his life had changed forever. If Destiny had a mate, could he be closer than she thought? Could he be in the next car over, just waiting for her to turn her head and see him?

Unable to resist, she looked inside the next car over. The driver was a woman.

That would be a no, Destiny thought, amused at herself.

As she drove toward the airport, she shook her head, chasing away those fantasies. *Sure* she was going to find her one-and-only, her destined true love, *tonight*. No, she'd be patient—she'd always been good at that—and content herself with the knowledge that mates actually were a real thing, and maybe someday, if she was very very lucky, in another year or five or ten or even fifty, she might meet hers.

It was only as she walked up to the airport that she realized that she had no idea what Ethan looked like. Sure, he was Ellie's twin, but they were brother and sister—fraternal twins, not identical. They might not resemble each other at all.

Destiny shrugged. With any luck, Ellie had called him back and told him to keep an eye out for a petite, curvy, African-American woman. If not, she supposed she could scrounge up some paper and make a sign.

Then she stepped into Passenger Arrivals, and laughed at herself. Of course. She could just look for the Marine. There he was, a strong-looking man in faded fatigues sitting on a military-issue duffel bag, with sandy blond hair in a slightly grown-out crew cut. His face was turned away because he was busy scanning the rest of the airport as if he expected an ambush. She remembered that from the Army, that constant battle-ready wariness. It took a while to wear off.

She walked up to him. He was on his feet and turning to her in a flash, moving with a fluid agility that made her briefly wonder if he was a shifter. No, couldn't be. He'd have told his twin. It was probably just a Special Forces thing. After all, they were the best of the best.

Their eyes met.

A jolt went through Destiny, like his intense gaze had physical form. His eyes were so beautiful—blue-green as a tropical sea, with golden lashes like the rising sun. Looking into them, she felt like she was recognizing him rather than seeing him for the first time, as if he were her long-lost best friend from childhood...

...*grown up hot*, she couldn't help thinking. *Look at those muscles! Yum.*

He was checking her out too, she could see, so she gave him the subtlest of shimmies to enjoy while she checked him out right back. He did resemble Ellie, though his features were hard and masculine where hers were soft and feminine. And his body, of course, was completely different, all hard-earned muscle instead of plump curves, with broad shoulders and biceps to die for. Destiny had always been a connoisseur of the male upper body, and Ethan's was *fine.* But the twins had the same snub nose and strong chin, and the same ready smile.

They didn't *quite* have the same blue-green eyes. Similar, sure. But Ellie's were just… pretty. Ethan's were extraordinary—the most beautiful eyes she'd ever seen on a man. Destiny couldn't stop gazing into them. Women must be all over him all the time. Or maybe not, if he did a lot of covert missions in the wilderness. Hmm…

Ethan offered her his hand. "Hi. I'm Ethan McNeil. Are you my ride? If you're not, can I help you with anything?"

If Rafa had said that line, it would've been a seductive double entendre. Ethan had a sexy voice, sure. But he just sounded friendly and confident. Like if she'd said she wasn't his ride but there was a creepy man following her and could she borrow his phone, he'd have handed it over, then gone and dealt with the creep himself.

"I'm Destiny Ford." She gripped his hand, giving him a little taste of her strength. She could never resist doing that to men when she first met them. It was such an easy way to sort out the men who were intimidated by or disliked strong women from the men who respected them.

Ethan smiled, clearly neither intimidated nor put off. "Good grip. You have got to be one of the bodyguards."

"Tonight I'm just your cabbie. Grab your gear. I'm parked right outside."

He bent to pick up his duffel bag. As he hefted it over his shoulder, his loose sleeves fell back, exposing tattoos in abstract patterns, stark black against his tanned skin. Destiny only caught a glimpse before the camouflage cloth slid down and hid them again, but she saw enough to intrigue her. He'd kept his hands, neck, and face clear of tattoos, in keeping with military regulations, but how many did he have under his uniform?

She hoped she'd get a chance to find out. She *liked* him.

As they walked outside together, she said, "It's about a three-hour drive to Hal's cabin. So are you more tired or more hungry? We could grab some food first. Or we could leave now and you could sleep all the way there. Up to you."

"The question is, are *you* more tired or more hungry?" Ethan asked. "And you don't have to do all the driving. I can pull my weight."

And there was yet another thing she remembered from the Army: the refusal to admit that you were tired until you actually collapsed from exhaustion, and maybe not even then. It was all coming back to her now. Ethan wouldn't admit he was too tired to drive unless he was actually worried that he'd fall asleep at the wheel, and given that he was a Recon Marine, he must be used to operating military vehicles on no sleep. If she said, "Yes, thank you, why don't you take a turn at the wheel?" he'd grab some bad coffee at a drive-through, drive the whole way without a single word of complaint, and get them to the cabin in total safety.

Well, she wasn't going to let him. He was back from the war; he deserved some good food and rest.

"*I'm* hungry," she said. "But I'm not tired. I was just leaving a club when Hal called."

Ethan gave another appreciative glance at her dress. "I wondered. I like dancing too."

Oh, she just bet he did. He was obviously the work hard, play hard type—like her. She was about to ask him if he'd like her to show him the local clubs later when he said, "I'm not sure how long I'll be staying at the cabin with Ellie, but when I come back, can I take you dancing?"

Destiny gave her hips a shake, making her sequined skirt flare out. "I don't know. Think you can keep up with me?"

"I think I'll have a hell of a lot of fun trying."

"You're on. Now are you going to tell me what sort of food you like, or shall I guess?"

"Guess. I've been eating MREs for six months. Anything not packaged in plastic and cooked with a chemical heater will be an improvement. Oh—that means Meals Ready to—"

Destiny swung out an elbow to jab him in the ribs. "I know what an MRE is, jarhead. I ate my share in the military police."

Ethan's amazing eyes widened as he once again looked her over, this time lingering on her muscles and the little scar on her shoulder, which he probably thought was a combat wound. (It was actually from her current teammate and former gangster Nick Mackenzie biting her, back when they were on opposite sides.)

Unlike some men—military men included—finding out that she'd been in the Army didn't make Ethan feel like he had to out-macho her. Instead, he grinned like she was… not his best friend, it was too sexy for that… like she was his *hot* best friend whose clothes he'd like to rip off so he could have his wicked way with her, immediately.

"You were an MP?" Ethan stuck out his hand. "Pleased to meet you, mudpuppy."

That nickname for the military police took her back—she hadn't had anyone call her "mudpuppy" in years. All those military nicknames, from "jarhead" for Marines to "mudpuppy" for military police to "squid" for sailors, the mostly-joking rivalries between branches… and, of course, the one thing everyone could agree on, which was the absolute awfulness of the military rations.

"What was your favorite MRE?" he went on.

"You mean, which was the least disgusting? I guess the maple sausage." She fished around mentally for another Marine nickname. It was a shame that most of theirs were so badass sounding. You could hardly tease anyone with leatherneck or devil dog. "What's yours, crayon eater?"

"Pork ribs. They really weren't bad if you ate them as soon as you heated them up." He sounded genuinely wistful.

Destiny vowed to get him to a good barbecue place, ASAP. And she knew just the one. If he actually liked the pork rib MRE, he'd think he'd died and gone to Heaven when she treated him to a meal at Aunt Lizzie's Back Porch.

She opened the trunk so he could toss in his duffel bag. Ethan looked inside, inspected her survival supplies, and laughed. "What are we, twins separated at birth? This looks like the trunk of my car. Only I have MREs instead of beef jerky and granola bars and dried fruit."

"I rotate my survival supplies to keep them fresh, so the edibles have to be things I actually like to eat."

"I only stock up on MREs that I actually like."

"Did you get your taste buds shot off in the war?" Destiny inquired. "I'm having second thoughts on the restaurant trip. Maybe I should go in and eat, and leave you in the car with a bone to gnaw on."

"If it's a pork rib bone..."

Destiny chuckled as she pulled out of the parking garage. She rolled down the window to enjoy the night air. The streets of Santa Martina were almost empty. Everyone was either asleep at home or dancing at a club. It had rained earlier, and the moonlight turned the streets to ribbons of liquid silver.

Ethan leaned back in his seat, relaxing, but his gaze was alert as he watched the city sights go by. When she turned on South Hanford, she caught his eyelids flicker in the slightest expression of alarm. Her own adrenaline instantly rose—had he seen something suspicious? But he said nothing, and as the one landmark on South Hanford came into view, she remembered that he must have been in Santa Martina plenty of times before to visit his sister.

Doing her best to keep a straight face, she pulled up at one of Santa Martina's few 24-hour restaurants (if you could call it a restaurant, which was debatable), a concrete block topped with a giant bacon-wrapped hotdog made of chipped, unappetizing-looking plaster.

"Big Bacon!" Destiny announced. "That'll hit the spot. It's a Santa Martina landmark."

"I know. One of Ellie's friends took me there once. A paramedic, Catalina. Do you know her?"

She shook her head. "But she's got good taste! Did you love it?"

Ethan's brow furrowed. He was clearly making a valiant effort to not insult her favorite restaurant. Finally, he said, "It'll be great to get some real American food. Just the thing to make me feel like I'm really back home."

Destiny had meant to string him along a little longer, but his attempt at tactfulness made that impossible. She burst out laughing. In between gasps for air, she managed to get out, "You call Big Bacon real American food? Which side are you on?"

"Just because I fight for the US doesn't mean I think it's perfect," Ethan said, trying and failing to glare at her. With a sweeping gesture that exposed another tantalizing glimpse of his tattoos, he said, "And there's the proof: the worst hotdog joint in existence, anywhere in the world. Did you know that during the Vietnam war, we had a hotdog MRE everyone called the Five Fingers of Death? I always imagined that it tasted exactly like Big Bacon."

"Maybe you should reconsider whether your sister's buddy is your buddy too."

"Catalina has a great sense of humor," he replied. "Like you."

Still snickering, Destiny got on the freeway and headed north. They were soon on the edge of town, where businesses and houses gave way to fields and clumps of trees. And something else that she bet Ethan didn't know about or he'd be looking excited right about now. Aunt Lizzie's was one of the best-kept secrets of Santa Martina. (Secret because locals didn't want it overrun by tourists.)

She took the exit that looked like it ran straight into a field, and began bumping along the dusty, unlit dirt road. Destiny snuck a quick glance at Ethan, wondering if he'd object or ask if this was another joke. Instead, he leaned back in his seat, utterly relaxed and ready to take on whatever was coming. Now that was a man with confidence.

Her headlights illuminated what appeared to be a barn, but warm yellow light shone through the windows and there were a few cars parked outside. Destiny pulled up beside them.

"Aunt Lizzie's Back Porch," she announced.

Ethan opened his door and took an appreciative sniff of the barbecue-scented air. Then, before she could move a muscle, he jumped out and run round to open her door for her. Not only that, but he offered her his arm.

Well, well, well. It had been a long time since any man had opened a car door for her. This night just kept getting better and better. She laid her hand on his arm, curling her fingers around his strong muscles. The moonlight bleached the color from him, leaving him a vision in black and white. He could have been a hero in an old movie, a soldier come home from WWII to find his girl still waiting for him.

I'd wait for him, Destiny thought. *Oh, I know it's too soon. But I've never felt this drawn to a man. This just might be my lucky night.*

CHAPTER 2

𝓔than felt as if he were in a dream as he walked through the night and toward the welcoming golden light, arm in arm with Destiny. One night he'd been slogging through the desert sand with a bunch of men who hadn't bathed in days, the next he was escorting the most gorgeous woman he'd ever seen on what sure as hell felt like a date.

She glanced up at the moon, and he took the opportunity to drink her in. Her short box braids tumbled back as she tipped up her face, extending her neck like a swan. The moonlight shone on her flawless dark skin and luscious full lips, and sparkled in her beautiful eyes. Everything about her was irresistibly sexy, from the impressive strength of her grip to the swell of muscle in her shoulders to her curvy thighs to cleavage that kept threatening to make him walk into a wall.

But there was so much more to her than looks. She was funny and playful and tough, easy to talk to and comfortable to be with. First dates always were a little too tense to be completely enjoyable, with the unspoken undercurrents of "does she like me?" and "do I like her?" But Ethan felt none of that. He was somehow both excited and relaxed, filled with happy anticipation and the pure enjoyment of the present moment. Everything about Destiny just felt so *right*.

They stepped into the restaurant. Ethan loved odd, out-of-the-way places. Little local secrets. And Aunt Lizzie's Back Porch was obviously that: an old-fashioned barbecue joint with rough slab tables, wooden benches, sawdust scattered across the floor, and the scent of smoked meat and sweet peaches filling the air. And open 24 hours, too, or at least extremely late. Just right for a man who got called to deploy at an hour's notice, and always seemed to return in the middle of the night. It was so exactly his kind of place that Ellie and Catalina must never have heard of it, or they'd have taken him there for sure.

The same brilliant smile that had caught his eye in the airport lit up Destiny's gorgeous face. "Nice, huh?"

"I can't commit till I taste the food," Ethan replied. "Who knows, it might be the Five Fingers of Death."

"Never thought I'd hear a Marine with such a sweet mouth," came the dry voice of an old woman behind him. "Or maybe you're too young. I was a nurse in Vietnam, and what we actually called them was the Five Dicks of Death. When I came home, I promised myself that I'd never again put anything in my mouth that wasn't delicious. And that's why I opened this restaurant."

Ethan felt a hot blush creep over his face. "I'm so sorry, ma'am."

"Aunt Lizzie," she corrected him.

"Sorry, Aunt Lizzie. I didn't see you. I was just kidding my —" *My friend?* Too soon. Besides, he was hoping to be more than friends. "—Destiny here. Food that smells this good has got to be *amazing*."

To his relief, neither Aunt Lizzie nor Destiny looked

annoyed at him. Destiny was rolling her eyes at him, but in an amused way.

Aunt Lizzie gestured them to a table. "Guess you'll find out. And welcome home."

"Thank you, Aunt Lizzie," he said, sitting down. "It's good to be back."

The menu was written on a blackboard. They both gave it a glance, then ordered.

As Aunt Lizzie walked away, Destiny kicked him under the table. "I can't take you anywhere, can I? Bring you to the best barbecue restaurant in Santa Martina, you stroll right up to the owner and say she serves the Five Fingers of Death."

"Five Dicks of Death," Ethan corrected. "Don't be shy, I'm a Marine."

Destiny kicked him again. "I'll have you know, I'm a nice old-fashioned girl."

"A nice old-fashioned girl with an M16."

"You wouldn't catch me dead with one of those. They don't go with *anything* I wear. Nowadays I carry a modular Sig Sauer. Fits right into my purse."

It was like a game or a dance, that easy push-pull flow of teasing between them. Like their wrists were tied together, so any time one tugged, the other moved. And once that image occurred to him, he couldn't help picturing it: a red ribbon binding his wrist to hers, with more ribbons trailing over her luscious naked body as they lay in bed together, teasing each other with the silken fabric…

Destiny snapped her fingers. "Now who's falling asleep? I said, what do you do in your spare time other than dancing at clubs and getting pranked with terrible hot dog stands?"

Jolted out of his fantasy, Ethan said, "Basketball. Hiking. Rock climbing."

"Good stuff," Destiny said. "Just what you'd expect from a

Recon Marine. And all of it requires a whole lot of room. What do you do to kill time when you're in your tent?"

"Play video games."

"Ah-ha! I knew there was something like that. And it's not just to kill time, right? You really love them, right?"

Caught out, Ethan admitted, "Yeah."

"I knew it. Nerd," Destiny said with satisfaction.

"It takes one to know one. What's *your* nerdy passion, nerd girl? A secret addiction to the *Twilight* books?"

"No way. They got werewolves all wrong, and there's no such thing as vampires."

If she knew that, she'd read them. All of them, from the sound of it. So his guess that she liked books was on the money. "Then what's your favorite thing to read?"

"History." She tossed her braids. "Not nerdy at all."

Ethan grinned as he saw the gleam in her eyes. It was the sure sign of a nerd thinking of their obsession. "Favorite time and place?"

"Oh, I've got lots. But let me tell you, there was incredibly cool stuff happening in Asia and Africa when Europeans were huddled in the dark gnawing on turnips and not bathing."

"Tell me one cool fact from one of your favorite periods."

"In India in the 1600s, there was a king named Shivaji who rebelled against the emperor. The emperor captured him and his teenage son and held them prisoner. But Shivaji was very popular, and the emperor was afraid that his people would rise up if he treated their leader badly. So instead of throwing them in a dungeon, he kept them under house arrest in a house befitting a king, but under heavy guard.

Shivaji pretended to be sick, and asked the emperor for permission to make donations to temples so the priests would pray for his recovery. The emperor was a little suspicious, so he gave him permission but doubled the guard on his house. Shivaji ordered two gigantic fruit baskets delivered to the house every day, so he could inspect them and make sure all the fruit was perfect, then sent them on to the temples.

At first the guards searched every basket, when they went in and when they went out. But they were enormous baskets and it was a giant pain to have to take out hundreds of mangoes and then put them back in. Twice. And if they bruised any fruit, Shivaji would complain to the emperor that the guards were disrespecting the priests and trying to sabotage his recovery. Finally the guards couldn't take it anymore and just started waving them through."

Ethan started to laugh, seeing where this was going.

Triumphantly, Destiny concluded, "And of course, Shivaji and his son were in the next two fruit baskets. Buried under a layer of perfect, unbruised mangoes."

"Awesome story," Ethan said. "History nerd."

Aunt Lizzie came over with an enormous platter and a pitcher of iced tea. "Here you go."

Steam rose up from the plates. Ethan applied himself to the food. The pulled pork was just the right balance of sweet and spicy, the ribs were smoky and juicy, the coleslaw was crisp and creamy, and the cornbread to mop up the sauce was sweet and crumbly and fresh out of the oven.

They didn't do much talking as they ate, but that was fine with him. Getting some food in his stomach made him feel more present, as if eating here in the US was what made him really believe that he was home again. It always took him a while to feel that in his bones as well as know it in his mind. The first few nights back, he'd wake up uncertain of where he was.

If Destiny was beside me, I'd always know, he thought.

Though that was hardly the main reason why he'd want to wake up next to her. She was gorgeous and sexy, funny and quick-witted, and they had so much in common and got along so well. He'd had so much fun talking to her, and it was weirdly hot to watch her eating, putting her meal away with none of the self-consciousness that lots of women had when they ate in front of a man, and yet so neatly that she had yet to get a single speck of sauce on her sparkly dress. But there was something else about her that he liked which was harder to identify. Something about her felt like... coming home.

Yeah. Definitely looking forward to that dance date.

Ethan didn't want to get ahead of himself. But he couldn't help hoping that they'd do more than just dance, and that it'd be more than just one night.

Being a Recon Marine made it hard to have anything last beyond a quick fling. He was gone most of the time, usually on almost no notice. When he left, he couldn't say when he'd come back, and when he did return, he couldn't say where he'd been or what he'd done. He had buddies in the Marines. And he had his sister, of course. But other than them, he didn't have any close relationships, let alone a serious girlfriend. What woman would be willing to put up with a man who was never around and couldn't talk about his life?

Destiny might, he thought. *She's a vet herself. She'd understand.*

But once he imagined an actual relationship with her, he couldn't imagine spending most of his life away from her.

A voice from deep down inside of him said quietly, *You won't be a Marine forever.*

Another, much louder voice snapped, *Once a Marine, always a Marine!*

Both were true. He'd always be a Marine at heart. But he couldn't keep deploying into combat forever. All else aside, eventually he'd be too old for it. And his term of service was coming up in two years. He'd have to decide then whether or not to re-enlist.

Maybe he shouldn't. There were plenty of civilian jobs that might suit him. He might enjoy being a bodyguard, like Destiny. He could talk to her about it—hell, he could talk to her boss Hal, see if there might be room in the agency for him some time in the future. If she knew he'd come home to her forever when his two years were up, would she wait for him? He had a feeling she would.

Now you're really getting ahead of yourself, he thought. *You haven't even gone on that first date yet.*

But he didn't feel like he was rushing. He felt calm and ready and brimming with excited anticipation, like he did every time he got that call to move out. Like he only had one life, and this was his chance to live it to the fullest. Only this time, maybe it was also his chance to share it, and find a connection like he'd never imagined he could have.

Aunt Lizzie served their peach cobbler with a glance and a wink at him, like she could read his mind.

"Everything was fantastic," he told her. "It was… The Five Pigs of Deliciousness."

Aunt Lizzie walked away, chuckling to herself. Destiny pulled a face at him. "Weirdo."

Raising his voice so Aunt Lizzie could hear—that woman obviously had ears like an elephant—Ethan said, "I mean, the Five Hogs of Heaven."

"Super-weirdo," Destiny said. "Thought you jarheads got down to business. Why are you sitting there babbling nonsense when the world's best peach cobbler is right in front of you?"

She leaned over the table, giving him a heart-stopping view of her generous cleavage, grabbed his fork, stuck it in his dish of peach cobbler, and offered him a bite. Feeling a little dazed, both by the view and by the gesture, Ethan opened his mouth and let her feed him the bite. The streusel topping was crisp and buttery, the peaches soft and sweet.

Maybe it *was* the world's greatest peach cobbler. But he suspected that he'd have thought the Five Dicks of Death were the greatest thing ever if Destiny was the one putting them in his mouth.

He took her fork and held a bite of cobbler to her lips. They parted, making him think how soft they'd feel if he felt them moving against his, and he slipped it into her mouth. She closed her eyes in bliss as she chewed. He couldn't help imagining how she might react to other sorts of bliss. Destiny seemed to be a woman who lived life to the absolute fullest, enjoying its pleasures and facing its hardships without a flinch.

She opened her eyes—her big, beautiful, deep brown eyes—and Ethan knew what she wanted. What *he* wanted. It wasn't too soon. It was exactly the right time.

He leaned across the table and kissed her. Her mouth was hot and tasted like peaches, and she grabbed his shoulders and pulled him a little closer in. Her soft little hands were deceptively strong, and he loved knowing that she wanted him even nearer. He could feel her passion in her tight grip, in the exploring flicker of her tongue, in the way she sighed into his mouth.

A rush of heat swept through his body, and he suddenly found himself picturing the back seat of Destiny's car. It was big enough for both of them, and they'd have plenty of privacy if they parked in the woods…

A sharp noise made them break apart, startled. It was Aunt Lizzie, banging a spoon on the table. "All the world loves a lover. But not on top of my tables, *if* you please."

They both leaned back hurriedly. Destiny's skin was too dark to show a blush, but if she felt anywhere near what Ethan did, she'd be fiery red right now. He was pretty sure he was. They mumbled their apologies, and Aunt Lizzie departed with a stifled snicker.

Ethan and Destiny looked at each other. Her lips looked fuller than ever, her braids were tumbling into her face, and her skin glowed with a light mist of sweat. She looked like they'd actually made love, not just kissed for a few seconds. Or maybe it had been a lot longer than a few seconds. Who knew how long Aunt Lizzie had been standing there trying to get their attention?

"You look like a maraschino cherry," Destiny said.

"Good enough to eat?"

"I guess I set that up. Let me re-phrase: you look like a five-alarm fire."

"Smoking hot?"

She kicked his ankle. "Shut up and finish your cobbler."

They finished theirs in record time, paid and said goodbye to Aunt Lizzie, and headed outside. The cool of the night made Ethan even more conscious of how hot he felt. His heart was pounding. He reached out for Destiny's hand, and was rewarded by a grip that he already felt like he knew by heart: small and strong, soft and warm.

"How about we find a nice stretch of deserted woods to park the car?" he suggested.

"Yeah." Her voice was husky, almost a purr. He'd never heard a woman sound like that before, and it set him on fire inside. "Yeah, let's do that. Not here, though. I don't know this area, and we might end up accidentally parked in Aunt Lizzie's backyard. Let's get a bit farther out of town. There's a bunch of dirt roads going nowhere that would be perfect."

She took the wheel, driving with one hand on his thigh. It felt like a hot coal, burning through his camo pants. He put his hand on her thigh, feeling her bare skin and soft curves. Ethan hoped he wasn't distracting her as much as her hand was distracting him, because if he was, she'd go off the road.

"You want me to move it?" he asked.

"Nah." There was that purr again. It made him so hard, he

didn't know how he was going to be able to stand the entire fifteen minutes or whatever he'd have to wait before she pulled over. "Nah, you leave your hand right where it is. You put it in my space, so it belongs to me now."

Ethan barely stopped himself from blurting out that all of him could belong to her, if she'd take him.

Too soon, he told himself.

That other voice inside him, the one that had pointed out that he couldn't be a Recon Marine forever, said, *Yeah. Wait a couple days. Or at least till tomorrow.*

She got back on the freeway and drove until the fields yielded to forests. Ethan breathed in the pine-scented air. Only twenty-four hours ago, he'd been humping a sixty-pound rucksack through Afghanistan, hot and dirty and exhausted but unable to relax in case he missed the signs of an ambush. He'd been so focused on the danger, he'd actually forgotten that he was going to go home the next day. Now he was driving through the woods, with the taste of peaches still in his mouth, to make love to the most incredible woman he'd ever met. And after that… who knew?

All it takes is an instant for your life to change forever, he thought. *One gunshot. One look into a pair of brown eyes…*

A movement in the rear-view mirror jolted him out of his musings and into full combat-readiness. A gun barrel had just poked out from the passenger window of the car behind him.

"Duck!" Ethan's hand slapped against his hip, instinctively reaching for his gun. Only then did he remember that was in his duffel bag in the trunk of the car.

At the same moment, Destiny yanked her hand off his thigh and swerved the car off the freeway, flinging him into the side of the car. "Get down!"

The familiar crack of a rifle sounded, and an equally familiar zing of metal told him that the car had been hit. To his immense relief, Destiny was unharmed. She floored the car along the rough mountain road she'd pulled on to. Ethan twisted around, with difficulty due to the jolting from the rough road, and saw that the shooter's car had followed them off the freeway.

Another rifle shot. This one missed.

Destiny had said she had a Sig Sauer in her purse. He rummaged inside, found and loaded the gun, and hit the button to roll down the passenger window.

"You drive," he said. "I'll shoot."

"Sounds good." Destiny whipped the car around a hairpin curve.

Ethan hoped the other car would go off the road, but it too had a skilled driver, and stayed on their tail. He leaned out the window, trying to steady his hand enough to hit *something* while the car was jolting over rocks or into ruts every few seconds. He fired, mentally crossing his fingers, and felt a rush of primal satisfaction when he saw the other car's windshield explode.

But the car kept coming at them. Just as he took aim to fire again, he heard another shot, followed almost instantaneously by a second bang. Their enemy had blown out their tire.

Destiny didn't panic as the car began to skid toward the cliff. Nor did she yank on the steering wheel, which would have made it worse. Instead, she took her foot off the gas and steered into the skid, obviously meaning to gently guide the car away from the edge once she had it under control. Even in the midst of the danger, Ethan couldn't help admiring her cool under fire.

But she was faced with an impossible task. There wasn't time to regain control of the car. It fishtailed, hit a rut, and skidded over the edge.

"Brace!" Ethan shouted as the car tumbled through the air.

An instant later, it landed with a tremendous crash, shattering the windshield. The force of the impact made him lose his grip on the Sig Sauer, which went flying through the broken windshield. Ice-cold water flooded in as the car began to slowly sink down. In the second it took him to realize that they must have fallen into a river or lake, the water inside the car was up to his ankles and rising.

He turned to Destiny. A fear colder than the freezing water gripped him when he saw her slumped over the steering wheel. If she'd been shot...

He felt for her pulse, and was tremendously relieved to find it strong beneath his fingers. Ethan lifted her gently, and saw blood dripping from a cut at her temple, and a matching smear of blood on the steering wheel. She must have hit her head in the crash.

The water was up to his thighs now. There was no time to waste. He unsnapped her seatbelt and his own, climbed on to the hood of the car, and lifted her into his arms. Her lower body was soaking wet and cold, but the rest of her was still warm.

He crouched atop the hood, looking and listening. By the bright light of the moon, he saw that they were in the middle of a lake in the woods, with trees obscuring the road they'd skidded off. As far as he could tell, they were as impossible to see from above as their enemies were to see from below. But the fall had been short, so it might not be hard for them to climb down.

Ethan desperately wished for a weapon, but the Sig Sauer was at the bottom of the lake and his own gun was in the locked trunk of a car that was sinking fast. He could retrieve his gun or get Destiny to safety, but not both. At least, not both before the car sank. Ethan took the keys out of the ignition and stuffed them in his pocket. He'd get her to shore, then dive for his gun. He looked for her purse in the hope of finding her cell phone, but it looked like her purse had also been thrown through the windshield when they'd crashed.

Carefully, he draped her across his shoulders. With his left arm, he held her arms and legs across his chest. Then he slipped into the icy water and began to swim, keeping himself more-or-less upright so she'd stay as dry as possible. She probably already had a concussion. It would be bad if she got hypothermia on top of it.

Ethan reached the shore, shivering. Maybe *he* should be worried about hypothermia. Well, if it came to that, he could make a fire by rubbing twigs together. Maybe. His wilderness survival training, not to mention his actual wilderness survival experience, had taught him that you could generally hike to somewhere with matches in the time it would take to light a fire without them.

He hurried into the woods until he was far enough in that he was sure he couldn't be seen from either shore or above, then laid Destiny down on a bed of moss and checked her again. The dappled moonlight showed him that the cut on her temple had stopped bleeding, and when he put his ear to her chest, he could hear that she was breathing steadily.

Relieved, he straightened up and considered his options. Scoop her up and start hiking? Leave her here, run back to the lake, dive for his duffel bag, and cross his fingers he got it out before the enemies returned?

It was only then that he realized that he didn't even know who the enemies *were*. He'd fallen back into combat mode so easily that it only now struck him how weird the whole thing was. They weren't in a war zone, and gangs didn't hang out in the middle of nowhere. He and Destiny didn't have anything valuable, so far as he knew, except maybe the car. But carjackers wouldn't shoot out the tires. Ethan didn't have any personal enemies, at least none who'd try to murder him rather than punching him in the face, and he couldn't imagine that Destiny did either.

But she was a bodyguard. She might have made some impersonal, work-related enemies. And then there were the gangsters Ellie was going to testify against. She'd told him they'd all been arrested, but had they really? Murdering the brother of a witness seemed like the sort of thing that could happen with organized crime, to send a message about the price of testifying.

Destiny's eyelashes fluttered. She put a hand to her head, then struggled to sit up. "Owww."

Ethan lifted her gently, letting her lean against his chest. Softly, he said, "Take it easy. The car went into a lake."

Destiny also spoke quietly as she asked, "The people shooting at us—where are they?"

"No idea. Gone, I hope, but I'm not counting on that. Any idea who they are?"

She shook her head, then winced. "Might be the same gangsters who went after your sister. But we've got other enemies. Where's my Sig Sauer?"

"At the bottom of the lake. Sorry. I could dive for it. But I think it'd be easier to get my gun. It's in my duffel bag. Which is also at the bottom of the lake, but in the trunk of your car, so it'd be easier to find."

"And my purse?"

"Also at the bottom of the lake."

Her eyes widened in alarm, and her hand flew to the neckline of her low-cut dress. She felt around her left breast, then pulled out a packet of pills sealed in plastic. Destiny peered at them, shook them, and looked relieved when she saw that they were still dry.

"What are those?" Ethan asked.

From her expression, it was obviously some private

medical thing. Before he could withdraw the question, she said, "Female problems. You don't want to know." She stuck the pills back into her dress—into her bra cup, he realized belatedly—then felt up her right breast.

"Ah-ha!" Destiny pulled out a tiny black thing, fiddled with it, then stuffed it back into her dress and grinned at him. "It's a mini-pager. Waterproof. I just sent an alarm to the entire agency. We should get some backup in..." She glanced upward, and an odd expression crossed her face. Then she shrugged, apparently trying not to laugh. "Possibly very soon."

That made him feel a lot better. Dismissing whatever in-joke she'd decided not to tell him—it was probably something about one of her teammates that would take way too long to explain, and then not be funny unless you already knew him—he said, "What's the soonest ETA, and what's the latest?"

"Soonest..." She again glanced up. "Twenty minutes, maybe. Latest, probably not more than forty-five. Hmm. That's not so good."

Forty-five minutes—twenty minutes—even two minutes —was a very long time when the enemy was armed and you weren't.

"I'd better try to get my gun," Ethan said. "Do you want to stay here, or come with me? I'm honestly not sure which would be safer."

"Come with. I'll keep watch from the shadows while you dive." Destiny looked down at herself, let out a soft groan of dismay, then said, "Well, it's pretty much ruined anyway."

Working quickly, she scooped up handfuls of mud and smeared them across her sequined dress, then over her silver shoes. Ethan watched in disbelief for a moment, then realized that it was camouflage. Otherwise she'd stand out like a woman-shaped glitter ball. He grabbed a palmful of mud and applied it to the hard-to-reach parts of her back.

"Thanks," she said. "I guess. That was my favorite dancing dress. 'Was' being the operative word."

"I'll buy you a new one," he offered.

She rolled her eyes at him. "How much do you think a dress like this costs?"

"Don't know, don't care. It was your favorite and I helped destroy it. I'll work some overtime if I have to."

She snickered. "Okay, then. We're going shopping when we get back. Maybe you can get a makeover while we're at it."

He helped her up, and was glad to find that she was much steadier on her feet than he'd expected. The cut on her head had stopped bleeding, and was smaller than he'd initially thought.

Destiny looked down at herself and sighed. "You plotted this entire thing as the lead-up to a mudpuppy joke, didn't you?"

"I plotted it because I thought it'd be hot," he said. "Mud is the new wet T-shirt."

She nailed him with a handful of mud, straight to the chest. "There. Now we're both hot."

As they walked through the woods, he noticed that she could move as silently and stealthily as he could. Not only that, but she made herself blend in with the shadows until he felt like if he looked away for a single second, he wouldn't be able to spot her when he looked back. That wasn't a skill he'd known they taught to military police, or to bodyguards for that matter. Maybe she'd done a whole lot of extra training on her own time and dime. Or maybe she was just that good. And she was doing it injured, and in high heels and a mud-plastered dancing dress.

He felt certain that he could trust her the same way he trusted his own men—that no matter what was thrown at them, she'd have his back just as much as he'd have hers. It wasn't something he'd ever expected to feel about a woman he was also dying to get naked with. And despite her mud-plastered dress, Destiny was *still* ridiculously sexy.

She's what I've always wanted, he thought. *I never knew till now.*

At the edge of the woods, they stopped and surveyed the lake. The car had sunk beneath the water, and everything looked peaceful in the moonlight. But if their enemies were lying in wait rather than gone, Ethan would be completely exposed once he left the woods to dive for his gun. And there wouldn't be anything Destiny could do to help, as she was unarmed herself.

But he wasn't afraid. Instead, he was filled with a cool, calm readiness. He gestured to her to stay where she was, concealed in the shadows. Then he ran out, moving as quietly as he could, and plunged into the lake.

Diving into freezing water was always a shock. But it was the sort of shock he was used to. He'd expected to have to feel around for the car, but though it was night, the water was clear and the car was cherry red. He could see it at the bottom of the lake, glowing like a coal in the refracted moonlight.

Ethan swam down to the trunk, keys in hand. This was the tricky part. If the trunk was watertight, the water pressure would keep it closed whether it was unlocked or not. But if it had filled with water, then the pressure would be equal inside and out, and he should be able to open it. He guessed. This wasn't exactly something he'd tried before. Carefully, he inserted the key in the lock and turned it. Nothing seemed to happen, but he put the keys back in his pocket, wedged the heels of his hands beneath the trunk, and shoved it upward with all his strength.

The trunk didn't budge. Frustrated, Ethan gave it another

shove, pushing until his shoulders burned and black spots danced before his eyes. But he might as well be trying to lift the entire car. There was no way he could get to his gun.

He turned his face upward. His exertion had burned through a lot of his oxygen, and his chest hurt. As he started to kick off the bottom, he was startled by the splash of something falling into the lake. It was one of Destiny's dancing shoes. Ethan froze as he watched it sink toward him, the mud coming off in clouds and leaving it shiny and clean.

She was warning him not to surface—and in a way that would have given away her location to any watching enemies.

He swam away as fast as he could. A second later, he heard gunshots, along with the splashes of bullets striking the water. They were shooting at him. Good. That meant they weren't shooting at her. The pain in his chest became an agony, but he swam on until he reached one of the clusters of reeds that edged the lake. Once he was concealed within it, moving very slowly to avoid making ripples, he lifted his face out of the water.

What he saw filled him with a protective fury. Two men stood in the clearing by the lake, both armed with pistols. One was scanning the lake, clearly trying to spot Ethan. And the other was stalking toward the part of the woods where Destiny had concealed herself.

Ethan longed to stop the man going after her before he got anywhere near her. But neither of the enemies were close to him. He'd be seen the instant he stood up from the reeds, and he'd be shot down before he could do anything. He forced himself to take a deep breath and think. Destiny had undoubtedly moved from her original position; she was a veteran and a working bodyguard, and he'd seen how stealthily she could move through the woods. Even injured, unarmed, and missing one shoe, she was perfectly capable of concealing herself. If they both stayed hidden, they could sit it out until her team arrived.

The man at the shore ruined that idea by firing into the clump of reeds closest to him. He systematically raked that area with fire, then started in on another clump. Ethan readied himself to dive again. This time he'd hunt for Destiny's Sig Sauer, which had to be somewhere at the bottom of the lake. It wasn't much of a chance, but it was the best he had.

A terrifying roar shattered the night. Ethan was hard to startle, but he barely stopped himself from jumping out of his skin. It was some big cat, and close. A cougar? Could they roar like that? It wasn't as if Santa Martina had lions…

The enemy at the lakeside stopped shooting. "What the fuck was that?"

The other man, who was near the edge of the woods, took a step back. "Must be a mountain lion."

The roar sounded again, making the enemies twitch nervously.

"Maybe we should get out of here," said the one who'd been shooting at the reeds.

"No!" the other snapped. "She's from Protection, Inc., and they're why Mr. Nagle is in jail right now. We're taking her dow—"

A tiger leaped out of the woods and took him down.

Ethan's jaw dropped. But he only let his shock stop him for an instant. As the other enemy started to swing his gun toward the tiger, Ethan charged him. The man heard him coming, looked round, and froze for a fateful second, caught between the man and the tiger. In that instant, Ethan punched him in the jaw, knocking him out cold.

The other enemy lay still between the big cat's massive paws. Ethan didn't see any blood. It seemed like both their enemies were unconscious, not dead.

The tiger stepped away from its prey. For such a huge beast, it moved with a strange daintiness. Ethan stayed still, his heart pounding. His enemy's gun was right there at his feet, but he didn't want to bet that he could stoop and grab it before the tiger could leap. Besides, he had no desire to harm the beast that had just saved his life. It was a magnificent creature, with its soft-looking fur and deadly grace. He'd always loved wild things; he'd hunted for food, but never for sport.

If he didn't attack it, probably it wouldn't attack him. Maybe it had been scared by all the shooting and had acted in self-defense. Or maybe it had cubs it was protecting.

Ethan and the tiger looked at each other. His pulse throbbed in his ears, but from excitement and awe rather than fear. He'd never been so close to a big cat before, not even at the zoo…

…of course. It must have escaped from a zoo. No wonder it didn't seem afraid of him. Very slowly, Ethan held out his hand. The tiger cocked its head as if it was trying to figure out what he was doing, but it didn't seem frightened or angry. He made the clicking sound that his sister's best friend, Catalina, used to talk to her housecats.

The tiger padded up to him and nudged his hand with its head. Barely able to believe this was really happening, Ethan scratched it behind the ears. Its fur was incredibly thick and soft.

"You beauty," he murmured. "I wish you were mine…"

The soft fur melted away from under his hand. Incredulous, Ethan stared into Destiny's merry brown eyes.

And a whole lot else. She was completely nude, and standing so close that he could feel her body heat. Between that and the tiger, his brain went into a total shutdown.

"You can let go of my ear now," she said.

"You're the tiger!" he blurted out.

"Yup."

"And you're naked!"

She looked down at herself. "Whoops. Better give me your shirt."

Ethan had been half-sure he was dreaming, but as he automatically moved to obey, the sensation of slimy cold cloth dragging over his face convinced him that no matter how bizarre the situation, he was awake and it was real.

He started to offer her the wet shirt, then thought better of it. "Take one of theirs instead. At least they're dry." He indicated the nearest unconscious enemy.

Destiny pulled a face. "Not quite. Got some tiger drool on it. *My* tiger's drool, but still. I'll take the other."

Dazed, Ethan watched her pad over to the enemy he'd knocked out and start stripping off his shirt. Her nude body was every bit as lushly tempting as he'd imagined—no, it was ten times more tempting. A hundred times. A thousand. The perfect globes of her breasts, the sweet roundness of her belly with its dimpled button, the delicious sway of her thighs, her absolutely spectacular ass that he was getting a truly incredible view of right now—

She twisted around and snapped her fingers. "Get busy, jarhead. These guys could wake up any second."

His face burning, Ethan started ripping up his own shirt, which was a lost cause anyway. He tied up the first enemy, then came over to help Destiny with the one who was now shirtless. To his regret, she'd already pulled on the shirt, which came almost down to her knees. But he comforted himself with the recollection that they'd been planning to duck into the woods to make love anyway. He'd see her naked again. Maybe even later tonight.

She rifled through the men's pockets while Ethan made sure they were securely bound, extracting their wallets and cell phones. He peered over her shoulder as she looked through their contact lists.

"Ah-ha!" Destiny indicated a number labeled 'Mr. N.' "I was right: they're from the same organized crime ring that attacked my boss and your sister. That's the private phone line for Wallace Nagle, the Godfather of Santa Martina. At least, it *was*. He's in jail now, so I guess his phone is sitting in some FBI evidence lockbox. Let me call Hal and tell him what's happened."

She dialed a number. "Hal? First off, I'm fine and so is Ethan. But we still need a pickup. My car's at the bottom of a lake, along with my Sig Sauer, one of my shoes, and all of Ethan's stuff. And my dress is a pile of shreds and spangles." She paused while Hal said something. "Yeah: he knows. I'll explain it all to him while you cancel the cavalry."

She turned to Ethan. "Let's go talk somewhere out of earshot."

"Sure." They collected the gangsters' weapons, and then he followed her along the shore of the lake until they reached a flat rock, far enough to escape prying ears but where they could still see the gangsters. Destiny plonked down on top of it, and he followed suit. There was a brief silence while they looked into each other's eyes.

So beautiful, Ethan thought. The tiger had the same soft brown eyes as the woman, though much bigger. The tiger *was* the woman; the woman was the tiger. He'd seen and even felt for himself that it was true, but it was still hard to believe.

Wryly, Destiny said, "Would you believe that the whole time I've been a shifter, which is my entire life, this is the first time I've ever had to explain it to a person who's never even heard of shifters before?"

Only then did Ethan realize what a sacrifice she'd made to save him. She obviously could have simply fled in her tiger form and kept her secret, but instead she'd come back for him. "Is anything bad going to happen because you let me find out? You're not going to get court-martialed or something like that, are you?"

Her laugh echoed across the still water. "No. There's no underground shifter government. We just keep it a secret for obvious reasons. Also, because there's a lot of rumors floating around that the actual government, or parts of it, knows about shifters and would love to find out what makes us tick. Like, by keeping us locked up in a lab and experimenting on us."

"I'll never tell a soul," Ethan said immediately. "But Hal knows? Did you tell him? Or is he a tiger shifter too?"

"Guess I might as well spill the beans on everyone," she said with a grin. "Hal's a shifter, yeah, but he's a grizzly bear. Ellie already knows. They were going to tell you when you arrived. Break it to you gently."

Now that the shock was wearing off, his mind worked quickly. "And the rest of your team?"

"Rafa's a lion, Shane's a panther, Nick's a wolf, Fiona's a snow leopard, and Lucas is a dragon."

"What?" Suspicious that he was pulling her leg, he was about to say, "He is not," when he remembered how Destiny had glanced upward as she'd estimated how long it would take for her teammates to arrive. "Lucas could fly here in about twenty minutes, huh?"

"Yup. You're quick on the uptake. I thought you'd be way more disbelieving. And way more weirded out. Though maybe you're just having a delayed reaction and will freak out later." Though her tone was light, her gaze dropped down as if she was genuinely uncertain how he'd respond. Her hands were flat on the stone, but the tendons stood out. He wondered if she thought he might suddenly recoil from her.

"Hey." Ethan laid his hand over hers. She twitched

slightly, but he kept it where it was. "Destiny, I can't pretend this hasn't been the biggest shock of my life. And to be honest, I'll probably wake up in the middle of the night tonight and think, 'Did that really happen?' But I know it did. And I'm not scared or horrified or whatever it is you're imagining. I'm just... surprised."

She looked up then, and the moon shone in her beautiful eyes. "You sure?"

"Positive, nerd girl." As he'd hoped, she made a face at him, and he felt some of the tension leave her hand. "You're a gorgeous, fierce woman, and you're a gorgeous, fierce tiger. Any man lucky enough to get with you will never sleep cold at night."

She snickered. "He wouldn't anyway."

They sat in silence for a while, with her soft hand warm under his. A feeling of utter contentment filled his heart. He had no need to rush anything. If he and Destiny didn't do anything that night but hold hands, that was fine. He and this brave, bewitching, literally magical woman had all the time in the world.

A shout made them both start. "Destiny? Ethan?"

She jumped up and waved. "Over here, Hal!"

An enormous man holding a flashlight in one hand and a gun in the other stepped out of the woods. Ellie followed him.

Ethan ran to meet his sister, sweeping her off her feet in a hug. She threw her arms around him and held him tight. He'd never admitted it to anyone, not even to her, but by far the hardest part of being a Marine was how little he got to see Ellie, and how much he missed her when he was gone.

"Hey," he said, setting her down. "Hear you went and got engaged to a grizzly bear."

"He's only furry sometimes," she said, smiling. Despite the

stress she'd been under, she looked happy and relaxed. It seemed like love agreed with her.

Ethan took a good long look at Hal the bear. Ellie might like him, but Ethan was going to make up his own mind. Still, he had to admit that the first impression was positive. Hal clearly knew how to use the gun he held, which indicated competence. Destiny respected him, which did as well. But most importantly, there was no mistaking the love in Hal's gaze when he looked at Ellie. That man would live and die for her, and lay down the world at her feet. That was good enough for Ethan.

Ellie and Ethan started to catch up with each other while Hal and Destiny conferred about the gangsters and her car. Hal called the police to come pick up the gangsters and take them to jail, and made another call to get her car winched out of the lake. They waited for the police to arrive, and then they all climbed into Hal's car to drive to the cabin.

Destiny squeezed into the back seat with Ethan. He nearly put his arm around her, then decided that he shouldn't without knowing if she wanted her boss to know. He wasn't even sure how he felt about Ellie knowing. It was all so fresh and new, he wanted to keep it between the two of them for now. With an inward start of surprise, he realized that the most they'd ever done was kiss, and that only once. How strange. It felt like they'd come so much farther than that already.

He didn't dare look her in the eyes, or he'd give it away for sure. It was killing him to keep his hands off her. But a delicious warmth kindled within him at her presence.

Soon, he thought. *Maybe not tonight. But soon.*

CHAPTER 3

At Hal's cabin, Destiny took a hot shower and changed into clean clothes from the stash of assorted clothing in the attic for the use of any shifters who'd gotten unexpectedly naked. After Ethan had taken his turn with the shower and emergency clothes, they all converged in the living room to sit by the fire and listen first to the story of Ethan and Destiny's adventure (leaving out the part where they'd intended to get it on in the woods), then to the story of how Ellie and Hal had met. Destiny had heard it before but not in much detail, so she didn't mind hearing it again.

Despite the loss of her car, her dress, her gun, her purse, and even her shoes, she felt strangely happy. She and Ethan had put away the very last of Nagle's gang and so protected her friends, and she'd just met a man whom she felt very confident was going to become much more than a friend. With any luck, and if Hal and Ellie fell asleep soon, tonight.

"...and there she was, sitting in the police station," Hal was saying. "But her head was down so I couldn't see her eyes. I introduced myself and she looked up, and when our eyes met—"

He broke off, shaking his head, his expression alight with what Destiny could only think of as glory. "It nearly knocked me backwards. And my bear roared, 'Mine!'"

"You were a bear?" Ethan said. "In the police station? A *talking* bear?"

Ellie burst into giggles.

"No, no," said Hal. "When you're a shifter, your animal is always with you. When you're human, it's a voice in your mind. That voice is the part of you that *is* the animal: your deepest, most instinctive, most primal self. And it's the part of you that recognizes your mate."

"Your mate," Ethan echoed. "What does that mean?"

"Your true love," Hal replied without a trace of embarrassment. "The person you're perfectly compatible with. The person you'll never fall out of love with."

Perfectly compatible, Destiny thought. *Sounds like me and Ethan.*

They had so much in common, with their similar sense of humor, taste for excitement, cool under fire, even their shared love for dancing. They'd both been in the military. Even though they'd only just met, they had worked as well together to protect each other as if they'd been teammates for years. And, of course, there was their absolutely *sizzling* sexual chemistry.

Could Ethan be the one? Destiny wondered. *My one true mate?*

For an instant, she was filled with certainty and joy. Of course he was. He had to be. It felt so *right.*

Then Hal spoke again. "People who aren't shifters can have mates too, of course—I'm Ellie's as much as she's mine —but they have to fall in love the regular way, over time.

Shifters recognize their mates the instant their eyes meet." He snapped his fingers. "Like that."

"Like that," Destiny repeated numbly, not even aware that she was speaking until she heard the words leave her mouth.

Hal nodded, then chuckled. "And, of course, my bear kept growling stuff like 'Protect our mate! Take her to our lair! Feed her nuts and berries! Catch her a nice fat salmon! Only the best for our mate!'" More seriously, he added, "But yeah, I knew then and there. It was absolutely unmistakable, the instant I looked into her eyes."

Destiny forced her glance at Ethan to seem casual, as if she was looking out the window at the stars rather than meaningfully staring into his eyes. But she did look into his eyes.

Nothing happened.

She felt like she'd been kicked in the gut. And then she realized something that made her feel even worse. She'd looked into his eyes before—she'd looked into them plenty of times in the short but eventful time since they'd met—and nothing had *ever* happened.

Well, no—not quite nothing. That first time they'd met, she'd felt a sort of jolt. And she was sure feeling a whole lot of things right now. But that jolt could have just been a whole lot of sexual chemistry, or the force of a strong personality. And her attraction could be because he was exactly her type: a gentleman and a soldier, sweet and funny and hot as blazes, and because they got along so well and they *were* so compatible...

But her tiger hadn't said a word. And she was the one who would know.

Maybe she'd been snoozing.

Hey! Destiny gave her inner tiger a mental shove. *What do you think of Ethan?*

Her tiger tilted her head, a big cat's equivalent of a shrug. *He seems nice.*

Nice, Destiny thought. *Ugh. Nice is for best friends and bosses and brothers, not for fated true loves.*

But she wasn't going to let her tiger off the hook that easily. She tried again. *Could he be my mate?*

Her tiger gave her that head tilt again. *Your mate? I don't know. How am I supposed to tell?*

Weren't you paying any attention to Hal's story? Destiny asked, frustrated. *Do you get a 'mine' feeling when I look into his eyes?*

Nope, her tiger purred, sounding so unconcerned that Destiny wanted to grab her by the ears and shake her. *Never felt anything like that. Still don't.*

And then, adding insult to injury, the big cat curled up and went to sleep.

A hand touched her thigh. Destiny nearly jumped out of her skin.

"Hey, space cadet," Ethan said. "Say goodnight."

Her head jerked up. Hal and Ellie had already stood up. She leaned against him with every line of her body signaling her absolute trust, and he had his arms around her in a gesture of protectiveness and devotion.

That's what mates look like, Destiny thought. Despite the fire, she felt chilled to the bone.

Hal and Ellie went off to their bedroom, leaving Destiny and Ethan alone together.

"You can take the sofa. There's a sleeping bag I can use." Ethan smiled at her. "Or we can wait fifteen minutes, then split one. What do you think?"

His blue-green eyes were hot with desire and the firelight made his hair shine like molten gold. She could feel the heat of his body from where she stood, as if the space between them didn't separate them at all. He reached out for her. All she had to do was stand there, and then he'd hold her in his strong arms and press his lips against hers and—

It was the one of the hardest things she'd ever done, but she held up her hand. "Ethan, wait."

He stopped. "Too tired? We don't have to do anything, you know. We could literally just sleep together."

About a million thoughts popped into her head at that:

He is nice. Not in a brother-boss-best friend way, in a good guy way that's exactly what I want in my mate.

If we can't make love, I'd rather cuddle up with him and go to sleep than not touch him at all.

If we did cuddle up, there's no way we'd get any sleep.

Hal and Ellie have all the luck.

Destiny didn't know how to explain—she didn't *want* to explain—but her only other choice was to lie, and she couldn't do that to Ethan.

"There's something I have to tell you. That stuff Hal was saying about mates? It applies to me too. I like you a lot, but..." She almost stopped right there, then forced herself to continue. "You're not my mate. I looked in your eyes, and nothing happened. I asked my tiger, and she said no."

"But..." Ethan looked both baffled and outraged. "I don't get it. Are you banned from having relationships from anyone but your mate? Hal's in his thirties—are you telling me he was a virgin until he met my sister a month ago?!"

"No. I mean, I don't know, we've never discussed it, but I assume not. I know he's dated other women before." She hurried to get off the topic of her boss's sex life. "And no, it's not banned. I'm not a virgin either."

"Then what's the problem? Okay, so maybe I'm not the love of your life..." A shadow of hurt flickered across his face, making her wince. He obviously didn't like that idea one bit. But determinedly, he went on, "So what? I'm not asking you for a lifetime commitment. I'm only saying, let's try it out. See how it goes. You know, the way everyone who's not a shifter does it."

Destiny was tempted. She was *incredibly* tempted. Sure, they could try it out. For all she knew, she wouldn't meet her mate for another fifty years. She might not even have a mate at all. Why not take what he was offering, and let the chips fall as they may?

But there was a great big glaring problem with that.

"Ethan, *you* have a mate." The words almost choked her, but she forced them out. "The perfect woman for you. The one you'll love more than you love your own life. And she's not me. She *can't* be me. If I were your mate, then you'd be mine, and my tiger would know."

"No." He was shaking his head, his expression set in absolute denial. "I don't have a mate. I'm not a shifter."

"All that means is that you probably won't fall in love at first sight. But she's out there somewhere. And when you meet her, you *will* fall in love. The sort of love that Hal and Ellie have. And that'll be it for you and me."

"No, it won't!" Ethan forced his voice down from a shout. In a low, intense tone, he said, "We could've both died tonight, and then what happens to this woman I'm supposedly meeting? To hell with her. I don't believe in her. Let's forget about things that might happen in the future, and take what we have in front of us. That's you, Destiny. I want *you*, and I want you *now!*"

Destiny wanted him too. She wanted him *now*. But her mind had leaped ahead to what would happen if she let him persuade her. It would be wonderful; she knew it. But sooner or later, he'd meet his mate. And then what? Would letting go of him be any easier six months or a year or five years down the road? What if they were married?

What if they had kids?

She felt herself pressing her fist to her chest, as if she'd been stabbed in the heart and had to stop herself from bleeding out. She sure felt like she had. But he wasn't a shifter—he *couldn't* understand the way she did. And that meant she had to make the hard decision for them both.

Her voice dropped so low that it sounded like a tiger's growl. "Fine. You don't understand what it means to be mates. I get it. This is all new to you. But here's the important thing. I'm saying no, Ethan. The answer is no."

Ethan looked like she'd kicked him in the stomach. He actually took a step backward, as if she really had. "All right. I *don't* understand. But you're saying no, so... I respect that. You ever change your mind, let me know. But I'm not going to keep hassling you when you want me to lay off."

"Thanks. You're a good guy. And I hope we can still be friends." She sighed. "If it's not too weird. And awkward. And frustrating."

Ethan straightened up, visibly pulling himself together. Putting on a mask of unconcern, he said, "Aw, no, mudpuppy, we can still be buddies. I've been turned down before. I'm a big boy, I can take it."

"Okay. Good. We're on, jarhead." Destiny blinked hard, forcing back the sting of oncoming tears. Making herself sound casual, she asked, "Hey, I never asked. How long are you planning to stay in Santa Martina?"

He shrugged. The easy flow of conversation between them had dried up, which hurt as much as everything else. "A couple weeks, a couple months. I go where they send me, when they send me. You know how it is."

"Yeah, I remember."

She retreated to the bathroom to brush her teeth and take her pill. She normally took them first thing in the morning, but it was almost dawn now. She swallowed it, then changed into a borrowed nightgown, hoping Ethan would be asleep or pretending to be when she got back. Sure enough, he was in the sleeping bag when she returned, his face buried in the pillow. When she turned out the lights and got under the blankets on the sofa bed, he waited ten minutes, then snuck out to the bathroom.

Destiny lay awake trying to argue with the feeling that she'd made the biggest mistake of her life. But was it so wrong not to enter into a relationship that she already knew was doomed? Sure, she'd dated men before without worrying about mates. But they'd been casual affairs: just for fun, nothing serious intended on either side. She couldn't imagine anything she did with Ethan not getting very serious, very quickly. And then, doom.

No. She was definitely doing the right thing. Sometimes that hurt and was hard, because life could hurt and be hard.

But if Ethan wasn't her mate, who in the world was?

After the trial at which Ellie's courageous testimony put all the gangsters in jail, Ethan deployed. He only had time to give Ellie a quick call, and then he was gone. Destiny foolishly, pointlessly, hopelessly missed him every single day that she didn't see his blue-green eyes. Six months later, he came back, and every single day that she did see him, she foolishly, pointlessly, hopelessly missed the relationship they didn't have, had never had, never would have. Missed *him*, even though he was right there. And then he deployed again, and she missed him again. More fool her.

And so it went. For two endless years, while she watched as one by one, each of her teammates found their mates. She was happy for them, of course, and not only because they'd found love. With their mates, they also found a missing piece of themselves, had some jagged edge smoothed out or some old wound healed. And the same was true of their mates. They'd all been made whole.

What's the piece I'm missing? Destiny sometimes wondered. *How would I change, if I ever found my mate?*

She asked her tiger, sometimes, but the big cat only gave her a lazy shrug. *How should I know?*

Every time Ethan returned to Santa Martina, tanned and tired and happy to see his sister, the pang of love and misery that stabbed through Destiny's heart felt like it would just about kill her. After the first time, she made sure she didn't catch his eyes until a few seconds had gone by; that one unguarded look of raw longing she'd caught the first time had nearly made her throw herself into his arms.

But where would that lead? To him meeting his true mate and realizing how trapped he was, and her pretending it didn't break her heart when they broke up—or worse, got divorced—so he could be with the woman he *really* loved.

No. Being with Ethan was a fool's game, doomed from the start, and Destiny's mama hadn't raised a fool. She'd enjoy his company when she got it, but only as a friend. And when the time came, she'd dance at his wedding and make herself look happy, and never let on that her heart was breaking inside. And that was that.

Until Ethan deployed again.

And didn't come back.

CHAPTER 4

Two Years Later

Ethan had spent the last six hours in a rough and dangerous borderland that could be concealing an enemy behind every boulder or within every ravine, trudging up and down hills with an eighty-pound rucksack on his back, and he had at least another six hours to go. There had been absolutely no sign of the terrorist hideout they'd been sent to find. He was convinced that some desk-sitter back at the Pentagon had mistaken a herd of stray goats for a band of armed men. It wouldn't be the first time. If so, it was lucky for the goats that they'd sent four Recon Marines instead of a stealth bomber.

He was hot, hungry, tired, and sure that it was all for nothing. But what bothered him was that he wasn't enjoying himself anyway.

I used to love being a Marine, Ethan thought. *What happened?*

He wanted to believe that it was because he hadn't yet gotten used to his new fire team. A recent series of accidents and ambushes had sent a lot of Marines in his unit to the hospital or worse. As a result, personnel had to be transferred in and shifted around. Ethan's old team had been broken up, and he'd ended up on a new team that consisted of three misfits plus him. He'd hoped they were only having a rough transition, but it had been a month now and they still didn't get along. And on a four-man team, that was one hell of a problem.

"… and that's how the ruby necklace of the Lady of the Kingdom of Albania got into the watermelon," Merlin concluded. His voice was getting hoarse. Maybe it was finally wearing out. But he took a drink of water, cleared his throat, and went on, "As for how I got involved, my great-grandfather once spent some time as a gardener in a nunnery…"

Merlin Merrick had been talking nonstop for what felt like the entire six hours. Ethan thought he'd started talking to try to break the ice, continued out of boredom, and was now well into seeing how long he could go before someone told him to shut up. To be fair, Ethan had initially tried to help out with the ice-breaking, then had gotten distracted by thoughts of Destiny and fallen silent, and, once he realized that Merlin had been carrying on by himself for quite some time, had stayed silent to see how long he could go before he either gave up or was shut up.

Yeah. This team *definitely* had a problem. And Ethan was forced to conclude that he was part of it.

Pete Valdez interrupted Merlin in the middle of a sentence. "Is it even physically possible for you to shut the fuck up?"

"Is it even physically possible for any of you guys to have an actual conversation, like normal people?" Merlin retorted.

If Ethan didn't like being part of the problem, then he had

to be the solution. He broke in. "Good idea. I'm starting it." He took a split second to consider topics, then settled on sports. What Marine didn't like sports? And, to be safe, he didn't start with Merlin. "Pete, what's your favorite sport?"

Obligingly, Pete asked, "To play or to watch?"

"To play."

"Does it have to be a team sport, or does anything count?"

"Anything counts," Ethan replied.

"Boxing," Pete said. Ethan was unsurprised. Pete was a good-looking guy, but he also looked like he'd had his nose broken a time or two, and his big knuckles were flecked with little white scars. "What about you, Ethan?"

Ethan almost said baseball, which was certainly the sport he was best at, or used to be, anyway. But it had too many bad associations to be his favorite, and it had been years since he'd played. "Basketball."

Grinning, Pete said, "I'd love to see you go up against Shaq, short stuff."

"Right back at you, munchkin," Ethan retorted. He and Pete were both six feet tall exactly.

Unexpectedly, Ransom Pierce spoke up. "Muggsey Bogues was five foot three, and he played in the NBA for fourteen seasons. So there's hope for you yet."

Ethan was relieved that nobody argued, as it wasn't as if they could check with Google. But Pete and Merlin either already knew about Muggsey Bogues, or had figured out that Ransom apparently had Google beamed directly into his head. He not only knew as much as a college professor, but with his lanky frame and angular face, he also looked the part.

Looks could be deceiving. Ransom was the deadliest sniper Ethan had ever known.

"My grand-uncle was only five foot two, but he set a world record for—" Merlin began.

Sensing yet another unlikely story that would fray Pete's temper, Ethan cut him off. "Never mind your uncle, what's *your* favorite sport to play?"

Merlin shot him a look from his bright blue eyes like Ethan was an idiot for not already knowing. "Gymnastics."

Once he'd said it, Ethan did feel like an idiot. Whenever they had down time near a tree or an abandoned building with sturdy girders, Merlin would start swinging on them like an acrobat. When they'd asked him about it, he'd first claimed to have been a gymnast in high school, then to have been an *Olympic* gymnast, then to have been the star of a series of Latvian movies about a superhero whose power was agility, and finally to have been raised in a circus. At that point everyone stopped asking.

"Of course it is," Pete muttered. "You were raised by chimpanzees."

Before Pete and Merlin could start in on each other again, Ethan said, "Ransom? What about you?"

Pete glanced at Ransom's rangy frame and said, "Marathons, right?"

Merlin nodded, for once in agreement with Pete. "Yeah, that's a runner's build. Long-distance, not sprints."

Ransom gave a shrug, neither confirming nor denying, and made no reply. Aggravated, Ethan almost said something —why the hell would your favorite sport be a secret?—before remembering that he was trying to avoid arguments, not start them himself.

He shut his mouth with a snap. Fine. Let Ransom be Ransom, with all the sudden silences and weird secrets that entailed. However frustrating he could be, he had a sixth sense for danger like none Ethan had ever encountered before. On his very first day on the team, he'd saved God knew how many lives by stopping their entire convoy, then calmly pointing out an IED trigger in the road that no one else had spotted, including the bomb-sniffing dog.

Ethan just wished Ransom was a little less of a riddle wrapped inside an enigma. Why was he so cool in the face of danger, but went pale and made an excuse to get away whenever he encountered any one of an array of random things? Ethan had been mentally keeping a list of the latter, in the hope of figuring out what made him tick, but had been less than successful at figuring out what dice, flickering fluorescent lights, and the book *Carrie* had in common. And, apparently, his favorite sport. Whatever that was.

Only then did Ethan remember his intention to get his team to have a normal conversation. But a Marine is nothing if not persistent. "Pete, what's your favorite sport to watch? Other than boxing."

"Baseball. I love going to ball games with—" He broke off. After an awkward pause, he said, "What about you? Other than basketball?"

"Soccer," Ethan replied, though what he wanted to say, or rather scream to the heavens, was "Why is everything a secret with *all* of you?!" Instead, he said, "Merlin? What's your favorite sport to watch? Other than gymnastics?"

With a gleam in his eyes that made Ethan instantly regret asking, Merlin said, "Buzkashi!"

"What the hell is that?" Pete demanded.

"It's like polo, but instead of a ball, you use a dead goat."

"Yeah, right," said Ethan.

"It's the national sport of Afghanistan," Ransom said. "There's a similar sport in Argentina, but instead of a dead goat, they use a live duck in a basket."

"Ever seen it?" Merlin asked hopefully.

In a tone designed to discourage further discussion, Ransom said, "I don't watch sports."

And that was the end of that. Ethan tried to decide if he'd

managed a full five minutes of normal conversation, then decided that except for his brief exchanges with Pete, none of it had actually been normal.

And even Pete, his ability to talk normally about sports aside, had some definite oddities. In some ways, he was like a lot of Marines, a regular guy who liked being outdoors and working with his hands. But he wouldn't talk about his past or his personal life, in a way that went way beyond private and into flat-out strange. He refused to reveal his hometown, he wouldn't say if he'd ever had another job, and once when Merlin had decided to kill time by polling them on whether they wanted to have kids, Pete had given him a look so murderous that even Merlin had shut up in a hurry.

He was fiercely protective of his team, though, whether he got along with them or not. And he was absolutely fearless in combat. Maybe too fearless. Ethan once had to physically drag him away when they'd gotten the order to retreat, and afterward Pete had given him a blank look and said he hadn't heard the order.

"He's a berserker," Ransom had said.

"I didn't go berserk," Pete had said, scowling at him. "I couldn't hear the command over the gunfire, that's all."

It *had* been loud, but everyone else had heard it. Something got into Pete when he fought, something even Ethan couldn't help finding a little scary. He'd looked up "berserker" afterward, and found that they were Viking warriors who were said to be possessed by bear spirits and went into combat without armor, relying on the sheer force of their battle rage to protect them.

Pete didn't look like a Viking, or at least not like Ethan imagined Vikings, as huge white guys with blue eyes and long blond hair. He looked as strong as he was, but he wasn't enormous, and his buzz cut and skin and expressive eyes were brown. Still, Ethan had wondered ever since if Ransom had been on to something.

At least Merlin, though as brave as any man Ethan had ever met, didn't make him wonder if he'd have to drag him from a fight. He sometimes creatively interpreted orders, but not in the heat of battle. And even when arguing, he never got angry. Normally Ethan would have appreciated having someone friendly on the team. He *did* appreciate it. Merlin just took it to extremes.

Ethan had once joked that Merlin could be airdropped into Afghanistan and meet his old buddy, a travelling rug salesman. They'd all laughed at that... until they'd been airdropped into Afghanistan and Merlin actually did run into an old buddy. He was a travelling pots-and-pans salesman, but close enough. They'd had a whole conversation in a language Ethan had never even heard of, but Merlin could speak fluently.

He knew so many languages that he should have gotten pulled out of combat duty and into translation—which, Ethan supposed, was why he'd never seen Merlin speak anything but English when any officers were in hearing range. And when Ethan asked him how he'd learned them, Merlin had claimed that his mother had primed him by sleeping with language lessons playing all night when she was pregnant.

But that was Merlin. He had a story to account for everything, but he told them with a wink that made it obvious that he wasn't even trying to fool anyone. If anyone called him on it, he'd just tell another ridiculous story. What was he trying to hide?

Then again, there was plenty that Ethan himself hadn't told his team. They knew about his brother-in-law Hal's security agency, and that Ethan sometimes helped them out. But they sure didn't know that Hal could turn into a grizzly bear. And he'd never mentioned Destiny at all. He told himself that she was none of their business, but the truth was that it hurt too much to talk about.

Destiny.

He tried his damnedest not to think about her, but the most ridiculous little things always managed to remind him. Just now, it was the rushing river beside them, and the mud that had spattered their boots and camo. It made him think of the mud they'd plastered over her dancing dress when they'd first met. He never had bought her that new dress—he'd offered again, but she wouldn't let him—and they'd never gone dancing, either. And they never would.

Why'd she have to be a shifter? Ethan thought for the millionth time, though now that he'd seen her tiger, it was hard to imagine her without it. *If she wasn't, she'd have never heard of mates, and we'd be together now.*

But then he thought, also for the millionth time, *It wouldn't have made a difference. You've seen her teammates fall in love, and call that being mated. When she said, "We're not mates," what she meant was, "I don't love you, and I never will."*

It had been two years since she'd turned him down. He'd have expected the pain to have eased by now. But it was still as sharp as if it had been two minutes ago.

It's ridiculous for me to be so hung up on her, he thought. *People move on from divorces. Why can't I move on from a woman I never even dated?*

"What about you, Ethan?"

Ethan had completely zoned out. "What about what?"

"You gonna re-up?" Pete asked, obviously repeating himself.

Ethan had been thinking about it, off and on, but he made up his mind at that moment. What was the point of leaving the Marines? He had nothing waiting for him in civilian life.

Oh, sure, he had Ellie, and soon he'd have nephews or

nieces or one of each. But Ellie was in Santa Martina, and there was no way Ethan could stand to live in the same city as Destiny, so tantalizingly close and yet so frustratingly apart. He'd have to live somewhere else and visit. And if he was only visiting anyway, he might as well stay where he was. There was nothing like getting shot at for distracting you from your problems.

"Three misfits plus me," Ethan thought. *Make that four misfits.*

"Yeah," Ethan said. "I'll re-enlist. What about you guys?"

Merlin ran his hand over his clipped blond hair. "I am *definitely—*"

Ethan's foot came down on a hidden gopher hole, and he stumbled. At that exact moment, Merlin let out a yelp, then reached over his shoulder to slap between his shoulder blades, like he'd been stung by a bee. At the same moment, Pete winced slightly and lifted a hand to touch his back.

"Ambush!" Ransom shouted, and gave Ethan a hard shove.

The last thing Ethan saw before he went tumbling over the edge of the ravine were all three of his men collapsing, unconscious or dead.

Then he hit the river hard enough to knock the wind out of him. The current was fierce, tumbling him head over heels. By the time Ethan had managed to extricate himself from his heavy pack, he'd been swept far downstream. He struggled to regain control, desperate to get back to his men, but he was no match for the white waters. The current tossed him this way and that, then sucked him down in an undertow until he thought he'd drown. He fought his way to the surface, and managed a single gulp of air before the rushing waters flung him into a boulder. He saw a bright burst of light, and then only darkness.

. . .

Ethan awoke cold and wet and confused. His head throbbed fiercely, there was a stabbing pain in his side, and it was hard to breathe. When he opened his eyes, he saw nothing but a brown blur, and he could hear nothing but a roar of white noise.

Then memory rushed back. The ambush. The river.

His vision slowly came into focus, though it was a few more moments before he could process what he was seeing. He'd been washed up against a rock outcropping at the edge of the river. Most of his body was underwater, but the force of the current was pinning him against the stone. A lot of tree branches and other debris had washed up with him, then piled atop him.

He started to pull himself out of the water, but dizziness swept over him as soon as he raised his head. Ethan lay back down. If he got partway out and then passed out again, he'd be swept away and drowned. He had to stay where he was until he got a little more strength back.

Ethan wasn't a medic, but he knew some basic battlefield medicine. He'd been flung against the rocks and hit his head hard enough to knock him out, and he was still dizzy. Concussion, for sure. Every time he took a breath, it felt like someone was jabbing a knife into his side, and the deeper it was, the more it hurt. He'd been instinctively taking shallow breaths to reduce the pain. So he'd also cracked or broken some ribs.

Bracing himself, Ethan deliberately took a deep breath to see if he could figure out how many. It was cut off by an excruciating coughing fit. An alarming amount of water ran out of his mouth. No wonder his chest felt so congested. How long had he been lying there, cold and wet and with his lungs half-full of river water? He was in excellent physical condition, but that seemed like a recipe for getting sick.

Ethan started to cough again. Then, over the roar of the

river, he heard voices, and forced back the cough with sheer willpower.

"He has to be dead," said a gruff male voice. "Let's go back, set the explosives, and call it a day. We got three out of four prime candidates. That's good enough."

"I agree," said a woman. "It's been almost four hours. We could blow the entire operation if we spend any more time here."

"We can't just assume he's dead without seeing a body." That was a slightly higher male voice. "I say we keep searching."

The gruff male voice spoke again. "Don't sweat it, Kritsick. Locals call this the Disappearing River: anything you throw in is never seen again."

The high male voice, who was presumably Kritsick, said, "And if he's alive and blows the whistle, this entire project will never be seen again."

"Ayers?" asked the woman. "It's your call."

A new male voice, deep and commanding, spoke after a brief pause. "Even in the wildly unlikely event that McNeil turns up alive, what does he know, really? Most likely, he'll report that one of his men shouted 'Ambush!' and pushed him into the river to save him. He'll be told that his teammates were killed in an explosion. That doesn't contradict what he saw. They'll still blame the terrorists the team was sent to search for. Maybe they'll give Pierce a posthumous medal for saving McNeil. Makes no difference to us."

"What if he saw the darts?" asked Kritsick.

"Unlikely," said the woman. "They're quite small."

"Even if he did, that part of the report won't go anywhere," said the gruff voice. "This is what our people within the military are for."

Our people within the military. Ethan's heart sank. He couldn't run back to the base and get help—anyone could be in on the conspiracy, even his own commanding officer. Ethan was absolutely alone, with no one he could trust but himself.

"Anyway, it doesn't matter what McNeil might have seen," the gruff voice went on. "He's dead."

"We're moving out," Ayers said firmly. "We need to set those charges. We're already hours behind schedule."

"Who's going to tell Lamorat we lost one?" Kritsick asked.

Lamorat, Ethan thought. *What a weird name.*

"I will," Ayers said. But it was only after a long silence. Ethan realized that they were all afraid of their boss, funny name or not. "Come on. We have to go."

Ethan lay still and listened to their retreating footsteps. The pain in his head made it difficult to think, but he willed himself to clarity.

"Three out of four prime candidates," they'd said. That meant the rest of his team must be alive, and intended to be used for… something.

Shane Garrity, one of Destiny's teammates at Protection, Inc., had once been in the Air Force. Ethan had only heard his story second-hand—Shane didn't like to talk about it—but he knew that Shane had been on a mission when he and his team had been knocked out with drugged darts, then kidnapped by a black ops agency called Apex. Their disappearance had been covered up with a false report that they'd been killed in action.

That sounded incredibly similar to what Ethan had seen and heard. The only problem with that theory was that he'd been under the impression that Apex had been destroyed by Protection, Inc. In fact, Ethan had helped out on one of those missions. But was Apex really gone? Or had it only suffered a setback and the loss of some bases?

Ethan bet on the latter. Those people he'd overheard had to be from Apex. But that meant his men were in grave danger. The Apex agents had called them "candidates," and Ethan had a terrible feeling that he knew what they were candidates for.

Shane hadn't just been kidnapped, he'd been tortured, experimented on, made into a shifter and given special powers in a process that few survived, and forced to become an assassin. He and one of his buddies, Justin, had been the sole survivors out of the eight airmen who'd been captured. The last Ethan had heard, Justin was still so traumatized by the experience that he was living in self-imposed exile, refusing Shane's attempts to bring him home.

Ethan had to rescue his teammates before Apex killed them. Or worse.

CHAPTER 5

*D*estiny couldn't believe how much Protection, Inc. had changed. Two years ago, the agency had been full of unhappy misfits. Hal had been a driven workaholic, Lucas had been brittle and arrogant, Nick had been in a permanent state of rage, Fiona had been snippy and secretive, Shane had been haunted and hollow-eyed, and Rafa had created an elaborate false front to disguise his loneliness.

Destiny had liked to think she'd been the only normal, cheerful person there. But now that years had gone by and everyone else had found their mates and sorted out their problems, she had to admit that she, like Rafa, had only been better than the others at putting up a false front. Like the old movie had said, they'd been dancing as fast as they could.

Now Protection, Inc. was full of happy people who'd found themselves when they'd found love, and the only unhappy misfit was her.

"I'm pregnant!" Grace announced, beaming. "Two months along!"

Destiny wasn't surprised. She couldn't tell from any change in her figure, but her purple curls had an extra shine and bounce, and she just seemed overall glowy. Even more than that, Grace's mate Rafa had recently acquired a permanent grin, so engrossed in some wonderful news he couldn't wait to share that Destiny was surprised he hadn't literally walked into a wall.

"That's great," said Hal. "Our twins and your child will be so close in age. They'll get to grow up together."

"Only six months apart," said Ellie. "Almost triplets!"

"Now that's what I call a pack," remarked Nick. Nudging his mate Raluca, he said, "If we got started right now, ours and theirs would practically be quadruplets."

"I am not getting pregnant tonight," Raluca said firmly. "First I finish my degree, then I launch my business. *Then* we have children."

Nick looked wistful, but said, "You're the one who gets pregnant. Your choice."

Raluca traced his silver dragon armlet with a slim finger. "Our children will have big brothers or sisters to look after them."

Nick glanced at Rafa and chuckled. "Watch out, man. Little brothers and sisters exist to annoy the fuck out of their elders."

"Not in this case," said Rafa. "I expect yours will acquire excellent manners... from their mother."

Nick grinned. "My mom had great manners. Doesn't always take."

As the rest of the bodyguards and their mates congratulated Grace and Rafa, Destiny added her voice to the chorus. She'd probably never have children of her own, but at least she'd have friends' kids to babysit and spoil. Ellie was only a month away from giving birth to twins.

She hoped Ethan would come back in time for the birth. Destiny had known he hadn't wanted to deploy again, though of course he hadn't said so. But she could see the weariness in his eyes. He hadn't looked like Shane or Justin, thank God, like he'd spent the last couple years choosing every night between nightmares or not even trying to sleep. But he'd looked like Hal and Rafa and Destiny herself had when they'd left the military to start Protection, Inc. Like they were... done. Ready to move on.

He *could* move on. His time was almost up. But when she'd asked him if he was going to re-enlist, he'd shrugged, then said, "Probably" without looking particularly enthusiastic about it.

And that was that. He'd be in for four more years. At least. Four more years of—

A sudden, overwhelming sense of danger swept over her, making her whip around and scan the office. Nothing seemed amiss. No one was there but her friends, and they were all laughing and talking. But rather than relaxing her, the sight only made her more tense. She wanted to scream at them that something was wrong—

"Are you all right?" Fiona murmured in her ear.

"Yeah, fine," Destiny replied automatically.

But the sense of danger didn't go away. Destiny tried to make herself think rationally about it. Unlike some people present, she hadn't been tortured or otherwise traumatized, and had never had a panic attack in her life. So was she getting a genuine premonition? Should she order everyone out of the office, in case she'd picked up some subliminal clues that someone had planted a bomb in it or something...?

But when she thought of that, she realized that she wasn't afraid for anyone there. She was afraid for Ethan. Though she had no idea why, she was convinced that Ethan was in terrible danger.

He's a Recon Marine, she told her subconscious or whatever it was. *He's in danger all the time. He can take care of himself.*

Her subconscious wasn't having it. Destiny's heart was hammering against her chest. Her palms were sweating. The drumbeat of *danger, danger, danger* was so loud in her mind that she could barely hear herself think.

"Excuse me," she muttered, and stumbled for the bathroom.

Once she was inside, she splashed cold water on her face and stared at her reflection in the mirror. Her eyes looked strange. Wild. The green shimmer was strong against the brown, like her tiger was staring back at her.

Suddenly worried, she dug into her purse and took out her pills. Apart from the emergency stash tucked into her bra, she kept them in a box meant for birth control, so she could always tell by checking the calendar if she'd forgotten to take one. She gave a sigh of relief when she saw that she'd taken one that morning. She wasn't due for another till tomorrow. So at least it wasn't that.

But then, what *was* wrong?

Ethan, that strange inner alarm informed her. *Ethan's in danger. Go help him, or he'll die!*

It didn't sound like her tiger. It wasn't a voice at all—it was a feeling, a knowledge, a compulsion that Destiny herself was translating into words. All the same, she asked her tiger, *Is that you?*

Nope, her tiger replied. *No idea what it is. I can feel it too, though. Shall we go check it out?*

If I can figure out where—

"Destiny?"

Destiny jumped about a foot in the air, dropping her pill box. Fiona snatched it up before it could hit the ground and handed it back to her.

"Thanks," Destiny said, replacing it in her purse.

"You're not all right," Fiona remarked. Her leaf-green eyes were narrow with worry. "Mind if Justin comes in? You look like... Well, you look like he used to, sometimes. He noticed, too. He's right outside the door."

"Yeah, sure," Destiny said, resigned. "Why not? It's a unisex bathroom."

Fiona opened the door, and Justin came in. He looked her over with his coal-black eyes, so startling against his copper-red hair and lashes. "Did something happen to you that I don't know about?"

"Happen to me?" Destiny echoed, bewildered. "Like what?"

"Something bad," Justin said succinctly. "You look like you're having a flashback."

"No. It's nothing like that. It's—"

Ethan, Ethan's in danger, stop wasting time and go rescue him, now, now, now!

The command had the force of a hurricane. She gripped the sink with both hands, as if otherwise she might be swept away.

"Are you sick?" Fiona asked. "Would you rather we stepped out?"

Destiny realized that Fiona thought she was about to throw up. She opened her mouth to deny it, then closed it again. She couldn't explain what was really going on, since she didn't understand it herself and it made no sense, but pretending she was fine was right out. On the other hand, there was one thing she could say with absolute truth.

"I don't feel good," Destiny said. Before Justin, a paramedic, could offer to poke and prod her, she added, "I'm fine. It's a female problem."

Fiona's worried expression cleared at that; she'd seen Destiny's pills many times before, starting at the time when she'd stayed at Destiny's house before she'd joined the team. "Female problems" tended to cut off discussion, even among women. But before her teammates could decide everything was fine and leave, another blast of alarm hit Destiny like a fist to the gut.

Ethan! Go help Ethan!

Destiny once again clutched at the sink, and once again looked up into her teammates' concerned faces. If she didn't let them do *something*, they'd never let her alone. "Could you drive me home?"

"Of course," Fiona said. "Justin, can you tell everyone Destiny and I had to go? Just say she wasn't feeling well."

"Got it," Justin replied.

Fiona escorted Destiny to her own car and got behind the wheel. Destiny was relieved to find that the sense of urgency faded once she got in the car. She could tell that it was still there, but it seemed to be abiding its time so long as she was taking some kind of action. She closed her eyes, hoping to discourage questions. But when the car stopped and she opened them, she found that she was at Fiona and Justin's house, not hers.

"I know it's nothing serious, but you don't look good," Fiona said. "I thought you'd better stay where someone can keep an eye on you. The dogs aren't allowed in the guest bedroom."

Destiny couldn't think of any reasonable objection to that, especially since the entire problem was unreasonable. She followed Fiona into the yard, where they were greeted by an overjoyed pack of dogs.

"Sit!" Fiona commanded. "No jumping!"

All six dogs obediently sat as Fiona took Destiny to the no-dogs-allowed part of the house, which consisted of a guest bedroom, Fiona's art room filled with paintings and strange glass sculptures, and Fiona's tech room filled with computers and electronics. Sit Fiona in front of a computer, and she could find out anything.

She could find anyone.

Ethan, Ethan, find Ethan!

Without intending to say anything at all, Destiny caught herself blurting out, "Could you find a Special Forces soldier on a classified mission? I mean, if you wanted to."

Fiona studied her like Destiny was a computer she'd just started hacking. "If I wanted to. Sure. Like a Recon Marine, maybe?"

"Yeah," Destiny admitted.

"Why? Ethan's been on classified missions before. What's special about this one?"

For the first time in her life, Destiny lied to a teammate. "Before he left last time, Ethan told me something that makes me think he might be in trouble. Because... because he should be back by now, and he isn't."

Fiona's leaf-eyes seemed to see right through her. "This sounds like something you should take to Hal."

"No!" Floundering, Destiny went on, "Uh, Ethan said it was classified, and not to tell the rest of the team, because he might get in trouble, and—

Fiona held up a slim hand. "Destiny. Stop. Don't lie, you're not good at it. What in the world is going on?"

Destiny bit her lip. Fiona was a close friend, but that only made it worse. A teammate whose opinion you respected was the last person you wanted to have find out that you weren't the steady, dependable woman she thought you were. She couldn't bear the idea of Fiona, of all her teammates, thinking Destiny was a freak and a lunatic.

The silence stretched out between them. Then Fiona said quietly, "I am the last person who should object to you keeping secrets. Pull up a chair."

Fiona sat in front of a computer and got to work hacking into military databases. Destiny, very conscious of her lack of a classified clearance, did not pull up a chair. Instead, she fell back on her training as a soldier and averted her eyes.

"Found him!" Fiona exclaimed. "He's in Pakistan, near the border of India. I've got the exact area here... Hmm."

"What's the 'hmm?'" Destiny inquired.

"That's all I can get," Fiona replied. "His team must be involved in something top secret. It looks like a lot of stuff about them was never even entered into a database."

"To protect it from people like you," Destiny said drily.

Fiona gave her a catlike smile. "Guess we'll have to investigate in person. Do you want the whole team—" Destiny frantically shook her head, sending her box braids flying. "How about just me, you, and Justin? Or just me and you?"

"Just me," said Destiny. Most likely she'd lost her mind out of sheer broken-heartedness, and she didn't want to drag Fiona into that. Not to mention that she didn't want witnesses to her embarrassment when Ethan turned out to be absolutely fine. "It's probably nothing. I'd feel weird dragging anyone else into it. I'll fly into India, and then see if I want to try crossing the border. If it nothing, I'll stay in India for a while. Sightsee, clear my head. You know."

"I do know. Justin and I cleared our heads sightseeing in Venice once. I'll tell the team you were stressed out and went on a trip to India. It won't be a lie. On one condition."

"What?" Destiny asked warily.

Fiona crossed the room, took a tiny piece of electronic equipment from a shelf, and handed it to Destiny. "Keep this on you at all times. It's a GPS transmitter." As Destiny opened her mouth to object, Fiona said, "I won't use it to follow your movements. I know this is private business, and I respect that. But if you're not back in a week and you haven't called in to confirm that you're all right, I'm coming to get you."

"Got it." Destiny clipped the transmitter into her bra, beside her emergency pills.

She borrowed Fiona's computer, found the airport closest

to Ethan's coordinates, and booked a flight. Fiona dropped her at the airport. Destiny didn't even have time to go home and pack. But her purse had a month's supply of pills and everything else a girl might need if she had to go somewhere suddenly, and she could buy whatever else she needed at the airport.

All the way to the airport, her mind kept fluttering around like a bird that had accidentally flown into someone's house, jittering from the conviction that she'd arrive and find that he was fine and she was insane and then she'd get arrested for trespassing in a war zone, the terror that he wasn't fine at all and she'd arrive too late to save him, and memories of kissing Ethan, eating barbecue with Ethan, standing back to back with Ethan with their guns drawn.

The hurt in Ethan's sea-colored eyes when she'd told him to stop asking.

Destiny knew *she* should stop asking. If she kept picking at the scab, the wound would never heal. But she couldn't help herself.

Is Ethan my mate? Destiny asked her tiger.

Stop asking me that, hissed her tiger. *If I ever spot your mate, believe me, you'll be the first to know.*

Destiny had heard so many variations on that reply over the last two years that it should have stopped making her feel like her heart had been ripped in two. But the pain was as sharp and fresh as it had ever been.

She boarded the plane bound for India. Maybe after this little vacation of insanity proved exactly how crazy her obsession with Ethan had driven her, she could finally let him go.

CHAPTER 6

*E*than lay curled up in a wooden crate beneath a whole lot of MREs (country captain chicken flavor, his least favorite) and tried to strike a balance between staying absolutely still, so he wouldn't knock them all over and alert the enemy that he'd smuggled himself into their plane, and moving just enough so he wouldn't get cramps, which would definitely alert the enemy that he'd smuggled himself into their plane when he tried to get out of the crate and promptly fell on his face. The hardest part was not coughing. Probably he wouldn't be heard over the noise of the engine, but he couldn't risk it.

Rather than risk being spotted trying to follow a minimum of four enemy agents, he'd tried to circle around in the opposite direction and get back to his men before they did. He'd succeeded in not being spotted, but failed to beat them there. Ethan had watched from a distance while the four enemies who'd gone searching for him had met up with the four who'd stayed to guard Merlin, Pete, and Ransom.

Any hope he'd had of ambushing them and rescuing his teammates died then and there: eight against one was bad odds to begin with, and hopeless when the eight were armed and he wasn't. Especially since his teammates were still unconscious and could easily be used as hostages to force his cooperation.

On the other hand, only two enemies were with the small, unmarked plane that waited nearby, and they were both hanging out in the cockpit. Ethan considered his options, then decided that his best chance at rescuing his men—and his only chance at getting to the bottom of it all—was to find their base. He'd ducked inside the cargo bay, made a quick weapons check and found none, and buried himself in the only real hiding space, which was a half-full crate of MREs. He hoped no one would get hungry enough to come grab one.

He'd also hoped that his teammates would be stashed in the cargo bay, but no such luck. Ethan hadn't dared to peek out, but while he'd felt the thump of feet and heard muffled voices, no one seemed to have entered the cargo bay at all.

It felt like they'd been flying forever before his ears popped, signaling the descent. He waited, barely breathing, as he heard the enemies disembark. Once again, to his frustration, he could hear voices but couldn't make out the words. And then both voices and footsteps faded, and silence fell.

Ethan forced himself to count to a thousand before he so much as moved. Then he extricated himself from the crate, taking care not to send MREs cascading to the floor. The cargo bay was dark and still. He tiptoed to the door and listened with his ear to it. Nothing. He opened it.

Darkness met his eyes, and he drew in a breath of warm, humid air. He blinked, trying to see by the light of the moon. He was on a small airfield outside a base designed to blend in with the surrounding jungle. The plane he was in had been painted dark green, with no identification markings. Ethan bet the entire place would be perfectly camouflaged from above, invisible unless you knew what to look for.

He dropped down and pushed the door closed behind him. Urgency warred with caution in his mind as he approached the hidden base, keeping to the shadows. As he grew closer, he saw that it was patrolled by guards. If he walked up, he'd be captured immediately. He needed to come up with a plan.

A wave of dizziness swept over him, making him stagger. He'd hoped that "resting" in the MRE crate would help him recover, but he felt worse instead of better. His lungs felt heavy and sodden, his hands were shaking, his head and side throbbed, and his legs threatened to give out from under him. He was in no condition to launch a one-man raid on this place.

Ethan returned to the plane, grabbed a few MREs, and headed out into the jungle. The moss-covered earth was springy, and his feet left no tracks. He wasn't sure what country he was in, but he was familiar with this sort of terrain. A brief search uncovered a reasonable hiding place, a shallow cave in a hillside with its entrance hidden behind a curtain of vines.

He crawled in, cooked the MRE with its heating element, and ate it, trying not to think about joking with Destiny about the Five Fingers of Death. That thought led to him having to try not to think about their visit to Aunt Lizzie's Back Porch, and then to trying not to think about their one-and-only, peach cobbler-flavored, across-the-table kiss.

No matter what happens to me, at least Destiny's safe at home.

Comforted by that thought, he fell asleep.

Ethan woke to a shaft of dappled, greenish sunlight. He lay still, listening, but heard nothing but the chattering of monkeys and screeches of tropical birds. He stretched out, wincing, and again evaluated his condition. He felt less on the verge of collapse than he had the day before, and he was certainly capable of operating with a headache and broken ribs. But he could feel a slight rasp in his breathing, and though he couldn't be entirely sure, he thought he felt warmer than could be accounted for by the tropical heat.

If I'm coming down with something, I have to move fast before it gets worse, he told himself.

He might not be a one-man strike-force just yet, but he felt up to doing some reconnaissance. Depending on what he discovered, he'd either sneak in and break out his team, or sneak in, find a radio, and call for help.

He peered out of the cave, taking care to keep unseen within the vine curtain. To his dismay, the area around the base was bustling with enemies. A second unmarked plane was coming in for a landing, and a medical team and a security team were waiting for it. When it landed, a man was removed on a stretcher. Ethan was too far away to see anything but that he was lying still and there was a whole lot of blood on his clothes. The medical team jumped on him, there was a brief flurry of action, and then the stretcher-bearers literally ran him inside.

Ethan had no idea who the man was, but a whole lot of unpleasant possibilities came into his head about why he was there and how he'd been wounded. Apex had screwed up the ambush, and he'd had a chance to fight back? He'd been wounded in combat, and Apex had taken advantage of the commotion to snatch him when he was helpless?

Apex had captured Shane by ambushing his team when they'd been in the middle of a firefight and he'd been distracted by trying to save the life of his buddy Justin, who'd been hit and was bleeding out. Destiny had told Ethan about it; Shane still didn't like to talk about it. Justin wasn't the only one who'd been left with scars.

I hope you make it, Ethan thought to the man he'd seen so briefly. *If you do, I'll get you out of there. I swear it.*

Then, to his surprise, more people got off the plane. They were a pair of big men holding a struggling woman. She was yelling so loudly that Ethan could hear the sound, though he couldn't understand the words. One of the men put his hand over her mouth.

Ethan tensed to run out, then forced himself to stay still. He'd be taken prisoner immediately, and then how could he help her? As he watched, she apparently bit the hand (Ethan heard an anguished yell, and the hand yanked itself away), stomped on a foot, and made a break for it—*toward* the base, not away.

That's weird, Ethan thought.

Her attempt was brave but hopeless. She was instantly jumped by the security team and dragged inside.

I'll get you out too, Ethan silently vowed to her.

Which meant that he now had five people to rescue, not three. Much as he longed to break in and free everyone instantly, that wasn't realistic. In fact, getting in the base at all didn't seem very realistic. Still, he had to try.

Ethan settled back down. He hated to keep the prisoners waiting for an entire day, but he had to make his attempt at night or he'd have no chance at all. With a badly wounded man to deal with, hopefully Apex would be too distracted to do anything irrevocable to anyone any time soon.

He ate another country captain chicken MRE, plowing through it with the reminder that he needed all the strength he could get. Then, exhausted, he dozed off.

He awoke with a start and a jolt of adrenaline, hearing the

soft footfalls of someone making a stealthy approach. They were coming closer. He snatched up a rock and crouched, ready to brain the first person to try to crawl into his hideaway.

The footsteps stopped.

"Come out with your hands over your head!" yelled a gruff male voice. Ethan recognized it as that of one of the Apex agents who had searched for him.

He kept silent, rock at the ready. Let them come to him.

"This is your last chance!" shouted the agent.

Ethan didn't move or speak. Inwardly, he cursed himself for not having gone farther away, or found a better hiding place, or one with a second exit, or—

A familiar metal object was tossed into the cave: a flashbang grenade. Ethan dropped the rock and dove for it, intending to throw it back at them.

It went off in his hand.

The brilliant flash of light blinded him, and the bang left him deaf. He fell to his knees, dizzy and reeling. He'd seen the effect of stun grenades before, and knew that the shock wave disturbed the fluid in the inner ears, giving people vertigo. But he'd never had one go off that close to him before. Though he knew why everything seemed to be whirling and pitching around him, he couldn't do anything about it but grit his teeth and wait for it to wear off. He couldn't fight; he couldn't even stand up.

Ethan was only vaguely aware of being pulled out of the cave, then dragged through the jungle. His ears were ringing like a fire alarm was going off in his head, and bright afterimages flashed every time he blinked.

By the time the dizziness wore off enough for him to become aware of his surroundings, he was halfway across the airfield. He stayed limp, hoping they'd think he was still incapacitated, while he took in the situation.

It was still day; he must have been found soon after he'd hidden. Or maybe he'd been so exhausted that he'd slept through the night and into the day. Not knowing which it was made him feel even more disoriented.

He was held by two big guards, who were accompanied by four more. More guards had gathered by the entrance to the base, which he was being dragged to. Once he was inside, he'd undoubtedly be locked up.

Right now, he was being hauled past the plane he'd smuggled himself into. He wished like hell he knew how to fly. He'd been offered flying lessons once, but—

He broke off that painful line of thought. No point dwelling on what was past and gone. He had to take the one chance he had, which was to try to escape on foot, *now*.

Ethan kicked out, slamming his foot into the side of the kneecap of one of the men holding him. The guard went down with a yell of pain. The grip of the other guard loosened as he reacted in surprise. Ethan punched him in the solar plexus, dropping him to the ground, then bolted for the jungle.

He made it halfway across the airfield before the guards caught up with him. Ethan went down under the weight of them, his face slamming into the concrete. The guards dragged him upright, then slammed him against the nearest plane. This time a guard held his feet. He struggled, but in vain. He was far outnumbered and still feeling the effects of the flashbang, in addition to his other injuries. Pain stabbed through his head, and he subsided, feeling dizzy and sick.

A tall man stepped in front of him, rubbing his chin. Glancing at the name on his uniform, he said, "Ethan McNeil."

Ethan recognized the voice. It was Ayers, the man who'd seemed to be in charge of the agents who'd captured his fire team. "We thought we'd lost you. Thanks for coming all the way here. Now we have the complete team, just like we'd intended in the first place."

"I've already radioed for air support," Ethan said. "You'd better start running now if you want to have any chance of getting away."

Ayers smiled. "Good try. But if you'd radioed anyone, we'd have detected it. Now, how did you get here?"

Ethan didn't reply.

"Kritsick!" Ayers snapped his fingers at the man beside him. "Hurt him."

Kritsick punched Ethan in the mouth. Pain exploded through his head, and he felt his lip split. Warm blood trickled down his chin.

You'll have to do better than that, Ethan thought.

Getting punched in the face was no fun, but it wasn't as if he'd never been knocked around before. In fact, that hadn't even hurt more than his head already hurt from the concussion. He was tempted to say so, but decided keeping his mouth shut was the better part of valor.

"Not like that," Ayers said, sounding exasperated. "You think a Recon Marine can't take a punch?"

Ethan saw something in his captor's eyes that unnerved him. It wasn't sadism; Ayers didn't seem to be getting any particular enjoyment out of the situation. It was a total lack of feeling. This was a man who might do absolutely anything to anyone without flinching or caring at all, so long as it got him what he wanted.

Still, presumably they wanted Ethan for the same reason they'd captured the rest of his team: to force him to work for them. They couldn't damage him too much, or he'd be useless to them. But that thought didn't reassure him. There was plenty of damage that could be done that wasn't physical and wouldn't impair his usefulness. You only had to take one look at Shane to know that.

Ayers leaned in close. As if he'd read Ethan's mind, he said, "We can break you without damaging your ultimate effectiveness. There's so much that can be done with very simple means. Water, electricity, loud noises. Or no noise, no light, nothing. Just you, alone in a dark silent cell, with no way to even tell how much time is passing. Everyone has a breaking point. We have your teammates, you know. How would you like to watch while I try to figure out theirs?"

Ethan's blood ran cold at the thought. He didn't particularly get along with them, but the thought of watching them being tortured made him feel sick. Trying for a bravado he didn't feel, he said, "Fuck those assholes. Do whatever you like to them. I don't care."

"Is that really how you feel?" Ayers rubbed his chin. "We could find out."

Some treacherous part of him said, *Just tell him you hid in the cargo bay. What does it matter?*

Another part forced him to keep his mouth shut. He'd been trained for exactly this kind of situation. Once you started talking, you didn't stop. The best thing to do was to delay that moment as long as possible.

The two men stared into each other's eyes, neither backing down. Finally, Ayers broke eye contact, shaking his head in disappointment. "Fine. We'll start with one of the simple means. Lay him on his back."

The guards forced Ethan down and pinned him to the ground. The concrete was hot against his back, the sky a sheet of blue-white glare. They were holding his head in place, so he closed his eyelids, all but a crack, against the sun.

Ayers knelt down beside him, fishing in his pocket. Despite Ethan's resolve, fear cramped his belly. He knew Ayers wanted him to wonder what he'd pull out, but that didn't make him stop wondering.

"What are you waiting for?" Ayers inquired, pausing in his

search. "Sooner or later, you'll talk. Might as well be sooner. No one's going to swoop down and save you."

I know, Ethan thought.

In the corner of his eye, he saw Ayers take out a pocket knife. Ethan took a deep breath, held fast to his resolve, and kept his gaze fixed on the sky. It was cloudless, featureless except for a black dot. He'd focus on that, no matter what Ayers did to him, and distract himself by trying to figure out what it was. Might be a hawk... No, it was too big for that. A hawk wouldn't be visible that far up in the sky. A vulture, maybe.

Sharp pain stabbed through Ethan's hand, jolting him all the way up and down his spine. He forced himself not to flinch. The black dot. It was getting bigger. The vulture must have spotted something. Another stab of pain. His jaw was clenched so tight, it hurt.

The black dot was even bigger now. It wasn't a bird at all. It was a small plane, coming in fast. A two-person plane, like Destiny occasionally rented to fly for fun. She'd taken him up for a spin once, and he'd had to sit on his hands to stop himself from leaning over and kissing her. She'd offered to teach him to fly, and he'd meant to take her up on the offer, but he'd deployed before he could get the chance.

The plane came close enough to hear the faint roar of its engine.

Ayers looked up, and unfeigned shock spread over his face. "That's not one of ours!"

A wild hope made Ethan's heart leap. Seizing the opportunity, he said, "I told you I radioed for help."

He had the satisfaction of seeing a flash of panic in Ayers's cold eyes. "Vega, Jeffries, get the prisoner inside and lock him up! Park, sound the alarm! Kritsick, get me an RPG! I'll shoot that thing out of the sky!"

Two of the guards yanked Ethan up. He fought as hard as

he could, kicking, head-butting, foot-stomping. Another two guards were forced to join the fray just to hold him in place.

The plane was a black silhouette against the brilliant desert sky, but he could see now that it had a single pilot. Ayers drew a pistol and took careful aim. With a burst of strength, Ethan got one arm loose and lashed out, knocking the gun from Ayers's hand. The shot went wild.

Another gunshot sounded, and one of the guards holding Ethan collapsed. As the grip of the other guards loosened in shock, Ethan broke free, snatched the gun from the downed guard's holster, and fired at Ayers. Kritsick lunged for him as he did so, grabbing for his gun. Ethan knocked the man aside, but his hand was jostled and he missed the shot. The bullet ricocheted off the concrete.

The plane was coming in for a landing. Ethan bolted toward it.

"Ethan! Hurry!" The pilot's voice was hard to hear over the roar of the engine, but he recognized it nonetheless.

It can't be...

But it was. As Ethan reached the plane, he looked up, incredulous, into Destiny's warm brown eyes.

CHAPTER 7

*D*estiny had followed that strange inner conviction all the way to India, where it had become a directional pull. *Ethan's in trouble*, it told her. *That way.*

If she was losing her mind anyway, she might as well be crazy in style. She'd rented a small private plane and started flying *that way*. She'd worried about crossing the border into Pakistan, but that wasn't where her directional sense led her. Instead, it sent her farther into India, and away from cities, towns, and villages. The terrain got wilder and wilder, shifting from scrubby hills to forest to jungle. And then the pull shifted as well, from forward to downward.

Here, that inner sense told her. *Ethan's here.*

And he was.

He was battered, bruised, and bloody. His uniform was torn and muddy, and he looked pale and exhausted. But he was alive.

She threw open the door and helped him scramble into the passenger seat. He slammed the door and turned around, firing his gun in rapid succession.

They were taking fire, too. What in the world was going on?

Well, she wasn't going to waste time wondering. Destiny accelerated for a take-off. "Buckle up!"

Ethan fumbled to do so. When she took a quick glance at him, she saw that he wasn't just distracted by providing covering fire; his left hand was bleeding. She snapped the restraint into place.

"Thanks, mudpuppy."

"Any time, jarhead."

The plane lifted off and began rapidly gaining altitude. Just a few seconds more, and they'd be out of range of gunfire…

"Evasive maneuvers!" Ethan yelled. "They've got an RPG!"

Adrenaline flooded her system as she swung the plane sharply around. Even a glancing strike from a rocket-propelled grenade would take down this little civilian aircraft. It was intended for fun, not for war.

A black streak of a missile barely missed the wing. She veered away. An instant later, the grenade exploded in midair in a burst of flame. The shockwave buffeted the tiny plane, knocking it off-course. She struggled to regain control.

"Veer left!" Ethan shouted.

Destiny tried, but the plane responded just a hair too slowly. The second grenade clipped the right wingtip, sending the plane into a spiral dive.

She couldn't pull it up. Nothing seemed to be responding. Her heart pounding, she began to pray aloud as she wrestled with the controls.

A warm, strong palm pressed into her back. Calmly, Ethan said, "You've got this, Destiny. We're out of range now. Just fly the plane."

Her panic receded. She *did* know how to deal with this. Taking a deep breath, she managed to get control of the plane and pull it out of the dive. Compensating for the damaged wing, she sent the plane skimming over the jungle, back the way she'd come. After a few tense moments, she was able to relax. The plane might not be in the best of shape, but it should get them back.

"No pursuit," Ethan reported as he peered back. "I think they might've had to go fetch the pilots, and by then we were out of sight."

"Who were those people?" Destiny asked. "They didn't look Indian."

"They're not," Ethan replied. "I'm pretty sure they're Apex."

"What?" She groaned. "Them again! I thought we were done with them."

"Not quite yet." He quickly described what had happened to him and his team.

"Those bastards," Destiny swore. "Don't worry, Ethan, we'll rescue your men before Apex can do anything to them. We'll call in my team as soon as we get to the airport. I don't want to risk it now. Apex is probably monitoring all frequencies, trying to figure out where we are."

"Good plan." He sounded more tired than relieved.

She glanced at him. He had his forearm pressed to his side, bracing it. She knew that position all too well. "Did you break some ribs?"

"Cracked, maybe. It's no big deal. I'll be fine once I tape them."

She also knew the automatic dismissal of any injuries that weren't literally incapacitating. He'd said he'd hit his head and been unconscious for a while after he fell into the river, so he must have a concussion too. Once they got to the airport, she'd radio Protection, Inc., then drag him to a doctor and have him looked over while they were waiting for her team to arrive.

"Any other injuries you haven't bothered to mention?"

"Well, this, but you saw it already." He held up his left hand. The fingertips were bloody and bruised. It looked incredibly painful.

"Did someone stomp on it?"

"Nah. Stuck a knife under my fingernails."

Destiny saw red. "Who did that?"

"Some guy named Ayers. He was the leader of the group that ambushed my team."

"I'll kill him," Destiny swore.

"My team, my hand. I get dibs."

"That's fair," she said reluctantly. "Man, Ethan. You've really had a rough day."

He chuckled. "It improved a lot once you showed up. Hey, how'd you know to come here?"

She was incredibly tempted to lie. If it hadn't been for the extremely recent proof that she was absolutely terrible at it, and also for the fact that she couldn't think of anything even remotely plausible, she would have. Instead, she confessed, "I know how weird this will sound, but I had a feeling you were in trouble, and I followed it here. I flew into India—"

"Is that where we are?"

"Yeah. I told my team I was going there on vacation. I didn't bring any backup because I thought I was out of my mind."

"Huh. Well, you were right. I'm glad you trusted yourself enough to come. Nothing like that ever happened before?"

She shook her head. "Not remotely. In fact—"

The engine sputtered, sounding like a car running low on fuel. Destiny checked the fuel gauge, and was baffled to see it reading almost empty.

"Can't be," she muttered to herself. "It should have enough for four more hours!"

Then, with a sickening lurch in the pit of her stomach,

she realized that shrapnel from the wingtip must have pierced the fuel tank. They'd been losing fuel as they flew, but it had blended invisibly with the water vapor and exhaust, so she hadn't noticed.

"Fuel tank's hit," she said. "I have to make an emergency landing. See anything flat?"

"Just a lot of trees."

"We've got about five more minutes," Destiny said, trying to keep her voice steady. They had very little chance of surviving a crash into a lot of trees.

She scanned for anything but the dark green of thick jungle. Then she spotted an area of lighter green. It might just be a different type of tree, but it was the only thing she saw that even had a chance of being flat. She turned the plane toward it.

The engine sputtered and choked. Her heart sped up as she realized that they were going to go down in that light green area, whatever it was.

"Ethan, brace," she ordered. "We're going down."

"But you—" he protested.

"I will too, but not yet. You brace now!"

"You can do this." He cupped her cheek in one warm hand, letting her draw strength and courage from his trust. Then he braced his knees and elbows, and buried his face in his arms.

She could see the light green now, a small glade within the jungle. It would be a hard landing to make and they'd hit some trees for sure, but it was just barely possible. Destiny kept her touch light on the controls, tempted as she was to grab them hard. The plane bucked and lurched, and would have thrown them both out if they weren't strapped in.

Lightly, lightly, she thought. *Skim like a seagull over the water...*

She'd lied to Ethan, she realized. She wouldn't be able to land the plane and brace at the same time.

Keep the nose up, and touch down lightly, lightly, light as a feather...

The plane slammed into the ground, skidded to the side, and crashed into the trees. Her shoulder hit hard, then her head. She wasn't knocked unconscious, but she was dazed, unable to react quickly. White smoke rose up from the engine, then a tongue of orange flame.

I have to get out, she thought. *I have to get Ethan out.*

But she couldn't move. It was as if she was locked into a straightjacket.

Ethan moved fast enough for both of them. He unsnapped his belt, reached over and unsnapped hers, and tried to yank her out of her seat. But she was stuck tight. Crumpled metal had folded over her chest and knees. Her arms were pinned, so she couldn't exert any leverage to free herself.

Swearing, he pulled harder. She didn't budge. Then he fumbled under the seat, yanked out a crowbar from the tool storage compartment, and used that to pry the sheet metal away from her body.

The flames were coming closer. The heat was searing. Sweat poured down her face and chest. The plane could go up in a fireball at any second.

"Get out, Ethan," Destiny begged him. "Forget me. Save yourself!"

"No!" Ethan yelled. "Never!"

He gave a desperate wrench with the crowbar, and the sheet metal moved. Destiny pushed with her feet as he wrapped his arms around her body and pulled. Her shirt tore and her skin was scraped, but she came free.

Together they leaped from the burning plane. Ethan tugged her toward the safety of the trees, but she saw her backpack dangling from the wreckage. It had survival equipment in it that they'd need. She grabbed it and yanked. It had been snagged on a sharp piece of metal and tore open, spilling some of its contents into the fire. She tucked it under her arm, clamping down on the torn part to prevent anything else from falling out, and bolted with him.

They got three steps into the jungle when the plane blew up. The shockwave of heated air knocked them both sprawling. Destiny looked back, worried that they'd have to get up and run if it started a forest fire. But the jungle was too damp for that, and there had been very little fuel left in the plane. The fireball went out, and the few patches of flame on the ground flickered, then died. In minutes, nothing was left but blackened metal and singed moss.

They lay in a tangle on the mossy ground, shaking with spent adrenaline. Ethan was pale beneath his tan, and the wounds in his head and hand were bleeding again. When he wrapped his arms around her, he left smears of blood on her skin.

"You're safe," he whispered. "You're safe. I thought you'd never come free."

"You saved me."

"*You* saved *me*."

She sighed, letting her head rest on his shoulder. It felt like something forbidden—don't touch if you can't commit—but his solid muscle and warmth was so comforting, and the rise and fall of his chest reassured her that he was safe and alive.

Destiny would have liked to lie there indefinitely, but they hadn't flown all that far, and if she'd seen a landing area, any pursuit from Apex could have too.

As if Ethan had read her mind, he said, "I hate to say it, but we'd better get moving. That wreck is going to look like a bulls-eye from above."

They reluctantly scrambled up. Ethan went back to the burned-out plane to see if he could salvage anything useful. While he was cautiously poking through the wreckage, Destiny did an inventory of what remained in the backpack. She still had several changes of clothes—the least important thing in it, though she couldn't help being glad that she wouldn't have to wear filthy rags around Ethan—a survival blanket, a compass, a lighter, a tiny sewing kit, a canteen, some granola bars, and a lightweight tin pot for boiling water. The medical kit was still there, but it had come open and most of the supplies were gone.

That was it. She'd lost her cell phone, most of her food and water, and her ammo box. The only bullets she had left were the ones remaining in the magazine.

And she'd lost her box of pills.

Her hand flew to her bra, where she always kept a few days' emergency supply in a watertight packet. Her shirt had been ripped open, and her bra was torn as well. Fiona's GPS transmitter was gone. And so were her pills.

The fear Destiny had felt at the thought that the plane would crash was nothing to the fear she felt now. She frantically patted herself all over, then retraced their steps from the plane at a crawl, searching for the little packet of gray-green capsules in the dark green moss. But it was nowhere to be found. It and the transmitter must have fallen to the floor of the plane when Ethan had dragged her from the wreckage, and been consumed in the fireball. Just like the box that had fallen from her backpack.

They were lost in the wilderness, probably being pursued by deadly enemies, and the one way her team could have found her had just been destroyed. And now the time bomb inside her had begun to tick.

Ethan looked up from his search of the wreckage. All he'd

found that had survived the fireball was the crowbar and a hammer.

"Think we can use this?" he asked, holding up the hammer.

"I guess we could hit someone over the head with it." She was amazed at how normal her voice sounded. Maybe she wasn't such a bad liar after all...

He frowned. "Destiny? Is something wrong? I mean apart from, well, everything."

She bit her lip. The absolute last thing she wanted him to know was what a freak she was—a literal freak, a freak of nature. But if she didn't tell him, he'd find out for himself, and that would be worse. She might even become a danger to him.

"I... I lost something." She indicated her torn shirt, only belatedly realizing that she was displaying quite a lot of cleavage. Ethan grinned. "Not my bra. My medication. I had some in my duffel bag, but it fell out. And some in my shirt, but that's gone too."

His smile faded. "Was that the, uh, female problem stuff? Is it dangerous for you to not take it? Or just unpleasant?"

He was probably imagining horrible cramps or nonstop bleeding. She *wished* it was just that. And she really didn't want to have to explain then and there. She could wait another day, at least. Probably a couple. Maybe by then they'd be able to radio for help, and he'd never need to know. "It won't kill me. Let's not talk about it, it's embarrassing."

"No problem. But let me know if you need, I don't know, a massage or a hot pack or anything. I promise not to ask any questions."

Good, he did think it was cramps. And also, how sweet of him to offer! She was tempted to request a massage, just because. "Thanks. Where are you going to find a hot pack in the jungle, jarhead?"

"A Marine can improvise. Got any MREs in your backpack? I could use the heating element."

"Ugh, no. I had some actual food, but most of it fell out. Want a granola bar?"

"I'm okay. I had a country captain chicken MRE earlier."

"Yecch. Better you than me. Want some aspirin?"

"Yes, please."

He looked over her half-empty medical kit with mild dismay, then shrugged and swallowed a few aspirin.

"The medical tape's still there," she said. "Shall I tape your ribs?"

He looked tempted, but shook his head. "Later. Let's get some distance between us and the plane first. The last time I tried to hide out from Apex, I didn't go far enough. And look what happened." He held up his bloody, swollen left hand.

Destiny inwardly renewed her vow to kill the bastard who had tortured him.

They began to make their way through the forest, not heading in any particular direction other than "away from the very conspicuous crash site." The jungle terrain wasn't easy to walk in. They kept having to step over fallen trees, walk around bushes, and shove through thick vines that hung from the trees like spiderwebs. Monkeys chattered and swung from the vines, birds chirped and sang in the trees, and black millipedes the size of snakes scuttled away from their feet.

Normally she would have enjoyed a good hike through rough and interesting terrain, especially with Ethan. But she had no attention to spare for anything but looking out for danger, worrying about the loss of her pills, and trying to get as far away from the crash site as fast as possible so they could stop and she could tend to his injuries as best she could with her limited supplies. From Ethan's silence, she suspected that he was equally wrapped up in worries, probably over his buddies.

After about an hour, she saw that he was pale beneath his tan, and had his jaw clenched so tight that it was probably giving him a headache. Despite the aspirin, he was obviously still in a lot of pain.

"Let's take a rest," she said. "Just a short one. Take off your shirt."

"You move fast," he teased, then gritted his teeth as he started to pull it off. It clearly hurt like hell for him to try to lift his arms above his head.

She helped ease off the shirt. His muscular chest and arms were covered with a striking pattern of abstract tattoos. But much as she'd wanted for years to get a look at him shirtless, she couldn't take the time to appreciate the view now. His side was covered with a huge bruise nearly as black as the tattoos, making her wince in sympathetic pain. No wonder he'd been clutching his side!

She taped his ribs, and was glad to hear him sigh in relief when she was done.

"Thanks," he said. "That's better."

All the same, he winced as he tried to get his shirt back on. She helped him tug it over his arms and chest. And there went her chance to look at them. Oh well. It would only frustrate her to look but not touch.

Ethan's voice interrupted her reverie on his body. "Hey—I hate to ask, but would you mind if I carried your gun? You can turn into a tiger, so..."

"Yeah, you're right. That evens up the firepower." She handed it over, wondering at herself as she did so. Tiger or not, she'd normally hate to go unarmed when there might be armed enemies after them. But giving up her weapon to Ethan didn't make her feel any less safe. In fact, she felt *more* safe knowing that he was watching her back.

"How far are we from civilization?" Ethan asked. "Apex doesn't count."

"No, I'd hardly call them civilized. By foot, at least a couple days. Hiking over this terrain, with hills and valleys and all, might be more like a week." Anxiety made her belly clench. A week without her pills!

He also looked worried. "I think we should go back. God knows what Apex might do to my men in a week. But I think we're only a day or two away from their base."

She calculated the time they'd spent in the plane, and nodded. "Yeah, I think so too."

"Between you and me and your gun, we could ambush some guards and break into the base. Even if we can't break anyone else out, if we get to a radio, we could call for help."

"Sounds good," she said with relief. One or two days without her pills—she should be able to handle that. And then he'd never need to know. "Let's make a wide circle, so we don't run into anyone who finds the crash site, and start making our way back to the base. We can camp out in the jungle tonight, and hopefully we'll be there the day after."

They used her compass and recollected flight path to figure out which way the base was, and set off. Despite the urgency of their situation, she couldn't help enjoying walking through the jungle with him. She could almost imagine that they were dating, maybe hiking on the adventure vacation she was supposedly on.

Yeah, she sighed to herself. *Wouldn't that be nice.*

They camped at dusk. Not daring to make a fire lest the smoke or light should draw pursuers, they shared out the granola bars and some water, leaving enough for the next day.

Destiny could have eaten their entire supply of granola bars and had room for more—she could've eaten a country captain chicken MRE, and been grateful to have it—but Ethan only nibbled at his, then set it aside.

"Don't save it for me," she said. "You need your strength."

"I ate earlier, remember? I'll finish it for breakfast." He stuffed it in his pocket, then leaned against a tree. "I'll take first watch."

She lay down beneath the survival blanket, but sleep didn't come easily. Every time she started to drift off, something would awaken her, some screeching monkey or yelping creature or worrying thought.

Tomorrow would be her first full day without her pill since she'd been eleven. She'd never had a problem taking them in the Army—she'd gotten a note from a helpful doctor claiming they *were* for female problems. Plenty of women took actual birth control pills for those exact reasons, and she wasn't the only one who was careful to keep extra stashes in case of emergencies. She thought nothing much would happen in one day, but the truth was that she didn't know how long she could go, and she didn't want to find out the hard way. Maybe she should tell him…

…only Ethan had enough problems, didn't he, without also having to worry about her? He should have been starving after hiking all day, no matter how much he'd eaten earlier. He was probably in so much pain that it had spoiled his appetite. She should have pushed him to take more aspirin. But they didn't have much left. Maybe he was right to save it for later. At least *he* had some pills, even if they weren't much…

Fear stabbed unexpectedly through her heart. What if she hurt him?

I won't, Destiny told herself fiercely. *I'll feel it coming. If I feel like I can't control myself, I'll just run off into the jungle. Anyway, it's just one day. Maybe two. That's all…*

"Destiny?" Ethan had his hand on her shoulder. The night

was dark, but she could see his pale face in the moonlight. "Your watch."

"Thanks. See anything?"

"A snake or two. Looked like they were headed out to cuddle up with you."

"Ugh!"

He chuckled. "I shooed them away."

"Appreciate it. Get some sleep. I'll keep the snakes off."

He curled up under the blanket. In the quiet of the jungle night, she could easily hear the slight roughness of his breathing.

He's not just injured, he's sick, she thought. Coming down with a cold or something. Not surprising after he got chucked into a river… Still, poor Ethan! He ought to be in bed with chicken soup. Once they finished their mission and got back home, she'd make him some herself…

…but no, he was still on active duty. He'd have to go straight back to his unit, with barely a chance to say goodbye, and definitely none to wait around for six-hour chicken stock to finish simmering on her stove.

She sighed. Well, he'd go straight to the infirmary, and be taken care of even if she couldn't do it herself. Destiny pulled the blanket a little closer around her shoulders and resumed her watch.

In the morning, Ethan once again tried to stuff his granola bar in his pocket. He caught her raised eyebrows and flushed, guilty as a kid with his hand in the cookie jar. "I'm just not hungry."

"You are *not* trying to hike all day on an empty stomach. You'll keel over. Look, I know you're not feeling great—"

"I'm fine," he said instantly.

She went on as if he hadn't spoken. "But you have to eat. Take some more aspirin."

He shook out a few more, swallowed them, then finished

the granola bar, chewing and swallowing as if he had a gun to his head. "Let's go."

They took a compass bearing, then set out. The jungle noises seemed oddly sharp, colors unusually bright, smells extra-distinct. Had everything been this... *vivid*... the day before?

You're imagining things, Destiny said to herself. She didn't dare address her tiger.

For a few hours, they made good time. Then she noticed that Ethan was slowing down. She took a closer look at him. He was sweating, which wasn't surprising in the jungle heat, but his face was pale.

"Let's take a break," she suggested.

"I'm fine," he said.

"You don't look fine, jarhead."

"I'm *fine*," he insisted, then broke into a coughing fit that nearly doubled him over.

"Sit down. You need a break."

"I'll be fine." He straightened up, swayed, then braced his feet firmly on the ground. "Come on."

"How much good are you going to be breaking into the base if you're sick and—"

His eyes widened in alarm at something he saw over her shoulder. "Drop!"

As he snatched her gun from his belt, she threw herself to the ground. There was a gunshot, the sound of something breaking, and a yell.

"Freeze!" a male voice shouted.

She looked up. One of the men who'd been manhandling Ethan at the airfield was holding a pistol on her. Ethan had her gun aimed at him. A tranquilizer rifle with a shattered stock lay on the ground between them. Destiny supposed Ethan had shot it right out of their attacker's hands.

"Good shot, Ethan," she said.

"Not really," he replied, not taking his gaze off the enemy. "I should've gone for his head."

"I guess you're from Apex," said Destiny to their enemy. "Give it up. You're outnumbered. Ethan's got a gun and I can turn into a tiger."

"Try it," the Apex agent replied. "I can shoot it in the head before it can spring. McNeil, drop your weapon."

"*You* drop *your* weapon, Kritsick," Ethan retorted.

Neither of them moved.

Rip his throat out!

Her tiger's snarl was so unexpected and vicious that Destiny barely repressed a start.

He's got a gun aimed at my head, Destiny replied silently.

Her tiger snarled again, long and low and predatory. *We can move faster than a puny human. Rip out his throat and drink his blood!*

Gross, Destiny replied. *Stop talking. You're distracting me. Don't worry, we'll get our chance to fight.*

Kritsick broke the silence. "Ever heard of a daeodon?"

"No," said Destiny. "Ever heard of a Sig Sauer? That's what Ethan has aimed at your head. He's a Recon Marine; he won't miss. Kneel down and put your hands on your head."

The Apex agent went on as if she hadn't spoken. "It's an extinct mammal from the Miocene era. A wild boar the size of a rhinoceros. They call them 'hell pigs.'"

"So?" Destiny inquired. "You got one on a leash?"

Kritsick bared his teeth in a nasty smile. "I'm a daeodon shifter. My hell pig gives no quarter. You two surrender now, and I'll take you in safe and sound. Make me show you my daeodon, and you come in trampled or chomped or tusked half to death. Or all the way to death. He's a little hard to control."

"Destiny?" Ethan called. "Is there even such a thing as extinct animal shifters?"

"I came across one once," she admitted. "A saber-tooth tiger. He was running a gang in Santa Martina. I've never heard of any other extinct shifters before. We only found out what he was when he shifted and bit Rafa. I shifted and bit him, and he took off. Never saw him again."

"Hugo O'Dell?" inquired Kritsick.

"Yeah," Destiny said. "That's the guy."

"He was one of ours. An early experiment, back when we were using common criminals." The agent gave a humorless chuckle. "He made the mistake of running away from us. We took care of him. Now do you believe me?"

"Who cares," Ethan said. "If you don't get down on your knees right now, you're a dead man. Your hell pig can't survive a bullet in the head."

"Sure it can," said Kritsick, and shifted.

One moment Destiny was looking at a man in jungle fatigues; the next instant, she was faced by the hell pig. Just like he'd said, it was a wild boar the size of a rhinoceros. But he hadn't mentioned the bulging armor plates around its face, the ivory tusks, or the maddened red eyes. She'd never seen anything like it, saber tooth tiger included. That had just seemed like an unusual type of big cat. This was a true monster, a prehistoric beast that should never walk the earth.

Ethan didn't flinch. His gun was already leveled at the beast, and he fired. There was no way he could have missed—not him, not with a creature that size and at that distance.

But the hell pig only shook itself. If the bullets had wounded it, Destiny sure couldn't see any blood. It let out a ferocious bellow, pawed the ground, and charged straight at her.

Destiny wasted no time waiting for it. She summoned her tiger—was it her imagination, or did the big cat seem to spring eagerly to the forefront?—and leaped over the charging daeodon's head. Four tiger paws landed on its back.

She tried to dig in her claws, but they scrabbled uselessly over its back. It seemed to have some sort of armor just below its skin. Her claws left bleeding scratches, but they were very shallow. She couldn't even get enough of a grip to hold on.

She bent her head and closed her strong tiger's jaws over the back of the hell pig's neck, and bit down as hard as she could. But her teeth met the same resistance her claws had. She left shallow scratches, no more.

The hell pig let out a bellow and shook itself. Destiny went flying, and slammed into a tree. The impact left her breathless on the ground.

The daeodon turned, swinging its heavy head from side to side. A long rope of saliva dangled from its tusked jaws.

Yecch, Destiny thought. *What's worse than getting tusked to death by a prehistoric pig? Getting drooled on by a prehistoric pig,* then *tusked to death.*

Ethan fired at the thing, three times in rapid succession. She hadn't been counting the shots, but he couldn't have many left. And he was wasting them. The hell pig just twitched its flanks like it was beset by flies.

She shifted back to her woman's form and shouted, "Stop! It has armor!"

Ethan stopped shooting. She was going to suggest that he climb a tree when he bolted toward her. The short run took way more out of him than it should have, leaving him gasping. But he stood over her, feet braced, face white, her Sig Sauer aimed straight at the hell pig.

The daeodon looked from him to her. Its little piggy eyes gleamed red with triumph. It snorted, then bellowed. And then two thousand pounds of prehistoric monster came straight at them, shaking the earth beneath its cloven hooves.

Because Destiny was so close, she could see the adjustment Ethan made to his aim. He breathed out, and didn't breathe in lest even that disturb his aim. Then he fired.

Two thousand pounds of prehistoric monster crashed down dead at his feet.

For a moment, even the jungle seemed to hold its breath with Ethan. Then he breathed in, and the trees exploded with the cries of birds and screeches of monkeys. She gave a quick glance at the hell pig to make sure it was really dead. It was. Ethan had hit it in the tiny, piggy eye—a one-in-a-million shot at such a small target, and a moving target at that.

"That was one hell of a shot," said Destiny. "Good work, jarhead."

Ethan started to reply, but a coughing fit cut him off. He took a step toward her, then swayed like he was about to pass out.

"Ethan!" She scrambled to put her arm around him and support him. He was still holding the gun, which she gently took from his hand and replaced in her holster. He leaned his cheek against hers. It felt like he'd just pulled his head out of an oven.

He took a deep breath, then straightened. "Sorry. I'm all right. Just got a bit dizzy for a second."

"You are absolutely not all right," Destiny retorted. "You're burning up. What do you have? Some kind of tropical bug?"

"I doubt it. It wasn't tropical where I came from." Reluctantly, he said, "When I got tossed in the river, I was unconscious for a while. I breathed in a lot of river water, and then I lay in it for hours. I guess I caught a cold."

"Uh-huh. That wouldn't give you a fever like that. I think it might be pneumonia."

Ethan stepped away from her, then staggered. He compromised by leaning against a tree. "Does it matter what it is?"

Destiny had obviously spent way too much time with paramedics: Shane and Justin and Catalina on her team, and of course Ellie. She'd learned more than she'd ever wanted to know about all sorts of nasty illnesses just from being in the same room while they were chatting. As a result, she had two different answers to his question, and she didn't like either of them.

"Yes, it matters. A cold will go away on its own. If it's pneumonia, you probably need antibiotics."

"Do we have antibiotics?"

She went to her backpack and rummaged through the medicine kit. "Not anymore."

Having to go through her clothes reminded her that she was naked. And she'd been cuddling Ethan while she was naked. She'd been so worried about him that it had barely registered, but one glance up at his appreciative face showed that it was registering with *him*. Her face flamed, and not from fever. She scrambled into some clothes.

"And the other thing," she said once she was dressed. "If it is pneumonia, that's serious. You need to rest, not trek through the jungle all day and then stage a raid on an enemy base."

He shrugged. "Whatever it is, we can't stay here. They've obviously tracked us down. What if the hell pig has ten little piggy buddies?"

"Can't be close ones, or they'd already be here." But she agreed with Ethan. "Let me grab his gun... oh."

Unlike ordinary shifters like herself, the daeodon shifter hadn't shredded his clothing when he'd shifted. His clothes were simply gone. The saber tooth tiger Destiny had fought in Santa Martina had also transformed without losing his clothes, and reappeared in human form fully dressed. Lucas, a dragon shifter, could do that too, and even take small items like his hoard bag—or a gun—with him. Sure enough, though the broken tranquilizer rifle Kritsick had dropped still lay on the ground, the pistol he'd held when he'd transformed was gone.

"Goddammit," Destiny muttered, returning to Ethan. "We could've really used the ammo. Though since you can drop a charging hell pig with one bullet, maybe we don't need a lot more. I still can't believe we fought a *hell pig.*"

"Me neither."

"And you're right, we don't want to meet his buddies, if he has any. Lean on me." She offered him her shoulder. When he hesitated, she said, "If I were sick, you'd let me lean on you, right?"

"Wouldn't have to. I'd carry you," he muttered, but put his arm around her shoulders. For the sake of his pride, she neglected to point out that with her shifter strength, she was quite capable of carrying him, though probably not for a long distance.

"I don't think we should head for the base," Destiny said. "Not quite yet. Not if they've got people this hot on our tail. We'd probably get caught in a pincer: one group behind us, and one group ahead."

"And I'm in no shape for it. I admit it. I'm not *that* proud."

"*That* proud is just another word for stupid." She pointed at a stream. "Let's get our feet wet. Kill the scent."

He nodded, and they took off their shoes, tied them around their necks by the laces, and waded into the stream. It turned into a wider creek, then split off into tributaries. Every time it forked, she took a branch at random. They were risking getting hopelessly lost, but they had to shake off their pursuit, and shifters were liable to track them by scent.

She was sure he was trying to take as much of his own weight as he could, but his arm was heavy across her shoulders, and his body was like a furnace. Every now and then, he broke into a cough that sounded like something was tearing inside his chest.

Despite the heat of the jungle, Destiny felt cold. Ethan was dangerously ill, they had no medicine, they were pursued by dangerous and powerful enemies, and they were hundreds of miles from help.

And she was about to lose control.

CHAPTER 8

*E*than's head was swimming, but he gritted his teeth and forced himself to stay on his feet. He might be useless when it came to protecting Destiny, but at least he wouldn't let himself become a liability. He was so focused on forward momentum that he almost pitched over when she came to a stop.

They were standing at yet another fork in the stream. One ran down a steep hill over a bed of slimy-looking green rocks. The other vanished into a dark, ominous-looking cave. He didn't like the look of either route.

"Downhill, we break our necks," he muttered. "Into the cave, and we get eaten by a grue."

Destiny's clear laugh made him feel better, just by hearing it and knowing that whatever else happened, she was at his side. "Why am I not surprised that you play dorky old computer games like Zork, nerd boy?"

"Why am I not surprised that you recognized the Zork quote, nerd girl?" Studying the routes more closely, he said, "There's no water coming out of the cave, so it has to go somewhere. I vote we face the grue."

"Better than the hell hog."

Destiny passed him her flashlight, and he lit the way as they ventured into the cave. The rippling stream echoed eerily across the black and empty space, which smelled strongly of earth and moss and bats. When he shone the light upward, a thousand pinpoint red eyes stared back at him, and the flock of roosting bats chittered angrily. He quickly moved the beam back down to the ground.

"Thanks a lot," Destiny said. "I'm much happier now that I know there's about a million rabid bats nesting ten feet over our head."

"Would you rather have them lurking on the ceiling and not know they're there?"

"Yes. Yes, I would."

They followed the twisty tunnel downhill until it suddenly dead-ended in a pool. Ethan shone his flashlight on a wall of solid stone.

"Oh, damn," she said. "Worst of both worlds: we have go back past the bats again, then down the slippery slope, *and* we lose time."

"That doesn't make sense," he said, more to himself than her. "Water flows in but not out. It has to go somewhere."

"Down? The pool must be deeper than it looks. Or maybe there's some tiny crack in the wall, below the surface, and it flows out from there."

"Or maybe that's not a wall," Ethan said slowly. "Let's keep walking. I want to see it closer up."

The cold water was ankle deep, then calf-deep, then knee-deep by the time they reached the wall on the other side. Ethan felt so hot that he would have expected it to feel refreshing, but instead he felt simultaneously overheated and chilled: a deeply unpleasant combination. The only sensation that wasn't awful was the warmth and solid strength of Destiny's body next to his.

He reached out to run his hand over the wall.

It went through.

He felt as well as heard Destiny's soft gasp. But it was one of wonderment, not fear.

The "wall," he realized, was made of some kind of hanging lichen the same color as the cave itself. It hung in long narrow sheets, like flypaper, but appeared to be one solid mass until you actually touched it. Now that he was pushing one sheet aside, he could see more of the forest, the stream running along the moss...

...and a glint of gold.

Not metallic gold, but a warm smooth amber shade. Gemlike.

A golden city lay before them, nestled into the cup of the valley. Slender towers, delicate minarets, homes and temples and palaces and streets, were all carved from the same lovely amber stone. Ethan's heart leaped. This was no simple village, but a sophisticated city. It would have cell phones, a hospital, hot food and warm beds...

And then he registered the lack of human voices and saw the empty streets. Rainbow-colored parrots flew in and out of windows, monkeys swung from the arched bridges, and a tiny spotted deer bolted down a street, its hooves clattering. But there were no people. The city was deserted.

Destiny exclaimed, "The Golden City!"

"You know where we are?"

"Not exactly. But I know what it is. Hundreds of years ago, a maharajah—that's an Indian king—had a dream of building a golden city in the wilderness. He hired all the best architects and city planners and stonemasons, and they built this city. He was going to move his entire kingdom here. But before he could, he dropped dead of a heart attack. His son thought the whole thing was weird and impractical. He not only scrapped the plans to move the kingdom, he was so embarrassed by his dad's weird idea that he destroyed the maps showing where it was and banned it from even being mentioned. After a generation went by, no one knew where it was. Explorers have searched for it. But we're the first people to find it!"

"That's amazing," Ethan said. "History nerd. And the other nice thing about it is that if no one's found it yet, it's invisible from above."

Destiny nodded. "I'm pretty sure I flew right over it, and I didn't spot it. It must be completely hidden by the tree cover."

"I don't suppose the maharajah put in any beds before he dropped dead?" Ethan asked hopefully.

"Let's find out."

They pushed through the vines and stepped into the Golden City. Once he was actually in it, he could see that it hadn't been lived in for many years, if ever. Dry leaves blew across the roads, flowering vines twined up the towers, and the patches of greenery that he supposed had once been parks or gardens were tangled thickets. Ornamental ponds and fountains were still full of water, probably replenished by rain, but it was green and murky. Huge, bulgy-eyed frogs sat on lilypads and hung motionless in the water, then leaped away with shrill squeaks and plops when they came close.

But the marble itself was perfectly preserved, without cracks and or stains. Many buildings were beautifully carved, and the fountains were decorated with statues of lovely women, handsome warriors, or wild animals. The humid air was scented with the perfume of tropical flowers and the tangy scent of ripe fruit.

Ethan forgot his illness and exhaustion, and felt that he was walking through paradise with the one woman he'd want to share it with.

"Mangoes!" Destiny exclaimed with glee, pointing to a

tree laden with orange-yellow fruits. "Oh, I haven't had a good one since I was eleven. The ones you get in the US are from Mexico, not India, and they're just not the same."

Leaving Ethan sitting on a bench of golden marble, she ran to the tree, swung up into the branches with agility that reminded him of Merlin, plucked a few fruits, gracefully dropped back down, and sat beside him.

"Think you could eat something?" she asked.

He'd had no appetite for days, and when he'd forced down the granola bar, it had felt like sandpaper on his sore throat. But Destiny had been right that he had to keep his strength up. And though he still wasn't hungry, the mangoes smelled wonderful. He nodded.

She took out a pen knife, neatly cut one up, started to offer him a slice, then pulled it back. "Your hands."

Ethan glanced down at his hands. His left was covered with blood, the fingertips still swollen and painful, and his right was black with soot from rummaging through the burned-out wreckage of the plane. "Can't be helped."

"Sure it can." Destiny sliced off a smaller piece. "Open your mouth, jarhead."

Ethan opened his mouth. Though he saw it coming, he still couldn't quite believe it when Destiny put the chunk of mango between his lips. He had a wild temptation to catch her fingers in his mouth... but no. She'd said no. Nothing had changed since then.

He'd eaten mangoes before, but Destiny had been right: the ones in America weren't the same. This was soft and silken in his mouth, ripe and juicy, with a peach-like scent like that long-ago cobbler, but with a sweet and tangy flavor that was all its own.

Destiny sat there and fed him the entire mango, bite by bite, before she even tasted her own. She was just showing him a soldier's camaraderie, helping out a buddy who was hurt, he supposed. It shouldn't feel as tender, let alone as sensual and romantic, as it did. When he imagined himself doing something similar for any of his men in a similar predicament, though, he immediately thought of three or four different ways he could get them some mango without letting it touch their filthy hands, starting with handing them the knife so they could use it like a fork.

"Thanks." He felt awkward, because what he really wanted to thank her for was the exact thing he couldn't mention: her treating him like a lover rather than a buddy. To cover it up, he said, "So you've been to India before?"

She shot him a strangely nervous look, then nodded. "My family visited once, when I was a kid."

"That's a long way to go for a family vacation. Did your family have friends here?"

"Umm." Once again, she gave him that furtive look. It didn't suit her. "Not exactly. More like friends of friends. Hey, let's see if there's any clean water. A bath and bed would hit the spot, right?"

Ethan nodded, a little bewildered. Why was she acting so weirdly evasive about a childhood visit to India? The only times he'd ever seen her be anything less than completely straightforward were when they'd first met and she hadn't told him she was a shifter—but that had made perfect sense in retrospect—and when she'd been forced to mention her embarrassing female problem.

Which also made sense, he supposed. Women usually didn't like to talk about their periods with men. He hoped she wasn't going to come down with excruciating cramps. Though if she did, he hoped she wouldn't be too embarrassed to tell him. Maybe he could rub her stomach or apply hot compresses or even just distract her with conversation—whatever would make her feel better.

But what could possibly be embarrassing or a secret about a family vacation twenty years ago?

And, he suddenly realized, why in the world had she hiked with him in an Indian jungle for two days without ever mentioning that she'd been there before?

"Ah-ha," said Destiny, interrupting his thoughts. "I knew it. We have an actual bath!"

Ethan blinked down at a shallow swimming pool divided by a delicate sheet of thin marble. It was fed by the stream, and the water was clear and inviting.

"How'd you know there'd be something like this?"

"They were popular in India at the time this city was built, so I figured a maharajah would put one in. Look, it even has a privacy screen, so we can both bathe at the same time."

"I won't peek," Ethan promised, and looked away. But Destiny stuck around to help him pull off his boots, which was hard to do when it hurt to both use your left hand and bend over. He shooed her away before she could do more. "I got the rest."

He had to peel off his clothes, which were covered in mud and blood and river gunk. When he saw the disgusting heap they made, he felt bad for Destiny for having to touch them —and him. That bath was coming not a moment too soon.

He slid into the water. It was lukewarm, a little cooler than the air, but incredibly refreshing. When he sluiced off all the mud and dust and blood and river water, he felt as if he was also washing away his pain and weariness, leaving him clean in every way.

He could hear the cheerful splashes of Destiny bathing beside him, and see the shadows of her curvy body through the paper-thin marble. No details, or he'd have felt like he was spying and turned away; just the shape and movements of a gorgeous, sexy woman.

A gorgeous, sexy woman who doesn't want you, he reminded himself. *So hands off.*

He pulled his filthy camouflage uniform into the pool and scrubbed it against itself, watching as swirls of mud were caught by the current and rinsed away, leaving the water in the pool as clear as ever. When he was finally sure it was as clean as he could get it without soap, he laid it out on a sunny patch of marble. It would dry soon enough, and in the meantime, he could just stay in the water.

"Ethan?" Destiny called. "I'm going to poke around a bit. Do some reconnaissance. I'm leaving you the gun."

"Sure," he called back. "I can't get out anyway without flashing you and all the monkeys."

Her laugh echoed in his ears as her footsteps receded.

"Ethan? Hey! Ethan!"

He woke up, startled, and floundered for a moment before he remembered where he was. "Yeah?"

Destiny was crouched by the side of the pool, carefully staring out and over his head. "Your clothes are dry now. I'll just turn my back."

Ethan dragged himself out of the pool, feeling like he weighed as much as the hell pig. It took forever just to get dressed, and he was trembling from exhaustion by the time he was done.

"Okay," he said, still sitting by the edge of the pool.

Destiny turned around, and seemed to see him for the first time. Creases of concern appeared around her beautiful brown eyes. "I wish I hadn't left you here. I didn't think you'd just sit in the water this whole time!"

"I didn't mean to. I dozed off."

That only made her look more worried. "Ethan… Don't take this the wrong way, but you really don't look good."

He opened his mouth to deny it, then reconsidered. She was his friend and his partner on this mission. She needed to know what he was and wasn't capable of. Pretending he was stronger than he was to save his pride could put her at risk.

"I don't feel good," he admitted

She squatted on her heels beside him and laid her palm on his forehead. It was cool and soothing. "You're so hot. Damn, I wish the med kit hadn't come open."

Absently, he said. "Wish in one hand, shit in the other. See which fills up first."

Destiny made a face. "What a charming image. You learn that saying in the Marines?"

"Worse. My dad." He wanted to bite his tongue as soon as the words were out of his mouth. As far as he was concerned, and definitely as far as Destiny was concerned, that asshole didn't exist. "Hand up?"

She put her arm around his waist, he draped his arm across her shoulders, and they stood together. The world swung around in a sickening yellow blur, then stabilized.

"I found a good place," Destiny said. "Secure. And not far. It even has beds!"

"With mattresses?" Ethan asked.

"Yup. They're kind of dusty, but I pulled a couple off and banged them around some, so they should be good." She met his incredulous gaze, and said, "I'm not joking. Apparently the palace got furnished first—which stands to reason, right? No gold or anything. Looks like the real valuables got cleaned out. But the furniture and some of the furnishings are still there. You'll see."

He knew she wasn't making it up, but he still didn't quite believe it until he saw it for himself. The palace was unmistakable for anything else, a beautiful confection of ornately carved towers and elegant domes, and surrounded by a moat with an actual drawbridge. The stream which flowed from the baths was channeled into the moat, though the water wasn't as clear as it was in the baths. Lilypads floated in the greenish water, and fish swam lazily within the depths. And—

Ethan recoiled. "Is that a *snake?*"

"Yup. Very poisonous. Don't fall in."

He looked back down, careful not to lean. Several white snakes hung in the water, writhing unpleasantly. As he watched, one made a sudden sideways dart and snapped at a big silvery fish three times its size. The fish thrashed for a few seconds, then went belly-up. The snake undulated up to it, unhinged its jaws until they were a gaping abyss lined with needle-sharp fangs, and engulfed the entire fish in a single gulp.

"Yikes," Ethan muttered. "Guess we won't be taking any refreshing swims around the palace."

Destiny grinned. "Maybe not around, but *in*. It has an indoor swimming pool."

"It does not—" Ethan began, then decided that he should believe everything Destiny said no matter how insane or unlikely it sounded. She hadn't steered him wrong yet. "Snake-free, I presume."

"Completely." She laughed. "It's not literally a swimming pool. It's a giant bath, like the one outside but fancier. But it's deep enough to swim in."

They crossed the drawbridge, and Destiny pulled it up after them. He would have felt guilty about not helping her, but it was on a pulley system that was clearly designed to be easy to handle from the inside. Besides, he liked watching the play of muscles on her shoulders and back. A light mist of sweat lay over her brown skin, making it gleam like polished wood.

I could watch her pulling weights forever, he thought. *I could watch her do anything forever. The way she moves is so beautiful. Like a dancer. Like a martial artist. Like a tiger.*

He needed to stop obsessing over what he couldn't have and count his blessings that he had her at all, even if it wasn't the way he wanted. She was the best friend anyone could ever want, and he could count on her to help him rescue his men. It was better to be able to look at her beauty, even if he couldn't touch, than to have never seen it at all.

Yeah. He'd just keep telling himself that.

CHAPTER 9

Once the drawbridge was up, Destiny relaxed a little. Even in the wildly unlikely event that Apex had tracked them to a city they'd only found by chance and no amount of deliberate searches had ever discovered, the water vipers would make short work of any rampaging hell pigs. Ethan had the safe place he needed to rest and recover.

If rest is all he needs, an uneasy voice within her muttered.

He looked terrible, pale and sweating and trembling just from the effort of staying on his feet. When she slipped her arm back around him, she could feel how hard he was working just to breathe. By the time she got him to the room that she suspected had been the maharajah's bedroom, she was practically carrying him.

She laid him in the bed, took off his boots and belt, then, suspicious that he'd been hiding an injury, his pants and shirt. The black bruise on his side had spread past the edges of the tape she'd laid across his ribs. Broken ribs, for sure. Internal injuries? Pneumonia, like she'd surmised? Some other infection? All of the above?

He shivered, and she pulled the covers over him. He lay

still, eyes closed, looking far more vulnerable than she'd ever seen before. Destiny stroked his hair, which was damp with sweat and very soft. He didn't stir. The air rasped in his throat.

She wished she knew more about medicine than what she'd learned in a basic battlefield aid class, plus what she'd picked up from her paramedic pals. Then again, she suspected that the problem wasn't her lack of knowledge, but her lack of supplies. What would Shane be able to do if he was here? He'd probably just know the exact name and dosage of the antibiotics he didn't have anyway.

No, said her tiger. *Knowledge is* exactly *what you need.*

Destiny jumped, startled and uneasy. Her tiger's voice had sounded so... forceful. Normally she was playful or lazy. Cranky, at most. And then there'd been those revolting demands to rip out the daeodon's throat and drink his blood...

Yes, hissed her tiger. *It would have been so satisfying. Next time, I won't let you hold me back.*

Forget about... Destiny didn't even want to think it. Any of it. *...all that stuff. What did you mean about me needing knowledge?*

Medicine doesn't just come from tablets. Those... The tiger snarled the next words with anger and revulsion. *...those pills of yours don't come from a factory. There's medicine all around you, if you just remember it. Remember!* The last word came out in a silent roar that left Destiny reeling.

She tried to remember the herb-gathering trips she'd gone on with Mataji. They hadn't been in this exact sort of terrain—her area had been less of a jungle, more of a forest, and Mataji had said that Destiny's own herb, *sherneend,* only grew atop a single mountain. But she'd pointed out other herbs that she'd said grew in the entire region.

Unfortunately, Destiny had been more interested in flying kites, catching lizards, and generally raising hell with Mataji's rowdy grandkids. Now she wished she'd spent less time gathering long seed-pods to dry into rattling brown swords to fight mock duels with, and more paying attention to the priceless knowledge Mataji had to impart. If she'd only known!

You do know, her tiger growled impatiently. *Focus your silly human rattle-brain, and remember!*

Destiny closed her eyes and tried to relax, letting the memories come. Mataji had been spry for her age, trotting briskly along in her slapping flat sandals, with the edges of her green sari forever threatening to drag in the mud but somehow always staying spotless. She carried a cane, but just used it to bang on the ground to get attention, or to point. Destiny pictured that cane pointing, and tried to see what it pointed at.

A low creeper with white flowers. Mataji had said the dried flowers eased menstrual cramps. That had embarrassed Destiny horribly at the time since her period hadn't even started yet, but it was kind of funny in retrospect given her go-to excuse for her actual pills.

A spiny red fruit that could be steeped in alcohol to make a liniment to rub on sore muscles. Destiny could use some of that right now, but it wasn't as if she *needed* it, and anyway they didn't have any alcohol.

Little brown seeds, to be chewed for toothache... A jagged-edged green leaf, to be crushed and applied to wounds... A yellow flower, for coughs...

The images came thick and fast, crowding at her mind. Her tiger was right. She did have everything she needed, at least as far as knowledge was concerned. She just had to go out and hunt for it.

Yesss, hissed her tiger. *Be a hunter!*

Right. Sure, Destiny promised, trying to keep her uneasiness out of her mental voice. *Let's go stalk the wild geranium.*

"Hey. Hey, jarhead. Wake up."

She had to shake Ethan before he opened his eyes, and even then it was a moment before they focused on her.

"Do you need me?" he mumbled.

I always need you, she thought before she could stop herself. *I need you more than I need air to breathe.*

She crammed that thought into a box and sat on it. "No, I'm fine. I have to go out and get something. I want to leave my gun with you, just in case. Okay?"

"Yeah." His eyes were already fluttering shut.

She laid it on a little bedside table within reach of his hand. Then, doubtful, she asked, *"Could* you shoot?"

"Always, mudpuppy." His voice was weak, but she knew it was the truth.

She took his hand and squeezed it. "I'll be back soon."

Destiny hurried along the streets. She barely noticed the beauty around her, she was so knotted up with ten different kinds of worry. What if she didn't recognize the herbs after all? What if they didn't grow here? What if she got the wrong ones, and poisoned Ethan? What if—

Inside her head, her tiger roared with fury. *Shut up! Shut up, and hunt! Then let ME hunt!*

Destiny rocked back on her heels, jolted out of her anxiety and into a whole new one. She was tempted to yell back at her tiger, but God knew what sort of fury that would unleash. Instead, she made herself reply calmly. *I am hunting. And I need hands to pick the herbs, and then I have to carry them in a backpack, and then I have to grind them or boil them or something. You can't do any of that. You want Ethan to get better, right?*

Yes, growled her tiger. *We will protect Ethan. Go, silly girl! Protect him, PROTECT HIM!*

The roar was loud enough to make her head ring. As she left the city and began to poke through the jungle outside, she couldn't help hoping against hope that Mataji had been wrong about the whole "only on a single mountaintop" thing and she'd find a nice patch of *sherneend*, gray-green and ready for picking.

With smug satisfaction, her tiger said, *You will find none of that here.* Then, an instant later, *Are you blind? There, there!*

And there it was: a patch of the little yellow-flowered herb that soothed coughs, almost invisible under a layer of dead leaves. Destiny picked the lot of it, then, rather grudgingly, said, *Thanks.*

Her tiger purred.

And then she saw the entire world with new eyes. It was as if she was looking at one of those magic pictures that looked like a bunch of random dots until you stared at it long enough, and then it became a vase of flowers. The jungle was no longer a hard terrain to be overcome, it was a supermarket with everything free for the taking. There were fruits and there were vegetables and there were spices, there was a tree whose twigs could be chewed and used as toothbrushes, there was a vine that could be stripped and dried and twisted into rope. And there was an entire pharmacy full of medicinal herbs.

Unfortunately, most of them weren't the ones she needed. She impatiently passed over leaves that settled upset stomachs and roots that cured athlete's foot, bark for headaches and berries for cramps and a flower that could be made into a rinse for oily hair.

What about that? asked her tiger when she hesitated over a plant with pale leaves and tiny purple flowers. *I don't remember that one.*

I think Mataji showed me that one when you were asleep, Destiny replied. *It'll make Ethan feel better, but...*

Then give it to him, her tiger growled impatiently. *Stop dawdling and pick it!*

Destiny didn't feel like getting into yet another argument with her tiger. She picked it. There was no harm in that. But she'd let Ethan decide whether or not he wanted to take it.

She also harvested a jagged-leaved herb she could crush and apply to his wounds. But she had no luck finding anything useful for fever or pneumonia. Maybe none of those grew where she was. Or maybe if she kept searching, eventually she'd find some… but when she checked her watch, she saw that she'd already been gone for hours. She didn't like leaving Ethan alone that long, especially when there might be enemies about, gun or no gun. Reluctantly, she headed back into the city.

As she turned a corner, she startled a big white deer. It leaped over a low wall, then bounded toward the jungle.

Destiny's tiger lunged forward.

No! Destiny shouted inwardly. *Not now. We can get a deer any time we want.*

Not food, her tiger snarled. *I want to chase. I want to hunt NOW!*

It felt like the beast would explode through her skin, tearing her to bits in an effort to set herself free.

Destiny found herself down on her knees on the hard stone streets, clutching her head in her hands and shouting aloud. "Stop! I have to bring the herbs to Ethan! If you take me over, he could die!"

Her tiger backed down with a final, resentful snarl.

Destiny got shakily to her feet. She could feel the beast within as a raging, uncontrollable presence, not only in her mind but in her body, in her entire being. She'd defeated the animal for now, but she had no confidence that she could do so again. It was stronger than she was. It always had been. And now she'd lost her only defense against it.

She hurried back to the palace, pulled the drawbridge, and went to check on Ethan. He was still asleep, and didn't even seem to have moved. She stood for a moment looking down at his sleeping face, at his sandy eyelashes, the nape of his neck. She had the crazy impulse to bend over and kiss it...

...which was *not* what he needed. Maybe if she was his mate, her touch alone might soothe him. But she wasn't, so it wouldn't, so she wouldn't.

Destiny practically bolted out of the room before she could change her mind. She found the palace kitchen, which had a lot of sealed jars she decided were better left unopened, and also pots and pans and a cooking hearth, which she used to prepare the herbs.

We could have fresh venison right now, sweet and tender, if you weren't so stubborn, growled her tiger.

We'll hunt for deer later, Destiny promised. *I don't have many outfits, remember? I want to undress before I shift.*

Why bother? Fur is better than stupid clothes.

Destiny didn't dignify that with a response.

She carried a tray up to Ethan, set it on the table by the bed, and shook him awake. "Hey, jarhead. Buddy. Ethan, come on. Wake up."

He was hard enough to rouse that she thought he'd been closer to unconsciousness than sleep. His blue-green eyes were glassy, his face flushed. "Everything okay?"

"Yeah, we're fine. I made you some herbal remedies. Here, take this. It'll help your cough." She gave him a spoonful of sticky syrup. Then she held up the mug of tea she'd made from the herb with pale leaves and purple flowers. "This one... Let me tell you what it is, then you decide whether or not you want to take it."

He rubbed his forehead like his head hurt. "That sounds

ominous. Are you not sure whether it's mushrooms or toadstools?"

Destiny rolled her eyes. "No, jarhead. I know exactly what it is. That's the problem. It's a… kind of a pick-me-up. It'll help with the pain, knock your fever down, give you more energy and a clearer head…"

"What's the catch?"

"It's not a cure, or even a treatment. It'll make you feel better for a little while, but once it wears off, whatever's wrong will still be wrong. Worse, probably, since you'll have been running around doing things when you should've been resting."

The moment she said those last words, Destiny wished she hadn't. Eagerly, Ethan said, "Run around? It could get me back on my feet? For how long?"

"No idea. Might be a few hours, might be a few days."

"Days, huh? Think it could last long enough to get me to the base?"

Destiny bit her lower lip. "I really don't know. Like I said, it could just be a couple hours. Or it could last just long enough to get you to the base, then you collapse once you're inside."

"I'll take that risk." He held out his hand for the mug.

"You sure?"

"Positive, mudpuppy. Hand it over." He struggled to sit up, then fell back. Destiny helped him sit up and lean against a bunch of brocade pillows, then steadied his hands around the cup. She'd found it in the kitchen; it was made of fine porcelain painted with a delicate pattern of jungle vines.

Ethan sipped the concoction and made a face. "Tastes like old socks."

"How do you know what old socks taste like?"

She thought he was going to say it tasted like old socks

smelled, but he chuckled and said, "Because Ellie stuffed one of hers in my mouth when we kids."

"Good lord. And here I always thought you were the hellraiser."

"Nah. Both of us." He gulped at the tea, obviously trying to drink it quickly enough that he wouldn't have to taste it. "Maybe she stopped after a while. I wasn't there."

Hoping to distract him from the revolting tea, she said, "How old were you when your parents split up?"

"Ten." Ethan took another gulp. "They split up me and Ellie too. Dad moved across the country and took me with him. Before that, she and I had been inseparable. After, we saw each other once a year at Christmas."

"That's rough. I can't imagine."

"Aren't your parents divorced too?"

"Yeah, but Dad moved literally three blocks away. I saw him nearly every day, stayed over every weekend. It was years before Mom re-married, but my little brother calls his father Daddy and my father Papa." Destiny hadn't thought much about what that must have been like from her parents' perspective, but now she realized how hard it had probably been. "Mom and Dad really knocked themselves out make sure we all stayed a family, even though they weren't in love any more. I don't think I ever told them how grateful I am."

"You should. Ellie and I would've given anything for that." Ethan tipped up the mug to get the last drops, swallowed, and shuddered. "Got anything to get the taste out of my mouth?"

He needs meat, raw and dripping with blood, her tiger advised. *I'll pull down a deer and rip out its heart. You can bring it to him, still warm and quivering. That will give him strength.*

Not enough yeccch in the world, returned Destiny.

She offered Ethan another cup, this one filled with fresh-squeezed mango juice. His hands were steadier now, and he was able to hold it without help.

"I have another herbal thing for your cuts," she said. "It should stop them from getting infected and help them heal faster. It might sting a bit."

He smiled. "I think I can grit my teeth and bear a little stinging."

She pulled back the covers and began gently smoothing the salve she'd prepared into the incredible array of cuts and scrapes that marred his smooth skin. He felt a little less hot; she hoped that was real and not wishful thinking.

Ethan sighed, but with relief rather than pain, and she felt his taut muscles relax under her fingers. "It doesn't sting at all. It feels good, actually... Hey, how'd you learn all this? This is way more sophisticated than anything I learned in SERE training."

"When looking for edible grubs, turn over rocks before shoving your hand under them?"

"Just takes one scorpion sting to teach you that lesson. And by the way, thanks for not bringing me grubs. I don't think I could stomach them." Then, his steady gaze fixed on hers, he persisted, "Listen, if I'm asking about something that's classified, just say, 'Forget it, jarhead,' and I'll never ask again."

"It's not classified." Destiny only realized that her hands were trembling when the salve smeared over his belly. She *had* to tell him. Otherwise, if she had to run, he'd think she'd been killed, or abandoned him. But the thought of him knowing just how flawed she was filled her with a horrible mixture of cold fear and hot shame. "I... I..."

"Hey." He laid his hand over hers. It *was* cooler: no longer fever-hot, just human-warm. But his blue-green gaze burned like a flame. "If something bad happened to you here... If someone hurt you when you were a little girl, that is nothing to be ashamed of. I'd never think badly of you because of something that was done to you against your will, or of something you did because you had to do it to survive…"

"No!" To her horror, tears had thickened her throat, making her denial come out in a gulp. "No, no one ever hurt me here. They *saved* me! It's me that's the problem, me that's weak, me that's—that's a danger to you, Ethan!"

The anger and passion faded from his eyes, leaving them soft and bewildered. "How could you ever be a danger to me?"

She had to protect him. This was the only way. At long last, she had to tell him the awful truth that meant he would never again look at her with trust, but only with fear. And, worse, disappointment. He'd only desired her because she'd let him believe she was desirable. And now he'd learn the truth.

Taking a deep breath, she said, "Because I was born wrong."

DESTINY'S STORY

You ever hear of a "throwback?" It's when you're born with some trait that your ancestors had, one that died out up until you. Like, Siberian huskies were bred from wolves, but that was thousands of years ago. Now they're just dogs that look a bit like wolves. You can tell the difference because huskies have blue or brown or black eyes, but a wolf's eyes are yellow or green.

But every now and then, a Siberian husky is born with yellow or green eyes. It's a throwback to its wolf ancestors. That makes it flawed. Defective. It's fine as a pet or sled dog, but it can't be exhibited at dog shows and they won't let it breed.

I'm a throwback. Like those yellow-eyed huskies. Born wrong.

Hundreds of years ago, my ancestors were tiger shifters. But I was descended from the ones who had human mates, and whose kids had human mates. Eventually, the ability to shift died out. By my grandparents' time, no one was still alive who could remember anyone who had been able to shift. By my time, it was a family legend that no one believed in any more.

Until me.

Thank God, I wasn't born in a hospital. My mother didn't like them. Didn't like doctors. Since there weren't any complications with the pregnancy, she hired a midwife and gave birth at home. It was all very gentle. I was put straight on her breast, and she held me until the midwife left. Then she handed me over to my dad to hold. I guess I didn't like that. I let out a howl, and I turned into a tiny tiger cub and bit him.

I didn't have any teeth yet, but I still can't believe he didn't drop me. Dad's a great guy. Mom took me back and cuddled me, and I turned back into a baby.

And that was how it went for my entire childhood. I got upset or angry or even excited, and I turned into a tiger. I calmed down, and I turned back into a baby or a toddler or a little girl.

It was lucky we had that family legend, because that gave my family some sort of vague idea of what was going on. No one thought I was a monster or a demon or anything like that. Once they knew the legend was real, they also knew that the people in my family who had been shifters had led normal lives. They hadn't been locked in an attic, they'd been dressmakers and firemen and soldiers and so forth.

My family figured that shifters must learn how to control the shift once they got old enough to understand why they ought to. So they told everyone that I had a problem with my immune system and couldn't have visitors, but I was getting treated and hopefully it'd be fixed when I was older. They figured that if shifting is like knowing not to take off your clothes in public, I'd be able to control it by the time I was five, and if it was more like learning to play a musical instrument well, I could do it by ten or so.

You see, they didn't know any shifters, or know how to find any. If they had, they would've known that shifters usually don't get the ability to shift until they're older. Nine or ten, usually. Sometimes not until puberty. As a toddler, at the very earliest. And even then, they can control it themselves, though whether or not they want to might be a different story.

Our house had a big backyard with a wall around it, and my family would sometimes sneak me into their van in the middle of the night, then drive out to the wilderness for a hiking trip. So I wasn't locked inside all the time. But I never saw anyone but my family or their very closest friends.

My family tried their best to make teaching me not to shift be a normal thing, like teaching me to read or not to throw tantrums. But I couldn't do it. It was like they were trying to teach me to fly by saying, "Flap your arms! Now lift off!" And I'd flap and flap and flap, and finally I'd start crying because it was the millionth time and I still couldn't get off the ground, and then they'd say, "Don't cry, honey, I know you're trying. You'll get it eventually."

But I knew I ought to be able to do it already. I felt like a failure.

By the time I was nine or ten, they'd figured out that there was a real problem. They'd been trying the entire time to get in touch with some other shifters, but since the entire existence of shifters is a secret, they'd had no luck. They have some pretty funny stories about all the weirdos and lunatics they met on the internet. My poor dad had coffee with a whole bunch of them just in case they were for real, but none of them ever got past his screening to meet me.

Finally, mom thought of trying something different. She pretended she was into genealogy, and she started tracking down every relative she didn't already know, no matter how distant they were. Finally, she found a branch of the family who were still shifters, and we met them.

It wasn't much fun, to be honest. They tried to be nice, but I could see how they looked at me: like I was a freak. And they had no idea what to do about me. Some aunt made a snooty remark about us being proof that she was right about 'keeping the blood pure.' Mom grabbed me and stormed out. Dad stayed long enough to get the names and phone numbers of every other shifter they knew, and then he thanked them for their time, told the aunt he hoped she was proud of herself for making a little girl cry, and left.

Then we spent a year contacting other shifters. After a while, word spread in the shifter community and *they* started contacting *us*. We got emailed by shifters from all around the world. Only they all said stuff like, "That poor child, I've never heard of such a dreadful situation, I don't have any ideas but let me know if there's ever anything I can do to help" and "I've never even heard of anything like this but my auntie in Beijing knows lots of shifter history, here's her email" and "I'm so sorry, in all my years I've never heard of such a thing, best wishes from Beijing."

It was horrible. I'd spent my whole life feeling like I was this freak and wishing I could find other people like me. Then I found them, and it turned out that I was even more of a freak than I'd realized.

Finally, we got emailed by a woman in India. She was a ratel shifter—we had to look that up, it's sort of like a badger—and she said she didn't know how to help herself, but she lived in a town that had a lot of shifters and some of the families had lived there for hundreds of years. She said she thought that if we showed up, the town could collectively figure it out. It sounded pretty unlikely, but by then we were so desperate, we decided to do it.

Then there was the problem of getting there. If I got on a

plane, I might shift on the way. They could sedate me, but then they'd have to explain why they were putting an unconscious girl on a plane. Finally, they emailed one of the "if there's ever anything I can do to help" shifters, who'd mentioned that he owned his own plane, and offered to pay him to fly us there. He refused to take any money from us and flew us there for free.

It was the first time I'd ever been on a plane. He saw how excited I was and invited me to come into the cockpit and see how it all worked. My parents were nervous about me turning into a tiger and crashing the plane, but he laughed and said he was an Army veteran and a lion shifter and he'd be ashamed of himself if he couldn't handle one little tiger cub.

I didn't shift once. I just sat there, completely entranced. He spent the whole trip teaching me to fly. When my parents were taking a nap, he even let me take the controls for a while. When we landed at the airport, he said he'd be happy to give me real lessons later. I said I was too young, but he said I could learn at any age and get my pilot's license when I was sixteen.

For the first time in ages, I felt like I had something to look forward to.

By the way, that Army vet was Al Flores, Rafa's great-uncle. He not only taught me to fly, he introduced me to Rafa and Hal. We eventually had yearly get-togethers to bond about being military shifters, which isn't that common. Al and I would rag Hal and Rafa over being in the Navy—Al called our get-togethers "kid the squids." And when Hal and Rafa decided to start Protection, Inc., I was the first person they recruited.

Anyway, after my family and I arrived in India, the woman who'd emailed us, Priya Desai, picked us up at the airport and drove us to her town. It was an eight-hour drive.

At first it was fun looking at the scenery, but after a while, I got so bored and antsy I turned into a tiger. Twice. So I had to spend a lot of the drive crouched on the floor.

But once we arrived, things picked up. It seemed like the whole town turned out to greet us. They didn't all speak English, so some of them just smiled. We got served really great food on banana-leaf plates, and some people gave me little gifts like a kite and a set of bead earrings and a painted clay tiger. I caught my mom shooting that guy a look like she thought it was tactless, but I loved it. I still have it.

Then this old lady marched up, grabbed my wrist, squeezed my hand so tight I thought the bones would crack, and tried to shove something on to my wrist. I turned into a tiger cub and hissed at her. She held up a set of iridescent glass bangles and said, "These are for you when you can wear them."

I tried to snatch them with my claws. When I was a tiger, I had no self-control at all. She held them out of my reach and told my parents, "Bring her to my house."

Dad said, "When she changes back?"

The old woman shook her head. "Now."

My parents glanced at Priya, who said, "That's Mataji. Go with her, she's the reason I thought we could help."

I'd shifted back by the time we got to her house. It was a really cool house. It had an indoor swing, a polished wood plank suspended from the ceiling with cloth ropes tie-dyed blue and green. Mataji sat in it and made it sway like a rocking chair. The rest of us sat on cushions on the floor.

One of her daughters brought us a tray of drinks and sweets and snacks. My parents sipped and nibbled to be polite, but I was a bottomless pit for sweet things and I tried everything.

"Have you heard of a case like our daughter's before?" Mom blurted out.

"Throwbacks, yes," Mataji said. "Shifters who can't control the shift, not exactly. I did some research before you came and I found one account of a boy who turned into a wolf, ran into the woods, and never came back. But it wasn't clear to me whether he stayed a wolf permanently, or whether he'd just run away from home."

"Do you have any ideas of how you could help her?" Mom asked.

"Let's not get ahead of ourselves. I need to ask you some questions first."

I could tell this was going to be one more horrible, frustrating disappointment. I tried to change the subject. "Can I try your swing?"

"Not yet. My grandfather made it, and I don't want to risk it getting clawed. You can swing all you please when you can be sure you won't damage it."

I knew where she was going with that, and so did my parents. Mom told her I desperately wanted to control my shift, but I just couldn't.

"I understand that," Mataji said. To me, she said, "I'm not trying to bribe you. I'm giving you some things to look forward to, so it'll keep your spirits up for a long, difficult process. Also, I imagine you have a lot of regrets by now. Don't you? Birthday parties you couldn't go to... Friends you couldn't make... Favorite clothes and toys you destroyed."

It was so true. I thought of everything in my life that had been ruined by me not being able to control myself, and I started crying.

Mataji went on, "So I don't want to add to your regrets. Not even by a few broken bangles." Then she gave me a sharp look. "Why didn't you shift just now? If you're upset enough to cry...?"

"I only just turned back into a girl," I said.

"So you don't do it too soon after the last time?"

I sniffled and nodded.

"How much time would have to pass before you can shift again?"

"I guess about half an hour."

"Hmm." Mataji rocked a little faster. "What's your tiger feel like right now? Why isn't she taking over?"

Why aren't you? I asked.

My tiger yawned. *Too tired.*

"She says she's too tired."

Mataji smiled. "Now we're getting somewhere. Who was the last known shifter among your ancestors, and how many generations lie between them and her?"

At that point, my dad couldn't take it anymore. "I'm sorry, Mataji. I don't mean to be rude, but we never really got introduced, except by name. Are you a... a pack leader? A witch—"

Mom jabbed him in the ribs.

"A wisewoman?" Dad corrected himself.

Mataji stopped rocking and raised her eyebrows at Dad. They were very impressive eyebrows. "First, 'Mataji' isn't a name. It's a polite way to address an older woman. Like 'Grandmother.' Second, I'm not a pack leader. I'm a mongoose shifter. We have families, not packs. Wisewoman? Well, I try to never stop learning, which is certainly a way to become wise. As for why Priya called you here, many herbs grow in this area, and I've studied their uses. It's possible that one of them or a mixture of several could help."

That got Mom excited. Remember how she didn't want to go to a hospital to have me? She's big on alternative medicine. She exclaimed, "I knew it! This is what we've needed all along. Ancient shifter wisdom, passed on through the generations..."

Mataji smiled. "In a sense. I'm a pharmacist. Plenty of drugs originally come from plants. Aspirin is from the bark of the willow tree. Digitalis, which you take for heart conditions, is from foxgloves. And I'm on an email list for shifters with an interest in shifter-specific medical issues, like dragonsbane poisoning. Let me ask you some more questions. Has Destiny ever bitten anyone in the family?"

"Sure," Dad said.

"Broken the skin? Made them bleed?"

"Not on purpose!" I said.

She looked at me. "That's not why I'm asking. Have you? Who?"

I hung my head and muttered, "All of them."

"Really!" For the first time, Mataji looked surprised. "And nothing happened?"

We all shook our heads.

"Ever bitten anyone who wasn't a family member?"

"No." I said bitterly, "This was practically the first time I've even met anyone who wasn't!"

Mataji got up and put her hands on my shoulders. She said, "Never bite anyone else who isn't a shifter already. It could kill them."

"What?!"

"When a shifter bites a non-shifter, usually they make them into a shifter," Mataji explained. "But some people are... allergic, essentially. When they're bitten, they don't shift. They die. I'm sure it's genetic, but we have no idea what gene is responsible, so there's no way to tell which will happen. *Never bite anyone who isn't a shifter.* Do you understand?"

Scared, I muttered, "Yes."

"Does your tiger understand?" Mataji asked sternly.

Do you? I asked.

My tiger didn't usually do what I told her, but she growled, *Yes. I will not kill anything but prey. Now let's leave this boring old woman, and run and hunt in the jungle!*

"What's she say?" Mataji asked. "Word for word."

I repeated it. Word for word, staring right at her.

But Mataji didn't get angry. She looked relieved instead, then chuckled. "She's a lively one. I can see why you're having so much trouble with her. Now, as to why your family didn't become shifters after you bit them, there's a third thing that can happen when non-shifters are bitten."

"What?"

"Nothing," she said simply. "It's quite rare. Much less likely than them dying. But again, it's a genetic trait. They're resistant to shifting. I think this explains your problem, Destiny. You inherited enough shifter genes to overpower the ones for resistance to shifting, but enough resistant genes to overpower the ones that would normally allow you to control the shift. I'm sure it's more complicated than that, but I suspect that's the essence of the problem."

"But you can't change her genes," Dad said.

"No, but many genetic diseases can be treated with medication." Once again, she looked into my eyes. "Are you willing to experiment on yourself?"

"Nothing dangerous," Mom said quickly.

"She's just a child!" Dad exclaimed.

"I'll be very careful," Mataji assured them. Then she turned back to me. "But I will be creating a completely new medication, and testing it on you. That *is* dangerous. It will probably also be long and tedious and frustrating. But this is your life. Your body. Your..." She smiled slightly. "Your destiny. You must be the one to choose."

I heard my parents protesting, but I wasn't listening to them. Instead, I remembered my first airplane flight, and how I'd been pushed back into the seat as the plane accelerated along the runway. And then the lift-off. I'd looked down, and I could see so much. The entire world was spread out below me.

If I stayed the way I was, I'd never see more of it than my parents' home and a few shifter towns like this one. The price of safety was never taking flight.

I stood up, turned my back on my parents, and looked into Mataji's eyes like she'd looked into mine. "I want to try."

Her first attempts didn't do anything but make me tired, or give me headaches or stomach aches. Then she started working with a rare herb called *sherneend*, which means "tiger sleep." It tastes disgusting to herbivores, but carnivores nibble on it sometimes. If they eat a little bit, it calms them down. If they eat a lot, they fall asleep.

At first all it did was put *me* to sleep. But Mataji kept tinkering with the dosage, until she got one that didn't affect me, but put my tiger to sleep. At first I was thrilled, because it stopped me from shifting when I didn't want to. But then I realized that I couldn't shift at all, even if I did want to. More than that, I felt like something was missing. I felt... hollow. Like the part of me that made me *me* was gone.

So Mataji adjusted the dosage again, until she got one that just calmed my tiger down. She was still there, but she wasn't so willful. I could get her to do what I wanted instead of what she wanted. Finally, *finally*, I could control the shift.

The whole town threw a party, Mataji's shifter scientist friends emailed her to tell her what a genius she was, and I got to wear my bangles and swing. It was especially fun because there were so many shifter kids in the town, and we had a whole jungle outside the town we could run around in and climb trees and hunt.

All of a sudden, I had a future. I could have friends. I could have a job. I could do anything.

As long as I took my pill every morning.

I don't control my tiger the way every other shifter in the world controls theirs, because it's natural to them. Because they're stronger than it is. It's not natural to me, and she's stronger than me. The only way I can keep control of her is by taking pills.

I tried to tell myself it didn't matter. Whatever works is whatever works, right? But in my heart, I always knew there was something wrong with me, and some day it would catch up to me. And it has.

Just when you need me the most, I'm a danger to you. Because I'm weak. A liability. A freak…

CHAPTER 10

*E*than had never seen Destiny cry before. He'd seen her upset and worried, like when her teammate Shane had been shot, but even then she'd stayed strong for his sake. She'd always been so cheerful and tough, it had seemed like she'd never had a moment of weakness or self-doubt in her life.

But then she'd told him her story. He hadn't interrupted, letting her get it all out, but he'd watched as she struggled at times just to get the words out. And now tears flowed down her cheeks as she sat there calling herself names. Weak. A liability. A freak…

"Whoa, whoa!" Ethan sat straight up, grabbing for her hand. "Destiny, you're none of those things. Don't ever call yourself any of that crap again."

She jerked her hand out of his grip. "But it's true. Everyone else can control their shift. I'm the only shifter in the world who can't do it unless I swallow a pill!"

"So what? That doesn't say anything bad about you. I had a friend in high school who had diabetes. Would you say he was weak and flawed and a freak because he had to give himself an insulin shot every day?"

"That's different."

"How?" Ethan demanded. "How is it different?"

"It's a shifter thing. You can't understand."

Ethan had developed a deep hatred of those words. They were the exact ones she'd used when she'd rejected him, all those years ago. It was true that he wasn't a shifter, and couldn't know what it was like to be one. All the same, it didn't seem like any other shifters, other than that one snob aunt, had looked down on Destiny for being the way she was. Instead, they'd done their best to help her.

He pictured her at eleven, and the image made him smile.

"What?" she asked suspiciously.

"You must've been an awfully cute little girl. You had an entire town bending over backward to help you."

"They were just nice."

He flicked her arm. "You were adorable. Admit it. Chubby cheeks? Little pigtails? Pastel plastic barrettes shaped like animals?"

She sniffled, swiped her hand across her eyes, and gave him a wavering smile. "Right on all counts. Four pigtails tied top and bottom with dangly pastel plastic balls. When I see photos of me, I want to pinch my cheeks."

"It was more than that, though, wasn't it? Sure, you were a cute kid. And it sounds like the shifter community likes to help each other out, and that one town was extra-nice, and Mataji obviously enjoyed a challenge. But you also had Al Flores offer you flying lessons when you were eleven. You had shifters all around the world emailing each other to try to help you."

"Like I said. They were nice."

"I'm sure they were. But I think they also saw something special in you. I think they saw a girl who was brave beyond her years, who'd spent her entire life locked up but jumped straight into an adventure the instant she got a chance, who'd been knocked down a thousand times and got up a thousand and one."

He laid his hand over hers. This time she didn't pull it away. She listened, her beautiful eyes huge and glistening, as if she wanted to believe.

Ethan went on, "Mataji told you straight-up that you were in for something incredibly difficult and dangerous, and it was your choice whether you wanted to risk it. You chose to take that risk. And you were only eleven! Yeah, you *are* different from most people. You're braver. You're tougher. You're more determined. Destiny, the only person who's ever thought you were weak or flawed was you. Everyone else saw a girl who was fighting so hard, it inspired them to go above and beyond to give her a chance."

She lowered her head. Her short braids swung forward, shadowing her face. "Maybe you're right. Maybe that's how other people saw me. But even if I *was* brave and determined and all that, it wasn't good enough. And it's still not good enough."

Destiny raised her head, and he saw something else in her eyes that he'd never seen before. It was fear. "Ethan, I'm losing control. I can feel it. I'm having to fight my tiger again, and it's harder every time. Sooner or later, I'm going to lose. It's angry. It's an animal that wants to hunt and kill. I can't risk it getting out around you. I think you should stay here, and I'll go to the base."

"What? No!"

"If I'm going to lose control, better there than here. My tiger could do a hell of a lot of damage to Apex before they take her down."

Ethan broke in, horrified. "That's crazy. I won't let you."

She spoke louder, ignoring him. "And if I lose control on the way, I won't hurt anything but deer."

"Destiny. Stop it. I'm not afraid. I've seen your tiger before."

"That was my calmed-down tiger! Not the one inside me now. That one's a predator. A *beast*."

"I'm still not afraid. I believe what you're saying, but I don't think you would ever hurt me."

"It's not me!" Destiny shouted.

"Fine!" Ethan yelled back. "But you're not going anywhere alone! We go together, or we stay here till the cows come home, or *you* stay here and *I* go. Actually, why don't I do that? You sit here, and I'll come collect you on my way back."

She stared at him, wide-eyed and alarmed. "Ethan, no! We're really pushing it even trying this mission with two people. With just one, it'd be a suicide mission."

"Exactly." He patted her shoulder. "So we go together. Trust me, mudpuppy. You and your tiger will be fine."

Instead of looking encouraged, she sagged with defeat. "You've never had an animal inside you. You can't understand."

Ethan wasn't sure which he wanted to do more, take her in his arms and comfort her, or shake her until she promised never to say that again. Since obviously he couldn't do either, he said, "I understand that you're the strongest, bravest person I know."

She gave him an incredulous stare. "You're the one who's strong and brave and, and perfect! I'm just good at putting up a front."

"Whoa. Have you really been thinking I'm perfect?"

With a shrug and a toss of her braids, she said, "Apart from being a total weirdo and secretly a Zork-playing nerd... Yeah."

Ethan opened his mouth, then closed it. He could prove

otherwise. Or he could tell her some other story about himself, one that did show some flaw in him that he didn't really care but that wouldn't be quite so... revealing. Then he was ashamed of himself for even considering it. She had bared her soul to him. He couldn't hold back with her, even if it did make her think less of him.

"Destiny, let me tell you about my parents. I guess they must've loved each other once. But I never saw it. None of us could do anything right as far as my father was concerned. If we set the table without being asked, he'd tell us the spoons were crooked. Then Mom would say they were fine, only she wasn't talking to us—she was glaring at Dad. She was contradicting him, not supporting us. Then in private she'd tell us how terrible Dad was and how much she regretted marrying him. This was when we were, like, eight. It was totally inappropriate."

Ethan stopped suddenly. He'd never told anyone about any of this—at least, not in more detail than "My parents divorced when I was ten. We're not really close." He'd always imagined that if he ever did, they'd give him a stare like he was way too old to still be bothered by stuff that happened when he was eight and he needed to man up. He knew Destiny wouldn't do that, but he worried that she'd pity him. He hated pity.

She didn't. The expression in her warm regard was one he could only interpret as sympathy, and the desire to ease his pain, even a pain years by gone. She turned her hand over so she could squeeze his. "That's terrible, Ethan."

"Ellie and I used to hope they'd get divorced," he went on. "Then they did. The first thing they both decided to do was move to opposite ends of the country. We ended up in custody court. To this day, I don't think either of them really wanted us, they just wanted to mess with each other. Ellie and I begged the judge to keep us together, but that asshole gave me to Dad and Ellie to Mom. Dad took me and moved to the East Coast."

"What was it like just being with him?"

"Same, only I was all by myself. I remember the day I learned to ride a bike—which a neighbor taught me, by the way. No congratulations. Just a critique of how much I was wobbling. I was a star baseball player in high school, and all he ever talked about were the games we lost. It made me feel like nothing was worth bothering with. I started cutting school, skipping games, flunking classes. I finally got busted for hanging around a liquor store trying to get people with IDs to buy me beer. In retrospect I think I was trying to get Dad's attention. I did, but it was the same kind of attention I got for everything else: telling me how much I sucked."

Destiny sighed. "Man, Ethan. I know Ellie was the one you really needed, but I wish I'd been there. We could've hung out and done stupid nerd stuff together. I know it wouldn't have helped with your dad, but at least you could've had someone to talk to."

He'd never before imagined knowing her as a teenager. The idea made his heart ache. His life would've been so different. "I wish so too. Anyway, big surprise, he didn't approve of me joining the Marines. Said I should've gone to college instead."

"I bet if you'd gone to college, he'd have said you should've joined the Marines." She sounded angry—on *his* behalf. That sure wasn't something he was used to.

"Yeah. I finally had to admit that to myself. It didn't matter what I did. Nothing would ever be good enough. Anyway, Destiny, I didn't tell you all this to make you feel bad for me. You thought I was perfect—that's how perfect I'm not."

"That's your parents. That's not you. What your family's like doesn't say anything about you."

"Doesn't it? Because that's not what I've heard. Everyone says you grow up to become your parents. Or if you want to know what someone's really like, pay attention to how he talks about his parents. Well, my mom is cold and bitter, and my dad's a fucking asshole. No matter what Ellie or I has ever done or said, neither of them has ever changed. I haven't seen either of them in something like eight years. Everyone says you have to forgive your parents and find some way to reconcile with them. So what does it say about me that I hope I never see them again?"

His voice rose to a near-shout. He shut up, hoping she wouldn't feel like he was yelling at *her.*

But there was no hurt in her steady gaze. Nor was there disappointment or disgust. "It says you're honest. It says you stand up for yourself. You didn't get the family you deserved, and that's a shame. But you know what would be even more of a shame? If you let 'everyone' override what you know is the right thing for you."

Ethan had heard something like that before, from Ellie. But she was his sister; she felt the same mixture of guilt and grief and anger that he did. When Destiny said it, he had to believe it, at least a little bit.

"And you are nothing like your father," she went on. Now it was her voice that rose in anger. "He tears people down; you build them up. He was cold and unloving and I bet he never told a joke in his life—"

"You got that right. Never laughed, either."

"And you're warm and funny and—" She broke off suddenly, as if she had decided against saying something, then said, "Is Ellie anything like either of your parents?"

"Not remotely." Ethan sighed. "It's not that I'm afraid I'm going to turn into them. It's that I'm afraid other people will think that if they know about my family. Especially if they came from a good one like yours."

Destiny's eyes shone as if she was holding back tears. She swallowed, but her voice came out thick with emotion anyway as she said, "You were right, earlier. I don't think I ever really appreciated how much people loved me, and how important that was. My family. Friends. Even strangers. You should've had that too, Ethan. I wish—"

Once again, she broke off.

"Yeah," he said. "Me too."

It was strange how safe he felt admitting his own vulnerability to her now. He loved her so much, he should have wanted to impress her with his strength. But some barrier between them had gone down, and he knew she wouldn't think less of him for his anger and his pain and his longing for a love he'd never had.

They were silent for a while. Then Ethan, restless, got out of bed and went to look out the window.

"Hey!" Destiny exclaimed. "You're better! That stuff worked!"

Startled, Ethan stopped and assessed himself. He'd been so absorbed in her story and then their conversation that he hadn't registered when it had happened, but he did feel much better. The pain was gone, he felt neither too hot nor too cold, and he could breathe easily. "Hey, yeah. Good job with the herbs. I can't believe you remembered all that from when you were eleven."

"You said it yourself, I was a kid genius."

"That's not exactly…"

"Kid. Genius. Your exact words. Play it back on video if you wanna prove me wrong."

Much as Ethan would have liked to stay where he was and kid around with her, he had a feeling a clock was ticking. "A few days or a few hours," she'd said. What if he collapsed in the middle of a fight because they'd wasted too much time here?

"We'd better get going," he said, trying to keep his unease from his voice, and picked up the gun.

"I found an armory in the palace. How'd you like a sword, jarhead?"

"Oh, man, seriously?" Ethan couldn't help grinning. "I've always wanted one. I used to play this video game, Final Fantasy, that had some characters with really big swords…"

"Nerd." She poked him in the ribs. "If you're hoping for something as overcompensating as Cloud's, one, not practical, two, you couldn't lift it, three, the armory doesn't have anything like that because *no one* could lift it."

"You not only know who Cloud Strife is, you know exactly what his sword looks like. It is *you* who are the nerd."

Destiny rolled her eyes. "Weirdo nerd."

They stopped by the kitchen first, where she stuffed some leftover herbs in her backpack, and then she led him to the armory. Ethan had seen a lot of impressive things recently that he'd have liked to spend more time looking at if he hadn't been too sick to really appreciate them (the palace) or if they weren't trying to kill him (the daeodon). But of them all, he most wished he could take his time and explore the armory.

It was a treasure trove of ancient weapons. There, neatly hung on the walls and arrayed in holders, were swords and daggers, bows and arrows, staffs and spears, and more unusual weapons like spiked maces, chains on handles, and tridents. With something approaching reverence, he took a beautiful sword from the wall and blew the dust from it. Its edge was razor-sharp, and the rippling pattern on the steel blade gleamed with highlights of blue and green.

Then he realized something odd. "These have been sitting here for three hundred years, right?"

"I think closer to two hundred, but yeah. Oh, you mean, why haven't they rusted to bits? They must've been done with this special process that a genius swordsmith of the maharajah's invented. Nobody's ever been able to figure out exactly how he did it. Everything else he made is in museums."

Ethan looked at Destiny and laughed.

"What's so funny?" she asked suspiciously.

"You are. History nerd."

"Weapons nerd." She nudged him. "Go on, get your stuff. I'll get some too. Then we can hit the road."

Ethan limited himself to that sword and a long dagger, but vowed to come back at some better time and take a longer look, though he regretfully realized that once they told anyone about it, everything would end up in museums. Or maybe the entire city would become a kind of museum. He liked that idea.

"You know how to fight with either of those?" Destiny asked. She had also taken a sword and dagger.

"Not exactly. I did some bayonet training, so hopefully that's close enough. You?"

"Same. Also, check these out." She held up her hand, which was adorned with a set of steel rings. Then she made a fist, and a set of claw-like steel blades appeared between her fingers.

"Are there any more?" Ethan exclaimed, delighted. "Gimme!"

She handed him a larger pair. He slipped them on his hand, admiring how they worked. They were like brass knuckles, but with blades. When your hand was open, the blades were concealed, only to jut out when you made a fist.

"*Waghnakh*," she said. "It means tiger claws. Let's hit the road, Wolverine."

They took off their tiger claws and hung them from their belts. Grinning, Ethan followed her out. But he couldn't resist turning in the doorway to take one last, longing look at the coolest room he'd ever seen.

The swords and daggers on the wall trembled, sending up the faintest of rattles.

"Destiny?" Ethan called.

But by the time she returned to his side, they were still. "What?"

"I'm not sure. Did you feel something like a tiny earthquake?"

She shook her head. "Did you?"

"No, but the weapons..." His voice trailed off as the weapons quivered again.

"Okay, that's weird."

They stood watching them. Once again, the rattling subsided almost immediately.

"You know, that reminds me of something, but I can't quite think of what," Ethan said slowly. He rubbed his forehead, trying to remember. "Things shaking... Maybe water quivering...?"

"The glass of water in *Jurassic Park*!"

Destiny grabbed his hand. Together, they ran to the window. But there was nothing in sight but the golden marble streets and buildings.

A reptilian screech broke the silence. Ethan whirled around. A pair of man-sized lizards lunged through the door, clawed hands outstretched and needle-toothed jaws gaping wide.

Ethan and Destiny moved as if they were a single person in two bodies. They leaped to either side of the window, putting enough distance between them that they couldn't accidentally cut each other, and drew their swords. In such close quarters, in a room made of stone, he didn't dare use his gun for fear of a ricochet hitting Destiny.

"Talk about *Jurassic Park!*" Destiny gasped. "Those are velociraptors!"

She was right. Ethan recognized them now. But they were much scarier in real life. The velociraptors were as tall as him and twice as long, mottled gray-green and scaly. Their slit-pupiled yellow eyes darted back and forth as Ethan and Destiny moved into their fighting positions. Then they shrieked again, a sound that made the hairs on the back of Ethan's neck stand up, and attacked.

He ducked a slash of claws that would have taken his head off and stabbed at the beast where he hoped its heart was. His sword glanced off a bony plate, dealing the velociraptor no more than a minor wound. It darted aside with terrifying speed, hissed, and snapped at him. Ethan evaded and bolted forward. He'd first thought he should have his back to the wall so nothing could attack him from behind, but he now realized that with an opponent as quick as the velociraptor, that only left him cornered.

He snatched up a nearby battleaxe and flung it at the dinosaur. The axe hit the reptile a glancing blow, doing little more than scratching its tough hide, but the distraction bought Ethan enough time to check on Destiny. To his immense relief, she was unhurt and holding her velociraptor at bay. She slashed at the creature, making it leap back with a screech, then ran to join Ethan's side.

"I'll hold them off," Ethan said, grabbing the chain with a handle from a nearby weapons rack. "You check for a clear retreat."

As Destiny turned, both velociraptors bounded forward, shrieking and snapping and slashing. Ethan stood his ground and swung the chain in a rapid arc, so fast that it seemed to create a steel shield before the attacking dinosaurs. One of them thrust its snout into the whirling chain, then drew back with a screech. The other one hung back, hissing angrily.

"We're clear!" Destiny called. "Keep it spinning and back away slowly, and I think we can slam the door on—"

The hissing velociraptor sprang forward, flinging its entire body into the whirling chain. It knocked Ethan sprawling. Dazed, he lay on his back and looked up at the dinosaur that stood over him. All he could see was its soft-looking underbelly and cavernous maw as it bent to bite off his head.

Gripping the hilt in both hands, he thrust his sword straight into its belly. As it screeched, he rolled to the side. Destiny grabbed him and pulled him to his feet as the velociraptor crashed to the floor.

"Where's yours?" he gasped.

She jerked her thumb at the second velociraptor, which he now saw also lay dead. "If there's any others, go for the back of the neck. Swing hard. I had to use both hands."

"Me too," said Ethan. "Let's get out of here. I don't want to get trapped again."

Together, they bolted out of the palace. The streets were as empty as when they'd looked out the window.

"Maybe that was all of them," Destiny said, a little doubtfully.

"I hope so." He kept his hand on his holster as they walked down the street and toward the jungle. Despite his victory over the velociraptor, he still felt far more comfortable with a gun. He was also uneasily conscious that he had only six bullets left.

Now that Ethan was feeling better, he could take in more of his surroundings. The palace was in the center of the city, surrounded by gardens and smaller buildings. Four slim and graceful towers stood at the north, south, east, and west edges of the city, about ten blocks from the jungle. They were watchtowers, he guessed, as they were the tallest buildings in the city. The tops were flat and turreted, large enough for four people to stand watch.

They had just passed the eastern tower when Destiny shouted, "Drop!"

Ethan instantly dropped to the ground. He grabbed for her, but she was already grabbing for him. Together, they threw themselves behind a low stone wall around a small ornamental garden. A black dart flew past them, through the open gate they'd gone through, and stuck quivering in a tree.

Ethan quickly scanned the garden. There was only one gate. They could easily jump over the wall, but they'd be seen immediately. Trying to escape seemed riskier than trying to take their enemy. Destiny settled down, no doubt coming to the same conclusion.

"You got good eyes," he murmured.

"My tiger warned me," Destiny whispered. "She smelled him."

"Ask her how many people there are," Ethan whispered back.

A moment later, Destiny said, "She says just one." Gloomily, she added, "Probably another hell pig shifter."

"Surrender!" shouted a male voice. Ethan recognized it as belonging to Ayers. "I'm not telling Lamorat I lost you *again!* I want to bring you in alive!"

Ethan also yelled, but a little softer, hoping to lure the man closer as he strained to hear. "Like I believe that, Ayers! Your scaly little buddies tried to bite our heads off."

"Yes, but I knew you wouldn't let them!" called Ayers. He did sound a bit nearer. Ethan crouched by the wall, Sig Sauer ready. "I sent them to draw you out. And those weren't shifters. They were real Achillobators. Animals."

Destiny made a beckoning motion to Ethan: she was going to help lure their enemy in. "Achillo-whats? I thought they were velociraptors."

"Achillobators," said their enemy loftily. "We recreated them from fossil DNA. *Jurassic Park* called them velociraptors, but that's not what they were. Real velociraptors are the size of a chicken."

"What do you mean, you sent the Achillobators?" Ethan called. "Are they trained?"

"I'm not just a shifter. I also went through the Ultimate Predator process, which gives you special powers. I can control dinosaurs with my mind. So you better—"

Ethan quickly peered around the edge of the gate. He spotted their enemy, a man lurking in the open doorway of a building, also peering out. They fired almost simultaneously, then ducked back. Ethan heard the crack as his bullet struck stone, and saw another black dart slam into the ground behind them.

"Surrender!" yelled Ayers again. To Ethan's disappointment, he was obviously unhurt. "Like I was saying, we don't want to hurt you. We want to give you powers greater than anything you've ever imagined!"

"And torture us and use us as slaves!" Destiny yelled.

At the same time, Ethan shouted, "If the process doesn't kill us, like it does most people!"

"We've got version 3.0 now! It's the safest yet," Ayers called. Ethan noticed that he didn't respond to Destiny's charges. "Also, Lamorat figured out that Ultimate Predator is more compatible with extinct and mythic shifters than with regular ones. It's so safe now, we've even started using it on ourselves. I assure you, I would never take undue risks with my own life."

And then Ethan saw Destiny do yet another thing he'd never even known she was capable of: she lost her temper. Her face darkened with blood, and she screamed, "Of course not, you fucking asshole! You only used it on *expendable* people like Shane—and Justin—and Cat—"

She broke off, her lips curling strangely. Her eyes were strange too: no longer brown, they gleamed green as a cat's, the pupils contracting into slits. Destiny snarled, a deep, guttural, terrifying sound.

No. Not Destiny. That had to be her tiger. Just like she'd said, it was taking control of her. At any instant, she'd shift against her will, and become the predator.

She'd been afraid that she'd hurt him. But he was afraid that she'd shift and attack her enemy. And then Ayers would shoot her down.

Ethan grabbed her and held her tight. She kept on snarling, but he didn't flinch. Pressing his body into hers, his cheek against hers, he whispered, "Destiny, hold on. I know you don't want to do this now. And I know you can keep control. Be the nerd girl I—" He barely stopped himself from saying, *"I love."* She didn't want to hear that.

"I'm friends with," he substituted. "Mudpuppy. Come on, mudpuppy. You can kill him as yourself. Get your own revenge for Shane and Justin and Catalina and all the rest. It'll be more satisfying. You know it will. You want my gun? I'll give you my gun."

The quivering, catlike readiness in her body eased. She stopped snarling, cleared her throat, and looked up at him. Her eyes were human again, the warm brown he loved. Trying to smile, she said, "Thanks. But it's *my* gun, jarhead. And I don't know how long that lasted, but you might want to use it now."

She was absolutely right. Reluctantly, Ethan let go of her, crawled further away, and peeked over the wall. Once again, there was an exchange of fire that did nothing but make them both duck back to their positions.

Destiny crawled to join him. She whispered, "Let's get him to talk some more. Then we jump the wall on the other side. If we're quick, he won't be able to adjust his aim in time."

Her mouth was so close to his ear that he could feel the movement of her lips. It sent a hot shiver of desire through him. It wasn't the time, it wasn't the place, and he wasn't the man she wanted. And yet he still longed desperately, impossibly, unhappily to take her in his arms again, but this time to kiss her. To strip off her clothes and see her naked body because she wanted him to, not because she'd had to shift and everything she'd worn had been destroyed. To get down on his knees and taste—

Destiny lifted her head and yelled, "I don't believe a word you said! I caught on to you when you said those weren't velociraptors. What did you say they were? Achilles Bats? I never heard of them. I bet you made them up!"

As Ayers shouted back, "You're just showing your ignorance," Ethan and Destiny began crawling across the garden, trying not to snap any twigs or rustle any leaves. When they reached the wall on the other side, they could still hear their enemy's voice, now too far away to discern the words but with the arrogant tone distinctly audible.

"Let's run for the jungle," Ethan whispered. "If he follows, we can ambush him. We can crawl behind the tower, then run from behind it."

Destiny nodded. They vaulted over the low wall, then immediately dropped down behind it and began rapidly crawling for the tower.

A shattering roar filled the air. The stone road shook, and half the fruit fell from a nearby mango tree.

Ethan glanced over his shoulder. He would have thought that after the hell pig and the Achillo-whatevers, nothing could shock him anymore. But what he saw froze him in place. Towering over the garden walls—over the trees in the garden—over the building they were headed for—was a Tyrannosaurus rex.

He'd seen them in pictures and movies, and skeletons at museums. But nothing had prepared him for the real thing. Its size alone was almost impossible to comprehend in a living thing. It was at least twenty feet tall and thirty feet long, from gigantic head to lashing tail. Every one of the glittering fangs that lined its gaping jaws was the length of Ethan's forearm. Its tiny yellow eyes gleamed evilly from a face covered in armored plates as it swiveled its monstrous head toward them.

Ayers was nowhere to be seen. But as Ethan met the intelligent gaze of the T-Rex, he realized that it wasn't another cloned animal. It was Ayers himself—in his shift form.

Ethan also realized that they'd never make it to the jungle. Long before they reached it, the T-Rex that Ayers had become would take two immense steps and squash them flat. Even Destiny's tiger couldn't run fast enough.

Ethan stood up straight and fired at a yellow eye. The T-Rex twitched its head, and the bullet bounced off its cheek. Desperate to protect Destiny, Ethan fired again and again in rapid succession, trying to get off his best shot before the dinosaur charged them. He'd hit the hell pig in the eye—surely he could make this shot!

But the eyes of the T-Rex were embedded in cavern-like sockets protected by scales as tough as Kevlar, and the dinosaur wasn't as reckless as the hell pig had been. It ducked and weaved, making itself an impossible target. Every one of his bullets bounced off its scaly armor.

Disbelieving, Ethan heard his gun click on an empty chamber.

"The tower," whispered Destiny. "It's our only chance."

He grabbed her hand, and they sprinted for the entrance. The T-Rex roared angrily, loud enough to make their ears ring. The thud of its footstep shook the ground, nearly knocking them off their feet. Ethan didn't dare look back. He put on an extra burst of speed, giving it everything he had. With his longer legs, he outpaced Destiny, so he was half-dragging, half-carrying her as they burst through the open doorway.

An immense reptilian snout slammed into the narrow doorway, shaking the tower. The T-Rex roared in frustration, sending a fog of hot lizard breath over them.

Destiny and Ethan began tearing up the spiral staircase that wound around the inside of the tower like a gigantic spring. The T-Rex couldn't get in, but the T-Rex was also a man with a tranquilizer rifle and no doubt a regular gun as well. But once they got to the top before him, they'd have a massive advantage. It was far too tall for the T-Rex to reach, and no one in their right mind would want to climb a narrow staircase to try to attack enemies above.

Once again, Ethan's legs gave him the edge in speed. There was just enough room for two to walk abreast, so he put his arm around her waist and hauled her up with him. They reached the roof in record time, then dropped down, gasping and panting. They'd just run flat-out up the equivalent of ten steep flights of stairs. Even for a Recon Marine and a shifter, that was a lot.

But they only took a moment to catch their breath before looking down. The T-Rex was still a T-Rex, stomping around the base of the tower and roaring impotently. Every time it thudded its foot down, the tower quivered.

Doubtfully, Destiny asked, "Think if we stay here long enough, he'll go away to call for backup?"

Ethan shrugged. "I'm hoping if we stay here long enough, he'll get frustrated enough to turn back into a man and try climbing the steps. Then we take him out the instant he pokes his head into reach."

The T-Rex cocked its gigantic head. There was a cunning gleam in its reptilian eyes that Ethan didn't like one bit. The dinosaur edged closer until it got a grip on the tower with its little front arms. They didn't look strong, but the entire tower shook hard enough to knock Ethan and Destiny into each other's arms.

She was very warm and very soft, and he regretted it very much when she untangled herself. But then the T-Rex shook the tower again, and they once again had to grab on to each other. This time she didn't let go, and he certainly wasn't going to. Stealthily, he lowered his head and inhaled the intoxicating scent of her hair.

"Of everyone I've ever known, you're the one I'd most want to have on my side when I'm out of bullets and treed by a T-Rex," she said.

"Same here. Also on the bright side, it is literally impossible for this situation to get any worse."

The T-Rex shook the tower and roared. There was a sharp bang. A hairline crack appeared in the marble beneath their feet, and a piece of a turret split off and shattered on the street below.

Ethan's belly tightened. He'd thought they were safe as long as they stayed where they were, but not if the T-Rex could shake the whole tower down like a Jenga stack.

Destiny's eyes glinted with a greenish spark that alarmed him; he'd last seen it right before she'd nearly lost control and become a tiger. "I could shift and jump down on it. If I landed on its back, I might be able to get my teeth around its neck."

His arms tightened around her in instinctive protectiveness. "Absolutely not. That thing is twenty feet tall and bullets bounced off it! It'd knock you off and stomp you flat."

"Got a better idea?"

"Anything that doesn't involve you committing suicide!"

Ethan thought for a moment. "I could jump down on its head and stab it in the eye."

"That's not better!"

The tower shook violently. There was another loud crack, and the split in the marble widened. Ethan thought frantically, but he couldn't come up with any better ideas. Stab in the eye it was. He let go of Destiny and stood up, drawing his sword.

"No!" Destiny shouted. She grabbed his arm, snarling. Her eyes were now green as the forest, the pupils contracted into slits. She was about to shift.

He sheathed the sword and held her tight. "Easy. Easy, history nerd. You can control this…"

A pterodactyl swooped out of the sky.

It was like some hideous cross between a giant bird, a giant bat, and a flying lizard, with immense yellow-green wings made of thin membrane. Its vicious fanged beak opened wide as it dove toward them. Ethan let go of Destiny, leaped to his feet, and whipped his sword from its sheath to slash at the diving pterodactyl. It veered away, but not before he clipped one of its wingtips. It let out a piercing shriek, then circled in the sky above them like a vulture.

The T-Rex gave the tower its hardest shake yet, knocking Ethan and Destiny sprawling. He heard crashes as pieces of it came off and smashed on the ground.

Okay, Ethan thought grimly. *I was wrong the first time. But now the situation can't get any worse.*

Shredded cloth flew out in all directions as Destiny suddenly became a tiger. Roaring ferociously, she leaped over the edge.

"No!" Ethan yelled. He rushed to the turret, his blood running cold with terror, just in time to see the T-Rex get a faceful of angry tiger.

CHAPTER 11

The tiger landed on the T-Rex's snout. Berserk with rage and predatory instinct, she forgot everything but the urge to attack. The tiger slashed and bit wildly, digging in her claws to stay on as the T-Rex bellowed and shook its head. She would bite. She would kill. She would drink the big lizard's blood and roar her triumph to the skies!

Waves of fury and bloodlust washed over Destiny like she was caught in a storm at sea, helplessly tumbled head over heels by something far stronger than herself. She felt tiny and weak beside her tiger's ferocity and strength. Besides, what good was Destiny? She was just a woman—a woman who didn't even have a gun. The tiger was what Ethan needed, not the woman.

Destiny tried to make her tiger lift her head so she could see how Ethan was doing. But Destiny wasn't in control of her body, and the snarling beast ignored her. The tiger, losing her grip on the dinosaur's snout, sprang forward and sank her teeth into the back of the great reptile's neck. Yes! Here was the place. Now she could kill her prey!

The T-Rex swung his great head in a panic, trying to knock the tiger off. Its head crashed into the tower, sending a huge crack up its side. But the tiger dodged the blow, then once again sank in her teeth, using all her strength to try to close her jaws.

Stop! Destiny cried. *The tower! Ethan's on the tower!*

That got through to the tiger, which glanced up. Destiny and her tiger felt the same jolt of protective fear as they saw Ethan atop the leaning tower, bracing himself with one hand on a turret as he fought the pterodactyl that swooped and dove above him. He slashed at it with his sword, but the flying reptile was fast, dodging his blows and snapping at him with its long toothed beak.

We will kill the big lizard, growled her tiger. *Then we will kill the flying lizard. That's the best way to help him!*

Not if he gets killed when the T-Rex knocks down the tower! Destiny shouted.

But her tiger, too filled with protective fury to listen, chomped down harder on the T-Rex's neck.

The dinosaur let out an ear-splitting roar of pain and rage, and threw itself against the tower, desperately trying to dislodge the tiger. Her claws lost their grip on its back, but her jaws held tight. Destiny could only watch in horror as more cracks opened in the golden marble of the tower, and it began to tilt inexorably toward them.

As the tower started to fall, Ethan dropped his sword, as if in panic, and tipped his head to stare up at the pterodactyl. Seeing his unprotected throat exposed, it dove in for the kill, claws first like a hawk dropping down on a rabbit.

Ethan leaped upward and grabbed its feet just as the tower toppled. Screeching, the dinosaur flapped its leathery wings in a frantic attempt to stay airborne, but Ethan's weight sent it spiraling down toward the ground.

Within the tiger, Destiny experienced the surreal slowing

of time she'd experienced before in combat, allowing her to see many possibilities in a split second that felt like an eternity. The T-Rex, distracted by her attack, was too busy trying to throw her off to notice that it was about to be squashed flat by a hundred tons of golden marble. But her tiger had sure noticed. Her muscles were bunched to leap off the T-Rex. And once she did, the T-Rex would look up and jump clear as well. Their one chance to kill it would be gone.

Not yet, Destiny told her tiger.

The big cat's instinctive fear of death was overwhelming. Her panicked shriek filled Destiny's mind. *Jump! Jump! Jump!*

Her tiger was too strong for her. She was going to jump off, and then the T-Rex would kill her. And Ethan.

She had to save him.

Destiny fought her tiger, locking her muscles in place and her claws into the T-Rex's neck. She watched, her blood like liquid ice in her veins, as the dinosaur thrashed and her tiger shrieked and the tower fell and fell as if in slow motion, blotting out the sky.

NOW!

Destiny released her hold on her tiger. The edge of the collapsing tower brushed against her tail as they jumped clear, then rolled head over paws on the marble street. A reptilian bellow was abruptly cut off as the tower smashed into the T-Rex with a tremendous crash.

Chips and fragments of marble flew out like shrapnel, and a cloud of golden dust rose up. When it settled, she saw a giant pile of shattered marble, and, protruding from opposite ends of it, a gigantic claw and the tip of a scaly tail.

But Destiny had no time to relax and be relieved. A furious reptilian screeching arose from the other side of the rubble pile, then a very human yell. She raced around it, intent on helping Ethan in his battle. She skidded around the corner, her paws slipping on the smooth marble, and found

Ethan and the pterodactyl engaged in a desperate struggle on the ground.

The flying dinosaur's toothed beak snapped, its razor-sharp talons slashed, and its immense leathery wings flapped wildly. It was so much bigger than Ethan that at first she couldn't even see him. Then both wings slapped into the ground at once, and she saw that he was astride the pterodactyl with his strong arms locked around its neck, his face buried in its back to protect his head from its beak and claws.

Before she could do anything to help him out, the muscles of his arms bulged. There was a sharp crack, and the pterodactyl went limp. He had broken its neck.

Ethan jumped free, standing with his back to her. Instantly, he bolted toward the tower, shouting her name.

Unable to speak, she roared. Ethan turned around so fast he almost fell, then ran to her. He dropped to his knees before her, stroking her and burying his face in her fur. When he finally raised his head, she saw that his cheeks were wet with tears.

"I thought you were dead," he saw, his voice raw and choked. "I was yelling at you to jump, but you didn't. I couldn't get free of that thing until it was too late."

She was a tiger—a tiger who couldn't even control herself enough to become human again—but he'd run toward her, not away from her, without even a second of hesitation. Even as she felt his arms around her, it seemed impossible.

As if he'd guessed her thoughts, he said, "I'm not afraid of you. I could never be afraid of you. Your tiger isn't a monster, it's a part of you—the part that's wild and fearless. Angry and willful and stubborn, maybe, but that's part of you too. That's okay. I'm like that too. If we weren't, we wouldn't be Marines and bodyguards, we'd be accountants or interior decorators or baristas. But no matter how fierce your tiger is, it's only as fierce as you are. She'd never do anything that isn't in your own heart. You'd never hurt me, so neither will she."

It's true, her tiger said. *I'd rather jump into the big lizard's mouth than hurt him.*

I believe you, Destiny replied. Though she couldn't speak aloud, she intended her words for them both.

It was no struggle to become a woman again. As she did, she watched as Ethan's expression changed from one of intense relief to one of mingled desire and guilt, as if he was looking at something he knew he shouldn't be. His face flushed pink, and he pulled off his shirt, turned his back, and held it out to her without turning around.

Only then did she realize that she was stark naked. Again. She snatched the shirt from his hand and pulled it on. He was tall enough that it functioned as a short dress.

"You can turn around now." Her own voice came out choked and thick as she added, "That was the best thing anyone ever said to me. Thank you."

Ethan swept her into his arms and held her tight. Only then did she relax and let go of the adrenaline rush of battle. He was so strong, and his muscular body felt so good against hers. For the first time in what seemed like years, she felt safe and protected. If another T-Rex came stomping in, they'd face it together.

"Don't ever believe there's anything wrong with you," he murmured. "You're perfect. And your tiger is perfect too. You just took down a fucking T-Rex!"

"It mostly took itself down, but I'll take the credit for distracting it," Destiny said. "But you! You took down a pterodactyl all by yourself. Bare-handed!"

With his face pressed against hers, she felt as well as heard his chuckle. "Is that more or less cool than doing it with a sword?"

"That is a question for the ages," Destiny said. "But you started out with a sword, so I'll give you credit for both."

He didn't reply. She was so happy that he was alive and she was alive and they had won and he was holding her that she assumed he was just savoring the moment, as she was. His skin was so warm...

No. Not warm. It was hot. And getting hotter by the second.

Alarmed, Destiny broke free of their embrace to look at him. Ethan's face was very pale, with a bright red flush along the cheekbones. As she watched, he broke out in a sweat.

"I think the herb's wearing off." He stopped to cough, a painful, tearing sound. When he spoke again, his voice was hoarse and weak. "Goddamn it. I didn't want to be a burden—"

Then his knees buckled, his eyes closed, and he started to collapse. Destiny leaped forward to catch him. He was a dead weight, nearly knocking her down. She staggered, then crouched and pulled him over her shoulders in a fireman's carry. Then she stood up, lifting from the knees. She could carry him, but he was much bigger than her, and heavy. She wouldn't be able to get him very far, very fast...

...but the real problem was that they had no good place to go.

I suppose back to the palace is the best of a bunch of bad choices, she thought. *With any luck, Ayers is the only one who managed to track us here, and now he's dead and can't report back. And anyone else who comes hunting us will find us just as easily in the jungle as in the city.*

She carried Ethan back along the streets. Her tiger's presence was strong in her mind as it paced back and forth, its tail swishing with anxiety and unfocused anger, but it didn't try to take over. Destiny was less worried now that it would attack Ethan, and more that it would decide to run off into the jungle to hunt when she needed to stay human to take care of him.

No, I won't, growled her tiger, sounding exasperated. *Would you run off when he needs you? If you wouldn't, I won't either.* After a moment, she added hopefully, *But fresh meat would give him strength. Shall we make a soft, safe lair, and* then hunt for him?

Let's see how he is when we get to the lair, Destiny replied. *But you're right, he probably could use some nice, nourishing venison broth. Though I don't think the lair will be safe if we leave him...*

Her tiger snarled angrily, as unable as Destiny was to see any way to keep Ethan safe if they left his side. For her own part, Destiny was afraid that he might not be safe no matter what she did. His skin burned hotter and hotter, and every breath sounded like it might be his last.

Weight or no weight, she flat-out ran back to the palace. She stopped at the drawbridge, listening for any sound of something inside.

Let me help, her tiger offered. *I can hear and smell better than you.*

You can't shift, Destiny warned her. *I'm still carrying Ethan.*

I know. Just let me come a little closer to the surface.

Nervously, Destiny didn't fight as she felt her tiger enhance her senses. Her hearing became much sharper, her sense of smell a hundred times more so. But hard as she sniffed and carefully as she listened, she heard nothing but the whisper of wind, the flutter of leaves, and the labored rasp of Ethan's breath, and smelled nothing but dust and herbs and Ethan's sweat.

She laid him down on the floor to pull up the drawbridge. When she stooped to pick him up again, fear struck through her heart at how pale and vulnerable he looked. They might be safe from enemies inside the palace, but his most deadly enemy was inside his own body, and there was no fighting that.

Just like me, Destiny thought, trying to keep the thought in the back of her mind, safe from her tiger's prying claws. *Neither of us has ever been afraid of what's outside. Only of what's inside...*

She picked him up and brought him back to his bed, where she took off his boots and belt and tiger claws, and tried to make him as comfortable as she could. Destiny hated to leave him alone, but all her supplies were in the kitchen. She left the tiger claws on the bed beside him, just in case; she couldn't imagine he'd be able to use them, but if he woke up, he'd at least know she was near. No one else would know to leave them by his hand as a defense and a comfort. Then she bolted out of the room.

She hurried around the kitchen, making use of the herbs she already had and cursing her inability to go search for more. But she didn't dare leave Ethan alone in the palace. She made some more syrup for soothing coughs and hot tea to keep him hydrated, feeling all the while like she was slapping a Band-Aid over a bullet wound. Then she cut up another mango, dipped some cloths in cool water, piled everything on a tray, and returned to his room.

He hadn't moved from where she'd left him. She set down the tray on the table and stroked the damp hair back from his forehead. His skin was like fire. He turned his head slightly, moving into her touch.

"You awake?" she asked quietly.

His eyes opened slowly. His blue-green gaze was glassy and unfocused.

"Ellie?" he mumbled.

"It's Destiny. Ellie's not here."

He didn't seem to hear her, and he obviously wasn't seeing her. "Ellie, call in to the base for me. Tell them I'm sick. I'm not…" He coughed painfully. "…not fit to ship out."

"I'll make the call. Don't worry about it." Destiny wiped the sweat from his face with a damp cloth, then coaxed him to take a spoonful of the cough syrup.

He swallowed it, then closed his eyes. She was debating whether it was worth waking him up to get him to drink some tea when he opened his eyes, pushed himself up on one elbow, and shouted hoarsely, "Valdez! Valdez! Stop fighting, we have to go back! Merrick, grab his other arm!"

"Ethan, you're safe in bed. You're safe!"

He didn't hear or even look at her, but kept on shouting orders from some battle long past until a coughing fit cut him off. When it ended, he slumped back into the pillows, exhausted.

"Oh, Ethan." Destiny stroked his hair, which seemed to calm him. She lifted his head so he could drink some tea. He took a few sips, then turned his head away. She went back to stroking his hair.

"What's it take, Dad?" he mumbled. "Straight As? A baseball scholarship? Or nothing? Nothing, right? There's nothing I can ever do that'll ever be good enough."

"You *are* good enough," Destiny said. But he obviously didn't hear her.

"Recon Marine won't be either," he went on, his voice very hoarse. "But that's not why I'm doing it. That's for me, not you. For me!"

He began coughing again. When he finally stopped, she tried to get him to take some more cough syrup, but he refused it. She set down the spoon before he'd have spilled it all over the bed. It obviously wasn't doing any good anyway.

She had never felt so helpless in her life. Ethan was trapped in nightmares and she couldn't do anything but sit there and listen. If only there was some villain or monster to fight! She'd rather face a million T-Rexes than have to sit by Ethan's side and watch him suffer, knowing all the while that all he needed was medical help that was just a short plane flight away, but might as well be on the moon for all her ability to get it to him.

"Destiny?" Ethan whispered, startling her.

"I'm here."

"I have to tell you something."

"Sure, go ahead."

He coughed. "I can't breathe. Help me sit up."

She lifted him and let him lean on her, with his head resting on her shoulder. The heat of his body made her break into a sweat, as if she was sitting by a raging fire. She wasn't sure if he was still delirious or not. He'd called her by name, but his gaze was unfocused and his voice was distant and dreamy.

"I've loved you since the day I met you," he said. "Every day, I wake up and think of you. Your beautiful eyes. Your laugh. Your hand in mine. Then every day, I remember that you don't love me and you never will. And every day, my heart breaks all over again."

"Ethan," Destiny whispered, then stopped, unable to say more. She knew he was speaking the truth of his heart, but she didn't know if he meant to tell it to her or if it was only his fever that had loosened his tongue. But more than that, his words broke *her* heart. Oh, she'd known he liked her a lot. That he had a crush on her. But how could he truly love her when she wasn't his mate?

But he did. She could hear every minute of that two-year heartbreak in his voice.

Before she could say anything, he went on, "Dad was right. I'm not just good enough."

"He was wrong!" She wrapped her arms around him and held him tight. "Of course you're good enough! You're brave and strong and funny and hot—you're everything any woman could possibly want. You're everything *I* want!"

Destiny heard her own words as if they had been spoken by someone else, allowing her to know the truth of them. Slowly, she repeated, "You're everything I want. You've always been everything I wanted. Ethan, *your* face is the face I imagine before I open my eyes, and then I see the empty pillow. It breaks my heart too. I love you. I've always loved you. I—"

She broke off. His lips were parted, his eyes wide and bright with astonished joy. The heat still came off him in waves and he might sink back into fever dreams at any moment. But she could see that right now, he was here with her. Whatever she said next, he'd hear and remember.

"I said no because I was afraid," she admitted. "I'm not your mate, so I thought one day you'd meet her and leave me. But—"

"I hate that fucking imaginary mate!" Ethan burst out. "She doesn't even exist, and she's still keeping you from me. If I ever do meet her, I'll show her the door so fast it'll hit her ass on the way out."

A snicker escaped from Destiny's lips. "You don't need to be mean to her. I'm sure you wouldn't be anyway. You're a gentleman."

"You're right. I'll very politely escort her out. And then I'll put out a restraining order on her, to make sure she stays out."

She laughed again, a little incredulously. No one would ever do that to their mate… but what *was* a mate, anyway?

"I kept telling you that you weren't a shifter, so you couldn't understand," she said. "But you understood better than I did. If a mate isn't the person you love with all your heart and want to spend the rest of your life with, then I don't want a mate. I want you. And I'm sorry I made you wait so long."

"You're worth waiting for. Destiny, you—" His words were cut off as he broke into a long, painful coughing spell. He covered his mouth with his hand.

When he finally stopped, gasping for breath, his hand fell to his side as if he didn't have the strength to hold it up any longer. Where his palm touched, it left red smears on the blanket. Slowly, she raised her gaze to his face. There was blood on his lips, too.

Until that moment, she had never truly known terror. Nor had she known despair. It was only then that she realized that Ethan had been right: she'd been knocked down a thousand times, and gotten up a thousand and one. But this was something she could never get up from. The man she loved was dying in her arms, and there was absolutely nothing she could do to save him.

He was also looking at the blood on the blanket. Without fear, but rather the cool evaluation of a bad situation she'd heard in his voice when they'd been in combat together, he said, "I think I'm going to die if I don't get help."

Wild ideas raced through her mind. "I could carry you to the Apex base and break in—"

"Destiny." He had to stop to catch his breath before he went on. "I won't make it. But shifters heal better. Bite me."

Never bite anyone who isn't already a shifter had been so ingrained into her that it hadn't even occurred to her to try it until he'd mentioned it. Cold fear struck deep into her heart at the thought of it. "Ethan, no! I'll kill you!"

With that same detached calm as when he'd mentioned it, he said, "You said that was rare." He pulled in a labored breath. "I hate to make you risk it. But it's my only chance."

Destiny felt paralyzed. If she bit him, she might kill the

man she loved. If she didn't, she'd be letting him die through inaction.

Her tiger surged up, trying to force her to shift. Destiny pushed back. There was a brief but fierce inner battle. To Destiny's own surprise, she won.

He wants to be a tiger, said the big cat inside her. *He needs to be a tiger. Set me free. He will recover, and we will all be free to hunt together, as we should.*

Destiny looked into Ethan's eyes, and saw the predator within him. Her tiger was right; all she needed to do was set his own beast free.

"You sure, jarhead?"

"I'm sure, mudpuppy."

She helped him sit up in bed, propped against the headboard and some pillows. Then she stepped back and pulled off her shirt—his shirt. It still smelled like him. She stood naked before him, the jungle air warm on her body and his regard hot on her skin.

When she reached into herself to become a tiger, she found that doing so felt different than it ever had before. When she'd been a child, it had always been completely involuntary and, once she understood that she should only do it when she intended to, a shameful proof of her weakness. Later, after she'd started using the pills, it felt like a simple physical action, like drawing her gun, with no sense of connection to the big cat within her.

Destiny had always known that her tiger was a part of herself. But she'd never truly *felt* it. First she'd fought her tiger, then she'd built a wall between them, and then, when she'd lost her pills, she'd fought her inner beast again. But now she felt attuned to that other self. She *was* her tiger.

When she'd been a child, her tiger cub had contained the full force of a strong-willed child's anger and frustration.

The little girl trying to suppress those feelings had never had a chance against the part of herself that expressed them.

But now she was an adult, and so was her tiger. She didn't have to fight herself in a desperate battle for control or lock up her feelings in separate boxes. She could accept all of herself, and just *be* herself.

I never got to grow up, her tiger said. *Those herbs kept me too quiet to grow or learn. I was always a cub at heart. Until you stopped taking them, and I began making up for lost time.*

Her tiger *had* been acting like a rebellious teenager, ever since she'd stopped the pills. No wonder she'd been so much trouble!

And now? Destiny asked, though she already knew the answer.

Now we are one, her tiger purred.

The shift felt as natural as breathing. Destiny avoided looking at Ethan's face; she was afraid that if she did, her terror of him dying would come rushing back. It was best to simply act, and do it quickly and without thought. She lowered her muzzle to the bed and bit his forearm just deep enough to draw blood.

Destiny became a woman again. She pulled her shirt back on with shaking hands, and turned back to Ethan. If anything was going to—to go wrong—it would happen very quickly. Her gaze focused first on the trickle of blood from his bitten arm, then moved to his chest. He was breathing. And he kept breathing. Was it her imagination, or were the harsh gasps of his breath softening?

"You did it." There was no mistaking it: his voice was stronger. "Destiny, you saved me."

The force of her relief made her weak at the knees. She dropped down beside the bed, laid her head on his chest, and let her tears flow. For the first time, she cried in front of another person and felt no shame. She had no need to put up a bright front of strength and cheer. Ethan would understand; Ethan loved her; Ethan would live.

He didn't tell her to stop crying. He didn't speak at all. He just held her, stroking her back and hair, while she let herself feel all the pent-up emotion of everything that had happened that day. Everything that had happened since she'd first met him, and turned him away for reasons that now seemed absurd. Who cared about mates when she could have Ethan?

She wept until her tears dried up, replaced with a deep sense of inner peace. At long last, she lifted her head, and looked into the blue-green ocean of his eyes without fear.

Mine, her tiger purred with immense satisfaction and absolute certainty. *Our mate.*

"What?!" Destiny burst out. "*Now* you tell me?"

Ethan looked equally amazed and baffled. "Is your tiger saying we're mates? Because mine is sure of it."

"So's mine." To her tiger, Destiny demanded, *Why didn't you say so before?*

With an air of injured innocence, her tiger said, *I didn't know before. I told you, I was a cub at heart. You can't know your mate when you're a child.*

Destiny repeated that, adding, "It was those pills! They didn't just give me control over my shift. They were stopping my tiger from growing up with me. Mate recognition doesn't kick in until you're old enough to do something about it."

"Mataji didn't know that would happen, right?"

"No, I'm sure she had no idea. And I did need them at the time. I just should have stopped taking them later, once I was more mature."

Unexpectedly, Ethan chuckled. "So, you're saying you *literally* had an inner child."

"Smartass." She poked his arm—not the bitten one. "You must be feeling better."

"I am." He was still fever-hot, but not blazing like he'd

been before, and his breathing had eased. His eyelids fluttered, then closed. He seemed to force them back open. "Sorry. I'm really tired."

She stroked his forehead. "Go to sleep. You need it."

"One thing first."

He reached up a hand, caught the back of her head, and pulled her down to him. Their lips met in a kiss that was short but felt eternal in the very best way, a kiss of both passion and comfort.

A kiss of love fulfilled at last.

CHAPTER 12

When Ethan awoke, a sense of happiness and wellbeing filled him even before he remembered where he was and what had happened. He drew in a deep breath, and it neither hurt nor left him feeling suffocated. He was neither burning up nor freezing, but pleasantly warm. His head didn't hurt any more. Best of all, his heart wasn't filled with loneliness and the bitter knowledge that what he wanted most, he could never have.

He reached out a hand, and felt Destiny's fingers curl around his.

"Ethan?" she said softly. "You awake?"

He opened his eyes. She was perched on the bed beside him. A shaft of morning sun fell across her face, catching the golden undertones of her skin. Her warm brown eyes were brimming with the same love for him that he felt for her.

Our mate, his tiger purred.

That new inner voice should have felt strange, but it didn't. Ethan could feel that his tiger was a part of him. He'd never denied the fiercer parts of his self, so having the wildest and most primal aspect of himself given a voice of its own felt natural. And calling Destiny his mate was only putting a name to what Ethan had always known.

He couldn't believe that they'd known each other for so long and spent so much time together without giving in to their feelings. To their desire. It burned in him like a wildfire, fierce and hot and unstoppable. And when he looked into her eyes, he saw that it burned in her too. How the hell had they both managed to control themselves for *two years?*

"You are the most stubborn woman on the face of the Earth," he said.

"Gee, you really know how to give a girl a compliment," she teased. "And same to you. Well, not the most stubborn *woman...*"

He sat up, laughing, ready to make some terrible joke about proving his maleness. She was laughing too. But the laughter faded as he put his hands on her shoulders. At that simple touch, the raw sexual heat that had always smoldered within them, banked and repressed and fought with all their might, burst into flames.

He'd meant to take his time and savor the moment. He savored the moment, all right, but the instant he touched her, he knew that neither of them were in the mood for any slow careful lovemaking. It was love, yes, but love like a fever, love like a fire, a love that was wild and fierce and never again to be denied.

He kissed her with the ferocity of two endless years of pent-up passion. She returned it with equal urgency, nipping at his lips as he nipped at hers. Her scent surrounded him, filling his senses and driving him wild. He pulled at her clothes, impatient to touch every inch of her smooth warm skin, to mark it with his own skin, his own scent, to claim her and make her his own.

But her strong soft hands were already inside his pants, stroking his thighs, on his rock-hard erection. His urgent need threatened to flare out of control, and he heard himself growl.

With a teasing purr, she stopped her explorations just long enough to allow him to strip her. He feasted his eyes on her delectably feminine curves, her irresistible scent. All of her.

"My Destiny," he growled. "Mine."

"Ethan," she gasped. "Ethan, oh, Ethan, finally—!"

He pulled her out of her chair and laid her down on the bed. And then he let himself feast for real, tasting her, savoring her, teasing her sensitive nipples and feeling them harden to nubs under his tongue. Her nails dug into his shoulders as he went lower, but the tiny pain only sharpened his pleasure. She responded to his smallest touch, moaning and writhing, losing control. He loved seeing, hearing, *feeling* her desire. Destiny wanted him, needed him, just as much as he needed her.

He licked at her inner thighs, and she instinctively opened herself to him, inviting him to taste her tangy sweetness. He did. Her clit was like a little pearl under his tongue, and he felt it swell and throb as he made her climax.

Then he could hold himself back no more. And she was ready for more, a woman to match his own desperate desire. Even as he raised himself over her, she was pulling him in to her. They came together as if they were made for each other. And, he realized, that was because they *were*.

"Now!" she called out. "Come on, Ethan, now, now, now!"

He filled her with a single thrust, sliding into her ready wet heat. Destiny looked into his eyes, making it a moment of intimacy and connection as much as physical pleasure. She met his passion with passion, his desire with desire, his love with love. It was everything he had ever wanted. *She* was everything he'd ever wanted.

"I love you," he gasped. "My mate!"

She cried out his name as she reached her second climax. He had never heard anything so sensual as his name on her lips, or seen anything so beautiful as her widened eyes. As his own ecstasy engulfed him, he held her close, glorying in the shared joy that had come to them at last.

Afterward, they held each other tenderly. Every curve of her body fit into every angle of his, like puzzle pieces.

Ethan would have loved to stay entwined with her for hours, if not days, but they had a much-delayed mission to go on. And if he was strong enough to make love, he was strong enough to carry it out.

Reluctantly, he sat up. "How long was I out? I mean before."

She snickered. "I know what you meant." Then, seriously, she said, "Just about twenty-four hours."

Destiny cut off his exclamation of dismay with a shake of her head. "You needed it, Ethan. Shifters heal fast, but not instantaneously. Did you want me to wake you up earlier, so you could jump out of bed, tear off to the base, and collapse halfway there?"

He couldn't argue with that. "When we get back to the US, we'll stay in bed all day. All weekend, even."

"I'll hold you to that."

They shared one more passionate kiss, and he swung his legs over the side of the bed and cautiously stood up. A brief moment of dizziness washed over him, then faded. As he got dressed, he took inventory of his physical self. His side ached a little, and he could feel that he wasn't quite up to his usual strength. But he was almost there. If he didn't push too hard getting to the base, he should be fine by the time he arrived.

Destiny handed him his sword and tiger claws. "Here you go."

"I thought I'd lost the sword."

"I went back to the tower and retrieved it. Mine too. And my tiger claws." Destiny patted her belt. "And I killed a deer for dinner. My tiger was beyond thrilled."

"We've got venison?" Ethan asked hopefully. "Or did you mean you ate it as a tiger?"

"Both. My tiger had some, then I cooked some for me and you." Quickly, she added, "Not from the part my tiger had chewed on!"

"Mudpuppy, I'm so hungry I wouldn't even care."

He accompanied her to the kitchen, where she retrieved some venison steaks she'd grilled over the fire, sliced up, and packed in a sort of lunch box of hammered bronze. Ethan's stomach growled as she offered it to him.

"It's not Aunt Lizzie's barbecue, but…"

He was too busy eating the juicy, savory meat to reply. Once his mouth wasn't full, he said, "You'd give Aunt Lizzie a run for her money."

Still eating, they walked out together. As they passed the fallen tower, Destiny said, "I know it wasn't our fault, but I feel bad about that."

"Killing the T-Rex?" Ethan asked.

"No, knocking down the tower. It's a historical monument. Or it should be, anyway."

"It still could be. I mean, the whole city. We could contact some Indian archaeologists…" Ethan noticed the huge claw and tail-tip poking out from the heap of marble. "…or not. I don't know if finding a fresh T-Rex could lead to shifters in general getting discovered, but maybe it's better not to take any chances."

Destiny contemplated the claw. "Yeah, I don't think we want anyone finding any dinosaurs. But Mataji knows a lot of shifters in India. I bet if I tipped her off, she could arrange for a team of shifters to come dispose of the dinosaurs, then have someone 'discover' the city. Bingo! Historical monument!"

"How do you dispose of a T-Rex?"

She grinned. "I think I'll let that one be someone else's problem."

When they reached the gates of the city and saw the jungle beyond, Destiny stopped. "We'd make better time as tigers. Want to take a walk on the wild side, jarhead?"

Yes, purred his tiger. *We will run and track and hunt with our mate.*

Ethan watched with enjoyment and barely restrained desire as she undressed and put her clothes and weapons in the backpack. He had to turn his back on her before he undressed himself. If they were both naked at the same time and watching each other, he'd either be unable to restrain himself, or she would, or they'd both lose their minds.

He packed up his clothes and weapons, then reached inside himself to find his tiger. Ethan imagined being bigger, furrier, hunting by scent and on four huge paws...

...and the world seemed to shift focus. He was on all fours, in a new body that felt lithe and strong and fierce. He could no longer see in color, but all sorts of fascinating and distinct scents surrounded him. Ethan turned to see Destiny's tiger watching him with brilliant eyes. He tried to smile at her, and found himself making a huffing noise instead. They padded up to each other, sniffing and nuzzling, then, for a brief wild moment, playfully nipping and rolling over together on the ground.

Then he picked up the backpack in his powerful jaws and they set off at a brisk lope. Their tigers had evolved to travel in this exact sort of terrain, and moved between the trees with far more ease than they could as humans, despite being far bigger. And it was a special kind of joy to run through the jungle with his mate beside him, tracking the acrid lizard smell of the Achillo-whatevers and the human scent of their controller back to the base.

We hunt, purred his tiger with satisfaction. *This is what we were always meant for.*

His mate hunted by his side. Ethan felt light as a feather, in body and heart and soul. The miles fell away behind them.

CHAPTER 13

They reached the jungle surrounding the Apex base as the sun was going down. The scraps of western sky between the leaves glowed like the heart of a fire. Destiny's keen tiger's nose could smell concrete, engine oil, fuel exhaust, and other odors that had no place in a jungle.

She and Ethan stopped, concealed by dense trees and hanging curtains of vines. Destiny nuzzled him, then nudged the backpack he carried in his mouth. He dropped it and became a naked man.

It was good to see him standing strong and confident, not even winded by their long run. She'd been so afraid for him. But that was over now. They were on a dangerous mission, sure, but Ethan did dangerous missions for a living. And so did she. They'd already beaten a T-Rex! She couldn't imagine that base holding anything that could scare her after that.

Once Destiny became a woman, she took a moment to unabashedly admire him. The stark patterns of his black tattoos covered his chest and arms, following and enhancing the natural angles of bone and swells of muscle. She feasted her eyes on his biceps, his triceps, his pecs, the light dusting of golden hair on his chest. She always had liked men with muscles, and Ethan was well-endowed in that department. In others, too. What a lucky girl she'd turned out to be.

"You look luscious," Ethan murmured.

"So do you. Being a shifter suits you."

"It's hard to believe I was ever anything else."

He bent down, and she tipped her face up. His strong arms encircled her, protective and loving. They came together for a kiss, breathing in each other's scent and warmth and presence. His body melded against hers in a perfect fit.

They opened the backpack and dressed quickly, then slung their swords and tiger claws on their belts. She left the gun in the backpack; it was useless without bullets. With any luck they'd soon be able to ambush a guard and acquire a new one. A tranquilizer rifle, preferably. They hoped to be able to get in, radio for help, break out the prisoners, and get out without raising an alarm, and gunshots indoors would certainly do that.

As they began stealthily making their way toward the base, a rustle of leaves made them freeze and drop their hands to the hilts of their swords. They relaxed as they saw the source of the noise, a tiny shape moving behind a bush.

"Just a squirrel," she said. "Or a little—"

The creature burst out of the shrubbery. It was so covered in clinging wet leaves and moss that Destiny couldn't tell exactly what it was at first, other than that it walked on two legs.

"Is that a chicken?" Ethan said doubtfully.

The whatever-it-was stopped right in their path, showing no fear of them, and hissed. Destiny imagined she could hear a note of indignation in the sound. Also, it definitely was not a chicken, unless it was a mutant chicken with a whole lot of teeny fangs instead of a beak. It shook itself, sending moss and leaves flying, and revealed itself as a dinosaur. A very small dinosaur.

Destiny and Ethan stared at the creature. It somewhat resembled the Achillobators that had attacked them in the Golden City, but apart from being much smaller, it was black rather than mottled green, and had a sleeker shape. Its color made it blend into the rich black earth of the forest floor, so much so that it was hard to get a good look at it, apart from the gleam of its white fangs and the glow of its yellow eyes.

"I think it's a velociraptor!" Destiny exclaimed. "Remember, Ayers said they were the size of a chicken."

The velociraptor, if that was what it was, let out another hiss. Then it suddenly began to grow. Ethan grabbed Destiny's arm, and they jumped back as the dinosaur went from chicken-sized to Ethan-sized in less than three seconds.

"What the hell…" Ethan muttered, drawing his sword.

So did Destiny. "Must be another Apex agent. We can't let it report back!"

The dinosaur leaped away, changing shape as it did. A blond man in desert camouflage fell over backward into a bush, exclaiming, "Oops, sorry!"

He sprang up, started to hold out his hand to them as if he was asking for a shake, then pulled it back as Destiny instinctively followed the movement with her sword. "I'm friendly! Ethan, tell her I'm friendly."

"He's friendly." Ethan sounded more resigned than relieved. "*Very* friendly."

"I meant to turn into a man, not a man-sized raptor," the blond guy said, as if that explained anything. "I'm still getting the hang of this."

"Who are you?" Destiny asked, bewildered.

Ethan made a gesture of introduction. "Destiny, this is

Merlin Merrick, from my fire team. Merlin, this is Destiny Ford, my..."

Destiny had to repress a snicker as she watched Ethan fish for an explanation that wouldn't keep them there all day. But Merlin was a shifter, he'd know what mates were... or had Apex only turned him into a shifter after he'd been captured? There was an easy way to find out.

"Mate," Destiny said firmly. "We're mates."

"Oh." Merlin blinked a pair of extremely blue eyes at her. "You don't sound Australian."

The snicker escaped. "I'm not. It's a shifter thing. It means..." Now it was Destiny who had to fish for an easy explanation. As the words left her mouth, she realized that she was repeating Hal's explanation to Ethan from those two very long years ago. "He's my true love. Shifters mate for life."

"Congratulations," Merlin said, as if that didn't seem the slightest bit odd to him. He seemed sincerely pleased. "And you fight with a sword, very nice. Do you play video games? Ethan's true love would definitely play video games."

"Merlin—" Ethan began, sounding exasperated.

It was obvious that the two of them had a lot of clashes under the bridge. Destiny decided to cut the argument off at the pass. "Let's do the pleased to meet yous later. Here's the important thing about me: I'm an Army vet, former military police—" She overrode Merlin's remark of "A mudpuppy, cool," by continuing, louder, "—a tiger shifter, and also I'm a bodyguard in a private security agency where everyone's some kind of shifter. If we can get into the base, I can radio them to come back us up. They don't know I'm here."

"Merlin, is anyone following you?" Ethan asked.

"I doubt it," Merlin replied. "I don't think they know I'm gone yet. I escaped about an hour ago, when I figured out that I could change my size and squeezed through a duct. I'd meant to make a wide circle through the jungle, in case they did check my cell and launch a search, and squeeze back in through some other duct that wasn't guarded." Proudly, he added, "I camouflaged myself so if anyone did see me, they'd think I was a... hmm..."

"A chicken-sized leaf monster?" Ethan inquired.

"Something more normal in a jungle than a stealth-sized raptor," Merlin concluded. "Listen, do you know where Ransom and Pete are?"

"No," said Ethan. "We were hoping you did."

Merlin shook his head. "I woke up in a lab. They weren't there with me and nobody would tell me what happened to them or you. A doctor said they'd put me through some process called Ultimate Predator 3.0. He said it would give me special powers, and once I got them, I had to work for them or die. Then they stuck me in a locked room. Someone really screwed up to give me shrinking powers, then put me in a room with vents."

"They didn't know what powers you'd get," Destiny said. "I have some friends who got caught by this same organization—it's called Apex—and they think the powers have to do either with your personality, or with what you want at the time you get them."

"Oh." Merlin nodded. "Well, I definitely wanted to get out. And here I am. Out!"

Destiny was relieved that he didn't seem particularly traumatized by his brush with Apex. Maybe it was because his stay at the lab had been too short for them to do anything horrible to him. But she hoped that the T-Rex shifter had also been telling the truth, and their new version of the Ultimate Predator process was less dangerous and damaging than the old one. If the worst that had happened to Ethan's other two teammates was that they'd become shifters and gained powers, well, Merlin certainly didn't seem unhappy about that.

Ethan gave Merlin an extremely brief summary of what had happened since they'd last seen each other. Destiny was impressed with Ethan's ability to explain everything that Merlin actually needed to know in about five minutes, mostly by dint of not stopping whenever he tried to interrupt with a question.

"I like your original plan," Ethan concluded. "Let's keep it. We circle around, and you squeeze into a duct and let us in. The three of us can take it from there."

Destiny was relieved to hear his obvious confidence in Merlin's abilities, since she didn't have any tactful way to check for herself. But any man Ethan trusted was good enough for her.

The three of them slipped through the jungle, working their way in the direction Merlin indicated. The sun set, and in the darkness of the night they could hide unseen in the cover of the jungle and survey the base. No one seemed to have discovered Merlin's escape yet; there was no commotion or search parties that they could see. And while the entrances were all guarded, no one was guarding the vents.

"Here we go," whispered Merlin. "I'll try and get out that door there."

He first became a raptor even bigger than the one they'd first seen, about the size of a small pony. Then, with an exasperated hiss, he shrank into his chicken-sized (or, Destiny supposed, velociraptor-sized) form. Like the T-Rex and daeodon shifters, he took his clothes with him when he transformed.

The raptor's sleek, black form was even harder to see now that night had fallen, and she almost lost sight of him as he darted out of the jungle and across the ground. He was briefly very visible indeed as he clambered up the green wall of the base, and then, with a lithe wriggle, he vanished into the duct.

"He seems to be taking everything surprisingly in stride," Destiny whispered.

"Merlin's like that," Ethan whispered back. "I'm appreciating it a whole lot more now than I used to."

They waited, watching the doors. If Merlin wasn't able to take out the guards himself, hopefully by stealth and in silence, they'd have to jump in and help him. And whether they did so as tigers leaping out of the jungle or sword-wielding humans charging out, it would be neither stealthy nor silent. And then they'd be dealing with a whole 'nother ball game.

A door opened, and a blond man dressed as a security guard stepped out. Destiny tensed, waiting to see if the other guards would recognize him, but they didn't. She heard voices, but not what they were saying. Merlin made an animated gesture and pointed. Both guards turned to look, and he neatly shot them both in the back with his tranquilizer rifle. He caught them as they collapsed and dragged them inside.

Destiny and Ethan ran out of the jungle and into the base. There they found Merlin shoving the unconscious guards into the nearest room, an office already occupied by another unconscious man in nothing but boxer shorts.

"Sorry they're not your size," he said to Destiny.

"I'll make do. I'm used to changing on short notice." When Merlin gave her a puzzled look, she explained, "You take your clothes with you when you shift. Ethan and I don't. I think it has to do with whether you turn into an ordinary animal or something... else."

"But why—" Merlin began.

"Later," said Ethan.

He and Destiny ducked into the office, where they

stripped the guards, put on their uniforms, and took their tranquilizer rifles and IDs.

As they were changing, Destiny chuckled. "'Later?' No one has any idea why mythic and extinct shifters can take their clothes with them!"

"You haven't had to work with him," Ethan said. "If I'd said 'nobody knows,' we'd still be out in the corridor listening to him coming up with a hundred reasons why."

While Destiny rolled up the bottoms of her pants, Ethan stashed their regular clothes and swords in the backpack. It was an unobtrusive black one, so hopefully it wouldn't attract any attention.

They stepped out into a white corridor lit by fluorescent lights, which seemed to be the standard design for Apex bases if her previous encounter with one was anything to go by. It probably was; Shane had said they designed them to be as identical as possible, so they could move drugged prisoners from one to another without them realizing they'd switched locations. And in that case, Destiny had a rough idea of where things were.

Before Merlin could say anything, Ethan said, "Good job, Merlin," then turned to her. "Lead on. And we shouldn't talk unless we have to."

Destiny led them in silence toward the area where prisoners had been kept in the base she'd been to before. She was nervous about her uniform, which was several sizes too big, but more nervous about Merlin, who could actually get recognized. But all they could do about either was to walk confidently, as if they belonged there, and trust in people's tendency to not pay close attention. Her heart sped up when they encountered another pair of guards, but they passed without more than a glance and a nod.

At last they came to a door labeled "Subject Thirty."

"That'll be Pete or Ransom," Merlin said. "My door said Subject Thirty-One."

Destiny frowned. Justin had been Subject Seven, and Shane Subject Eight; Subjects One through Six had been the airmen who had been captured with them, and hadn't survived the experiments. Carter Howe, whom Fiona and Justin had rescued from the Apex base in Alaska, had been Subject Nine. Presumably the saber-tooth tiger they'd fought had been another subject. But who were the rest of them? Would the T-Rex and daeodon shifters even be counted that way, since they were Apex agents themselves? Destiny's stomach roiled at the suspicion that most if not all of the other twenty subjects were dead.

Ethan used his stolen ID to open the door. A quick glance showed them a small cell occupied by a single man dressed in desert camouflage, sitting on a cot. Destiny was chilled to see that he had a collar around his neck with an electronic lock and a disc of silvery metal that emitted a very faint glow.

"Ransom!" Ethan called softly.

The man didn't move or even look up.

"Come on!" Merlin urged.

Ransom didn't respond. With a sinking feeling, Destiny beckoned the other men inside. She used her ID to close the door behind them.

"Careful with him," Destiny said as Merlin started to hurry toward him. "He might be…" She didn't have time to explain exactly how damaged Shane and Justin had been from their experiences at Apex; Merlin had never met either of them, and Ethan didn't know Justin and had only met Shane after he'd had a year to somewhat recover.

"Think of it like he's just been through a really traumatizing combat experience," she said at last. "Don't grab him."

Merlin, who had been starting to do exactly that, pulled his hand back.

Ethan knelt down in front of him. "Hey. Hey, buddy, it's Ethan. Can you talk to me?"

Ransom slowly looked up. Destiny hadn't gotten a good look at him before, but now she saw that he had a lean and angular face, with auburn hair and high cheekbones. He was handsome, she supposed, or would be if not for the hollow-eyed stare that she remembered all too well from Shane and Justin.

"You're too late," he said.

"What do you mean?" Merlin asked. "What did they do to you?"

Ransom didn't answer. His gaze drifted away from their faces, then sharpened as he seemed to track something moving across the room behind them. All three of them whipped around, snatching for their tranquilizer rifles. But nothing was there. Puzzled, Destiny turned back, and saw Ransom continuing to watch whatever invisible thing he was seeing until it apparently stopped right behind her.

"He's coming closer," he said.

The hairs on the back of her neck stood up. Crazy as it was, she couldn't bear to stay there, feeling like a cold hand or slimy tentacle might grab her from behind at any second. She edged aside. Ransom continued to watch the space where she had been.

"What are you looking at?" she asked.

He gave her about the bleakest stare she'd ever seen. "Everything. Even when I close my eyes. I'll never see darkness again."

"You guys," Merlin broke in. "He's obviously been drugged."

Destiny sure hoped that was all it was. But she couldn't help looking at Ethan, who gave her the briefest head-shake: *don't say it.*

"Yeah," Ethan said. "That's right. Ransom, whatever you're

feeling is temporary. It'll go away once whatever they gave you wears off."

"It's not going to 'go away.'" There was an edge of bitter mockery in his voice. "I was already standing on the edge of a cliff. They pushed me over. I'll never stop falling."

"There's no point talking to him," Merlin said impatiently. "He's completely off his head. He probably won't even remember any of this tomorrow. We'll just have to cross our fingers he doesn't say something weird to the first guard we meet."

Ransom shot Merlin an irritated look. As if annoyance had broken through his haze of despair, he said in a much more normal tone, "*You're* the compulsive talker, not me."

"Guys," Ethan broke in. "We have to get out of here. Now."

"Wait," Destiny said. "That collar. Is it going to set off an alarm or… something… if you walk out wearing it?"

Or explode, she thought. From the expression on Merlin's face, she was pretty sure he was thinking the same thing.

"Or explode?" Ransom asked, as if he didn't particularly care. He shrugged. "No idea."

"I wonder why you have one and I don't," Merlin said.

Examining the collar, Ethan said, "Whatever it's for, we'll have to get it off later. I think it'll take special tools."

His expression didn't betray anything, but Destiny knew him well enough to guess that he was thinking, *And a bomb defuser, just in case.*

He helped Ransom up and led him to the door. Ransom didn't lean on Ethan, like a drugged or wounded man would do, but walked haltingly, using him as a guide like a blind person might. In fact, if she hadn't seen him focusing on her face earlier, she might have thought he *was* blind.

He doesn't need to say a thing to give us away, Destiny thought. *The first guard we meet is going to take one look at him and raise the alarm.*

Merlin, obviously thinking the same thing, said, "Maybe we should leave him here, find Pete, radio out, and collect him on the way back. I could stay with him."

Destiny's tiger put in, *No beast should be left locked in a cage.*

Destiny had to agree. "No. God knows what might happen to him—or you—if we do that."

Ethan backed her up. "We all stay together. If anyone tries to stop us, *we* stop *them*."

With a final dubious glance at Ransom, Merlin raised his ID and opened the door. To Destiny's immense relief, the collar did not explode, no alarms went off, and the corridor was empty. They looked for more rooms with "Subject" labels, but found only offices, storage areas, and unmarked empty cells. The corridor ended in a heavy, reinforced door.

"He's here," Ransom said.

A tremendous roar shook the air. Something crashed into the door, denting it and cracking the wall around it.

They all jumped backward, raising their tranquilizer rifles.

"Merlin, get Ransom back!" Ethan shouted.

Merlin tried to pull him away, but Ransom dug in his heels. His mouth moved, but whatever he was saying was drowned out in the roar and crash as the thing behind the door smashed through it and burst into the corridor.

It was a bear. But not one like any Destiny had ever seen. Calling this beast a bear was like calling the daeodon a hog, or the T-Rex a lizard. It was bigger than a polar bear, bigger than a grizzly. Even in the wide, high-ceilinged corridor, its sides brushed the walls and the fur of its back touched the ceiling. Its shaggy brown fur covered everything but its dagger-like claws, its gleaming white fangs, and its black eyes. Like the daeodon, this was a beast from another, more primal era.

"A cave bear," Merlin said, sounding awed.

The bear roared, and both the sound and its glittering eyes were filled with such terrifying rage that all of them instinctively flinched back. For the first time in her life, Destiny knew in her bones what it felt like to be the prey and not the predator.

Then her training took over. She fired her tranquilizer rifle, aware that Ethan was standing right beside her. She heard the puff and hiss of their shots, and saw the darts strike home.

The cave bear roared again and shook itself. The darts clattered to the floor. Destiny wasn't sure if the bear's fur was too thick for them to have penetrated or if they had but didn't affect it, but all they seemed to have done was anger it even more. It came for them in a shambling run with the inexorable deadliness of an avalanche.

"Tigers?" Ethan asked.

"No room!" Destiny gasped. But her own words gave her an idea. "Quick, in here!"

She grabbed Ethan's arm, beckoned frantically at Merlin and Ransom, and ducked into the nearest storage room. They all piled inside. The cave bear plunged after them, but stuck at the shoulders. But it kept trying, roaring and slapping at them with its immense paws. It was a small room, and they were only a few feet away from it.

"So much for stealth," Merlin said glumly. "Though on the positive side, we should get reinforcements any second now."

Sure enough, they heard yelling and pounding footsteps outside. The cave bear withdrew from the room. There was another roar, then a few screams that cut off almost instantly. A moment later, the cave bear roared once more, and stuck its head and paws back into the doorway. There was blood on its claws and muzzle.

In the brief moment of silence between roars, a quiet voice spoke. It was Ransom. "It's Pete."

"Then why's he attacking us?" Merlin began, then cut himself off. "Wait, never mind, they probably drugged him with the same stuff they drugged you with. Hmm. That's not so good."

"I'm not drugged." Ransom's gaze was more focused now, and he sounded a lot more coherent. "And neither is he."

"Oh?" Merlin stepped up confidently, though Destiny noticed he didn't come within range of the cave bear's paws. "Hey, Pete, you need to turn back—"

The cave bear roared at the top of its lungs, baring its fangs and slashing wildly at Merlin.

"Back off, Merlin, you're just pissing him off," Ethan said.

"Same as always," Merlin sighed, but retreated.

Destiny nudged Ethan. "You try. Remember how you talked me down when I was losing control? Like that."

Ethan gave her a doubtful glance. "I knew you wouldn't hurt me. I'm not so sure about Pete. He wouldn't do it on purpose, but..."

"Then don't cuddle him," Destiny advised.

Keeping his posture relaxed and his hands open at his sides, Ethan said, "The battle's over, Pete. Come back now. Come on, buddy, you can do it. You're a Marine, so be a Marine. Stand up on two legs and talk to me..."

The cave bear was suddenly gone. A dark-haired man in camouflage stood in the doorway, then staggered and leaned against it.

"Good to see you back with us." Ethan stepped forward and laid a comforting hand on his shoulder.

Pete jerked away as if Ethan had touched him with a lit cigarette. Then, brown eyes wide, he looked around the room. His gaze settled on Destiny. "Who's she?"

"Destiny. My—" Ethan paused, obviously not wanting to repeat the "She doesn't sound Australian" exchange, and settled on, "She's private security. I'll explain later. Did you see a radio anywhere? Any sort of communications?"

Pete shook his head. "No, but I saw another prisoner. He was in the infirmary, handcuffed to a bed."

"Oh, good!" Ethan exclaimed. When everyone gave him a funny look, he said, "I think I saw him being brought here. I'd meant to rescue him anyway. There was a woman, too."

Pete shrugged. "I didn't see any female prisoners. Just him."

"Let's run for it," Destiny said. "Once Apex figures out that the cave bear isn't on the loose any more, they'll swarm this place."

"This way," Pete said.

They followed him at a run, Merlin guiding Ransom. Alarms were going off all over the building. A guard poked his head and rifle barrel out of a room, but Destiny nailed him with a tranquilizer dart to the gun hand before he could get off his shot.

"Good one," said Ethan.

"Next one's yours, slowpoke," Destiny replied.

He grinned at her. Despite the danger, she felt exhilarated rather than afraid. Danger was her home turf. It was literally her job. But facing it with Ethan at her side gave her a completely new sense of fulfillment.

Pete snatched up the unconscious guard's tranquilizer rifle, then kept running. He stopped at an entrance with deep claw marks in it and the wall and the floor around it. The door had been ripped off its hinges. "Here."

"What hit this place?" Merlin asked.

"I did," said Pete shortly. "I came through as a cave bear. The doctors and nurses and guards abandoned the prisoner and ran." He frowned. "I hope I didn't hurt him."

"Don't you remember?" Destiny asked.

Pete shook his head. "Just bits and pieces."

They went into the infirmary, Pete staying just inside the room to guard the open doorway. The infirmary had been completely trashed, with beds overturned and pill bottles rolling all over the floor.

It was empty except for the prisoner, who was sitting up in bed. He was African-American, handsome and burly, with silvering hair and a short beard covering his strong jaw. Destiny could see the edge of a bandage where his hospital shirt had been pulled low over his chest. He wore the same collar Ransom had, and was handcuffed to the bed. But despite all that, not to mention having just been trapped with a rampaging cave bear, he didn't look frightened or helpless. Instead, he was patiently using the IV he'd apparently just pulled out of his arm to try to pick the lock of the handcuffs.

When they came in, he spoke, it was in the tone of a man used to command. "I'm Roland Walker, United States Army. Are you the rescue team?"

"Unofficially," Ethan said. "Most of us were captured too. But yes, we're here to get you out of here."

"You know how to pick a lock with a needle?" Merlin asked, sounding impressed.

Roland shook his head. "I have no idea how to pick a lock with anything. But the bed's bolted to the floor and I can't reach anything else, so I thought I'd give it a try."

"I can pick locks," Merlin volunteered. "But I need a piece of wire or a paperclip or something like that."

"Of course you can," Pete muttered from the door.

Destiny and Ethan started opening cupboards and drawers, helping Merlin search.

"Here." Ransom walked straight to a drawer, opened it, and held out a paperclip.

"Thanks." Merlin took it and got to work on the handcuff lock.

As he did so, Ethan quickly introduced everyone, then asked Roland how he'd ended up in the base.

"I was in the US, driving on a country road," Roland said. "I was on leave, but I'd gotten a call to come back to the base. In retrospect, it had to have been a setup. A tree was down across the road, but it had been cut, not fallen naturally. I realized that it was an ambush. I went into reverse and stepped on the gas, and just then I saw a car coming off a dirt road. I would've T-boned it and maybe killed the driver. So I swerved, went off the road, and rolled my car.

"The woman who'd been driving came out to help me. I was in bad shape. I think she saved my life. She took my hand and told me she wouldn't leave me. Then these men came up. They had tranquilizer rifles. I knew they must've set the ambush, and I told her to run. But she didn't. She stayed. The last thing I saw was her grabbing a tree branch from the ground and threatening them with it. A branch against guns!"

For the first time, his confident tone wavered. "The next thing I remember, I was here. And she was gone. Nobody would tell me what they'd done to her."

"Do you remember what she was wearing?" Ethan asked.

"Blue jeans and a white shirt," Roland said instantly. "She was a tall, slim black woman, about my age. Did you see her?"

"I think so," Ethan said. "I couldn't see that much detail, but the clothes match, and she was as tall as some of the men. I saw a man carried off a plane in a stretcher—I assume that was you. The woman fought some of the guards, and then they dragged her inside."

Roland eagerly leaned forward. "Have you seen her since?"

They all shook their heads.

"If she's a prisoner here, we'll find her," Destiny said. "We found you and Pete—well, Pete kind of found us. You too, actually."

Roland looked at Pete with a complete lack of recognition, then shook his head. "Sorry. I must've been asleep or unconscious."

When Pete said nothing, Merlin chimed in, "He was the bear."

Roland looked politely disbelieving. "The grizzly bear? I assumed they were doing animal experiments, and one escaped."

"Didn't they put you through Ultimate Predator yet?" Destiny asked.

"That bull—" Roland began, then, to her amusement, changed it to, "That absurd bit of psy ops? Yes, they did. I suppose it's to test whether prisoners can be brainwashed into believing something as ridiculous as a procedure that gives them powers and turns them into some kind of were-animal."

"It's not psy ops," Destiny replied. "It's real."

His forehead creased with incredulity. "They actually think it works?"

"No, I mean it really does work." Frustrated at his visible disbelief, she tried again. "Why do you think they'd go to all the trouble of kidnapping people and building a secret base if it didn't?"

"The military has been known to pour a lot of money and effort into things that don't work," Roland said drily. "Invisible aircraft. Mind-control. Clairvoyance. In the 60s there was a project that employed hundreds of people and ran for years, consisting of a bunch of guys out in the desert trying to kill goats by staring at them and breaking their noses trying to walk through walls."

"I can't demo right now," Merlin said, indicating the

handcuff lock. "And Pete shouldn't. Ransom, do you even have a shift form?"

Ransom didn't reply. He was off in his own world again, watching something far away.

"So somebody's going to have to strip," Merlin concluded.

Roland's eyebrows raised nearly high enough to lift the ceiling. Ethan and Destiny looked at each other, then Ethan started to pull off his shirt.

"Incoming!" Ransom pointed toward the door Pete was guarding.

"I don't..." Pete began, then stiffened. Softly, he said, "Yeah, I hear footsteps. Very quiet. They're trying to sneak up on us."

Ethan and Destiny stepped up to the door with their rifles ready; they couldn't risk becoming tigers and getting taken down with a dart.

Pete glanced at them. "The darts don't affect me. I could go after them as a bear."

"No!" exclaimed everyone but Roland, who practically had *What gang of lunatics have I fallen in with* hovering over his head.

"I could attack them as a raptor, then come back and finish with the handcuffs," Merlin volunteered.

"Will darts bounce off your skin?" Destiny inquired.

"Umm." Merlin scratched his chin. "I guess we'll find out. I could be a small one, so I wouldn't be hard to carry if they don't...?"

Destiny rarely snapped at people, no matter how stressed out she got. She prided herself on calm under pressure. But she couldn't help hissing at him, "You're not going to stop anyone if you're the size of a chicken!"

Merlin seemed unperturbed. "Ever had a chicken fly into your face?"

The enemies attacked before she could reply. Destiny,

Ethan, and Pete ducked back against the walls as tranquilizer darts hissed into the room, smacking into walls and bedframes.

Merlin and Roland also ducked, but they were both in the line of fire and had no way to shield themselves. A dart missed Roland's chest by a fraction of an inch, and another stuck in Merlin's loose sleeve before clattering to the floor. The three at the door returned fire, but it was only a matter of time before both Merlin and Roland would be hit.

"Merlin, how close to done are you?" Ethan called.

"I need another minute!"

"We don't have another minute," Roland said grimly. "All of you, get out. Someone can come back for me later."

Nobody budged.

"Pete, can you—" Ethan started to say, then broke off. Pete was no longer by the door, or anywhere in sight. "Goddammit."

"You can talk him down later," Destiny said, softly and for his ears only. "It probably is our best chance."

"Yeah, but—" From the frustration on Ethan's face, she was getting an idea of what it had probably been like to work with these guys. Brave and competent as they were, teamwork didn't seem to be their number one skill.

A familiar roar, followed by familiar cut-off screams and the sound of stampeding feet, sounded through the room.

"Pete," said Merlin unnecessarily.

There was a moment of silence, which was broken by the click of Roland's handcuffs opening.

"Okay, Merlin," said Destiny. "Chicken time!"

With his total lack of offense showing in his quick grin, the man vanished and a raptor stood in his place. It wasn't chicken-sized, but more like a medium dog. It grew to the size of a large dog, shrank back to medium, and then seemed to give up. It darted out the doorway.

"So," Roland said, a glint of ironic humor in his eye. "Guess the folk here were doing more than staring at goats."

The raptor returned. It shrank to the size of a chicken, gave an irritated hiss, then turned back into a man.

"Enemies are dead or gone," Merlin reported crisply. "And so's Pete."

Ethan sighed. "Let's go after him."

"That way." Ransom pointed. Then he turned to Roland. "Can you walk?"

Roland stood up, then swayed. Ransom stepped up close, silently offering his shoulder. Roland accepted his support, and they all went through the door.

Ransom, now walking easily, led the way. He stopped only briefly, to confiscate a tranquilizer rifle from a dead Apex agent and remark, "Not much range on these things. But the armory would have sniper rifles. If we keep heading in this direction, we'll get to it."

Ethan murmured into Destiny's ear, "You ever get the feeling like you've completely lost control of a situation?"

"All my life," Destiny replied softly. "It's okay, jarhead. We've got allies, even if they weren't the ones we meant to get and they're a little… new to this sort of thing."

They turned a corner, and almost tripped over a dead saber-tooth tiger. Pete was kneeling beside it, bleeding from slashes in his face and arms. He didn't look up at them until Ethan knelt down in front of him and called his name.

"I went to ambush those guys, and then…" Pete's voice trailed off as he glanced around. "Is that a *saber-tooth tiger?*"

"A saber-tooth tiger shifter," said Ransom. "You killed him."

Pete looked from him to the others, bewildered. "Is this a different part of the base? How'd I get here?"

It was only because Destiny knew Ethan so well that she knew how frustrated he was. But his voice and face remained calm as he said, "As a cave bear, apparently. Listen, Pete, you *cannot* turn into it again. And don't just go off without telling anyone. We need to work together if we want to get out of here in one piece."

Pete didn't argue, but the set of his face and shoulders was distinctly stubborn.

"Ethan's right," Roland said. "We do need to work as a team. All the same, I owe you. You gave us our chance to escape. Thank you." He offered Pete his hand.

Pete took it, then jerked his hand away as if Roland's touch was red hot. "Sorry. Hurt my hand."

There was no time for bandages, and Pete wasn't bleeding badly. Still, Destiny took a quiet look at his injuries for future reference when they did have time, and was puzzled to see that he had no blood or bruises or swelling anywhere near where Roland had touched. And apart from when he'd pulled his hand away, he didn't seem to be in any pain.

They came to a door at the end of the corridor. It led to a warehouse, with a lot of construction equipment and multiple doors out. Thankfully, it was empty. They scanned it for hidden Apex agents or traps, but saw none.

Just as they reached the middle of the warehouse, one of the doors slid open, revealing a bunch of Apex agents with tranquilizer rifles. Destiny, Ethan, and the rest dove for the nearest cover, which was a forklift and a bunch of crates. The hiss and clatter of tranquilizer darts filled the air.

Destiny scanned their surroundings. There was one door they could get to without going into the line of fire, but it was all the way across the warehouse. They'd have to run for it before the Apex agents figured out what they were doing and cut them off. She gestured to catch everyone's attention, then pointed to it and mouthed, *Ready, set*—

The door slid open. A cacophony of roars, hisses, and shrieks arose as a multitude of monsters were revealed.

Destiny caught sight of a huge wormlike thing with a gaping mouth lined with fangs, a mangy rat the size of a Buick, and things she couldn't even begin to identify: creatures with stings, chitin, and tentacles dripping slime. And then the whole pack of them came charging and slithering and leaping across the floor toward them.

Ethan and Destiny fired their tranquilizer rifles at the creatures. But while both of them hit their targets, the monsters just kept coming. It seemed like they, like Pete's cave bear, were either armored or immune.

Ethan's security guard uniform exploded off him as he became a tiger. With a snarl of protective fury, he leaped in front of Destiny and stood guarding her.

Merlin tossed his rifle to Roland, who caught it one-handed, then became a full-sized raptor.

Roland joined Ransom in returning fire at the Apex agents, while Ethan's tiger and Merlin's raptor faced the monsters.

Fight, growled Destiny's tiger, on fire with anticipation of the battle. *Fight for your mate!*

Destiny had no argument there, but she was gripped more by fear than by eagerness. Trapped between monsters attacking them and agents shooting at them, they were both outgunned and outnumbered. Even Pete's cave bear would be hard-pressed to fight the immense lumbering thing at the rear of the pack, a monster like some hideous cross between a giant scorpion and a cobra.

Destiny became a tiger. To her keen tiger's senses, the monsters seemed even more unnatural than they had to her as a human. They were deeply, profoundly *wrong*—soulless things that should not exist—and they horrified her tiger as well as enraging her.

But Destiny didn't let herself get swept away by her tiger's perceptions. She turned to Ethan and they nuzzled each other. She could feel the bond between them, alive and humming with love. Even if this whole adventure ended in their deaths together in this cold underground place, it would be worth it for those few days when they'd finally broken down the barriers between them and loved each other with their whole hearts. And Ethan didn't have to speak for her to know he was thinking the same thing.

Side by side, they braced for their last stand.

CHAPTER 14

*E*than's mind knew that they were probably all going to die, but he still had hope in his heart. He couldn't despair as long as he had his mate by his side.

Before the monsters could reach them, the constant hiss and clink of darts stopped, replaced by the solid thuds of bodies hitting the ground. He whipped his head around and saw, to his astonishment, that all the Apex agents lay sprawled on the ground. They seemed to have been shot with darts from behind, as there was no blood and he could see a dart or two sticking up from their backs. But no one stood behind them.

Ethan almost jumped out of his skin when Shane Garrity, the panther shifter bodyguard from Destiny's team, seemed to materialize beside them. "Hey, Destiny. Did you get bored with us and find yourself a new team?"

Destiny let out a snort, then butted Shane's leg with her head, as if to say, *Stop talking and start fighting.*

"Who are you?" Roland demanded.

"Friends!" The unfamiliar male voice echoed along the walls of the corridor. "Hold your fire, it's Protection, Inc.!"

The first to run in was a man Ethan didn't recognize, tall and lithe, with brilliant copper-colored hair. The redhead took one look at the incoming monsters, became a snow leopard, and leaped into the fray.

A gray wolf plunged through the door, snarling, and joined battle. A moment later, it was followed by a leopard. Ethan knew who they had to be based on the shift forms of the other bodyguards on Destiny's team. The wolf was the ex-gangster Nick Mackenzie, and the leopard was Ellie's best friend, Catalina Mendez.

Ethan's heart lifted as he too joined the fight. Destiny was at his side, protecting his back just as he protected hers. They fought alongside the snow leopard, the wolf, the panther that Shane became, and Merlin's raptor. Both Ransom and Pete were laying into the monsters with the butts of their rifles, Ransom as calmly as if he squashed giant tentacled roaches with a repurposed tranquilizer rifle every day, and Pete with a fury that made even the monsters take one look and scuttle or lurch or crawl away.

Roland, who wasn't in any shape for running around, had discovered the sword in Ethan's backpack. With his back braced against the forklift, he used it to neatly dispatch any monster that came within range.

Within minutes, all the monsters were either dead or fled. Against all odds, they had won.

Ethan wanted to shout out his thanks to the team and his joy to Destiny. Except he couldn't shout, because he was a tiger. What came out was a ferocious-sounding roar. Everyone stared at him. Sheepishly, he picked up his backpack in his jaws and padded to the other side of the forklift. Destiny followed him. They became human again, and quickly dressed. She was panting slightly from the exertion, her skin misted with sweat. Heat rose from her body, along with her irresistible natural scent.

Ethan didn't even try to resist. Seizing this brief moment of privacy, his heart singing with love and his body thrumming with adrenaline, he pulled her into his arms and kissed her. From the avidity of her response, she felt the exact same way.

A polite cough made them spring apart. The Protection, Inc. shifters must have gone back to the corridor to shift and get dressed, because they were emerging from it clothed and in human form. They had a perfect view of Destiny and Ethan.

Catalina grinned at Destiny. "Don't worry, it's nothing I haven't seen before." Then she winked at Ethan. "You, though... *that* was new."

"Hope you enjoyed it," he said, trying not to blush. Destiny kicked his ankle. "I mean, hope you didn't enjoy it." She kicked him again. "What?!"

"Stop talking, jarhead. You'll only dig yourself in deeper," Destiny advised him. To Catalina, she said, "Man, it's good to see you."

Nick, the ex-gangster werewolf, looked around incredulously. To no one in particular, he remarked, "What the fuck is going ON in this fucking place? Fucking monsters?" His gaze settled on Merlin, who was rapidly going from pony size to chicken size and back again. "Fucking *dinosaurs*? Are you fucking serious?"

Merlin finally managed to become a man. His security guard's uniform was streaked with green slime.

"Yeccch," he remarked, vainly trying to wipe it off and only succeeded in getting it on his hands too. "I'm jealous of you guys who don't bring your clothes with you."

"Don't be," the copper-haired man advised him. "The only thing worse than monster slime all over your clothes is monster slime all over *you*."

"Good point." Merlin stuck out his hand, then hurriedly

withdrew it. "Sorry. Anyone got any wet wipes? I'm Merlin Merrick. Pleased to meet you."

"I'm Justin Kovac. I have a medical kit in the corridor. Have someone else open it and take them out for you, if you don't mind. I doubt that stuff's sterile."

"Wait, *you're* Justin!" Ethan blurted out. "Sorry, I didn't recognize you."

He'd only met Justin once before, for about thirty seconds, and he'd been distracted at the time by Shane having just gotten shot in the chest. The last Ethan had heard of him, he'd been so traumatized by his experiences with Apex that he'd dropped off the map and was refusing to contact anyone, even Shane.

"Yeah, I get that a lot. I'm Protection, Inc.'s newest bodyguard. And Fiona's mate. Lot of stuff happened while you were overseas." Justin's look of amusement faded as he went on, "Looks like a lot of stuff happened to you, too. So you're a tiger now. Did Apex have time to put you through Ultimate Predator, or did Destiny get to you first?"

Ethan rushed to reassure him. "Apex never had me. At least, not for more than about fifteen minutes. Destiny made me a tiger. She had to, to save my life. I was sick..." Everyone was listening to him with bated breath, except for Destiny, of course, who was watching her teammates with bated breath to enjoy their reactions. He joined her watch as he added, "And we're mates!"

A flash of astonishment crossed Shane's imperturbable face for about a millisecond, then was gone. "Congratulations. I always thought you were."

"You did not," Destiny said, giving him a playful shove.

"Fucking awesome!" Nick exclaimed. He slapped Ethan on the back hard enough to nearly knock him over, then turned around and gave Destiny the exact same whack.

Catalina flung her arms around Destiny and congratulated her, then gave her a poke in the chest. "Why'd you wait so long, you weirdo? You must've known he was your mate ever since you met!"

"I didn't!" Destiny protested. "I was taking a medication that turned out to block my ability to sense my mate."

Catalina, a paramedic, nodded wisely. "Those unexpected side effects can really get you. A lot of meds have ones that doctors don't warn you about."

"Ah-ha," said Justin, amusement dancing in his dark eyes. To Destiny, he said, "So *that's* why you rushed off after Ethan. The mate bond told you he was in danger."

"It couldn't have," she said. "We weren't bonded yet."

Justin shrugged. "I knew when Fiona was in danger before we even met."

"Oh, so Destiny's your girlfriend?" Pete gave them a surprisingly sweet smile. "Good for you, man."

"Mates are more than that," Nick said. "I'm mated too. It's true fucking love. Unbreakable. Forever."

"There's no such thing," Ransom said flatly. Then, obviously realizing he'd been rude, he shrugged and said, "Just speaking for myself."

"Congratulations," Roland said. But though he sounded sincere, his mind was obviously on other things. Urgently, he addressed the other members of Protection, Inc. "Did you see any other prisoners? Any women? A tall woman, African-American, middle aged? Beautiful..."

"No, sorry," Justin said.

Reassuringly, Catalina said, "But if she's here, the others will find her."

"Others?" Destiny asked.

Nick nodded. "We split into two teams. Lucas, Rafa, and Fiona are the other one. They're tearing it apart, looking for prisoners and booting everyone out. When there's no one left inside, they'll blow the place sky-high."

"It'll be Fiona's third time," Justin said fondly. "She's gotten a taste for it."

"What about Hal?" Destiny asked.

The other Protection, Inc. members shot Ethan slightly guilty looks, then turned to each other. Apparently Shane was silently appointed as the bearer of the news, because he said, "Hal's not here. Ellie went into labor right when we were gearing up to go. She's absolutely fine—Catalina checked her—but he couldn't leave her to give birth alone."

Ethan groaned, feeling the emotional weight of all those years apart. "I did, though."

Destiny put a hand on his shoulder. "Ellie will understand. Anyway, sooner we're out of here, the sooner you'll see her. Let's get going."

They headed back out into the maze of corridors, with Justin leading the way. As they walked, Ethan said, "How'd you all find us, anyway? We kept trying to find a radio to call you, but we never did. And Fiona's GPS was destroyed when our plane crashed."

"Yes, but her computer had recorded its last location, so we knew your last known area. And I can track people. It's one of my Ultimate Predator powers." Justin's expression darkened, then cleared. "I didn't ask for it, but it comes in handy. I already had a lock on her, so once we got close, I just pointed the way. Hold out your hand."

Ethan offered his free hand to Justin, who clasped it for a moment, then released it.

"There," Justin said. "Now if you get in trouble and need help, I can always find you. *We* can always find you."

Though Ethan had felt nothing special at the physical touch, Justin's words went to his heart. He'd joined Protection, Inc. for several missions, but he'd never been a real member of the team. Now Justin was, and Ethan still wasn't... but the team could always find him now. It made him feel like he belonged, in a way that was different from how he and Destiny belonged together. As if he was part of a family that was suddenly much bigger than just him and Ellie.

"Thanks." His voice was roughened with emotion.

Rather than pretending not to notice, Justin said, "Yeah. It takes some getting used to. But it's worth it."

Nick caught Justin's elbow as he started to turn a corner. "Wait. Go the other way."

"What's there?" Shane asked.

Nick sniffed the air. "Not sure. It smells interesting, though."

"Dinosaurs?" Merlin asked eagerly.

"This whole place smells like reptile. Nah, this is something else. Maybe…" Nick sniffed again. "Cats?"

With equal eagerness, Catalina said, "Oh, let's go look. Maybe they're experimenting on cats. We should rescue them!"

Ethan couldn't help noticing the distinct split between the people giving Catalina looks of total disbelief (Pete and Ransom), doubt (Roland), and genuine enthusiasm at following her lead (Shane, Justin, Destiny, Nick, and Merlin). Personally, he was in favor of rescuing the cats, especially now that he was one himself, always assuming they didn't turn out to be Apex agents in saber-tooth tiger form.

They turned in the direction Nick had indicated, now following his lead. Needless to say, it was yet another white corridor.

"A maze of twisty passages, all alike," Destiny remarked.

"I know what ancient text game that's from," replied Ethan. "Nerd."

"Double nerd."

"Super-nerd."

"Ultra-nerd."

"Hey, nerd-mates," Nick interrupted. "It's here."

He stopped in front of a door. While everyone fell into defensive positions, Ethan used his security guard ID to open it.

Nick sniffed the air and told them what Ethan could already see. "No humans inside."

They hurried inside and locked the door behind them. As Catalina had guessed, it was full of cages sized to fit cats or dogs. They were made of thick bulletproof plastic webbed with hair-thin strands of faintly glowing silvery metal that made it difficult to see what was inside any of them. The latches on the cages were made of the same metal.

As they peered at the cages, trying to see inside, a few sad meows arose.

"I knew it! Poor things. We have to rescue them." Catalina reached for the latch of the nearest cage.

Shane caught her hand. "Hold on. That same metal is on their collars." He jerked his head at Ransom and Roland.

Catalina froze, hand in mid-air. "What do the collars do?"

Both men shrugged.

"Neither of you can shift, can you?" Destiny asked. When they shook their heads, she said, "Maybe these are imprisoned shifters."

"No," Ransom said. "They're animals."

"How do you know?" Justin asked.

"That's his power," Merlin said. "He… knows things. Right?"

Ransom gave a reluctant nod.

"Are the animals dangerous?" Merlin asked.

Ransom frowned, as if struggling to put what he saw or knew into words, and finally said, "They won't hurt us."

"I hate to rain on the pet rescue parade," Pete remarked. "But I don't want to be juggling a bunch of loose cats if we get attacked."

Merlin, who had been prowling around the lab, raised his head. "I found some carrying cages. We can stash them in there."

As if in response, a chorus of plaintive meows arose, and also several canine whines.

"Dogs!" Justin said indignantly. "No way we're leaving helpless dogs for Apex to experiment on."

"Or helpless cats!" added Catalina. With that, she opened the nearest cage.

It contained a fluffy black kitten with enormous yellow eyes and wings like a Monarch butterfly, striped and spotted in black and orange. It blinked at her, gave an excited squeak, and flew into her arms. She instinctively caught it. The flying kitten rubbed its head against her chest and began to loudly purr.

"What the..." Pete began.

"No weirder than dinosaurs and monsters and shapeshifters," Merlin said with a shrug.

"Yes, it is!" Pete said to Merlin. "This is the weirdest yet."

"It's definitely the cutest yet." Destiny reached for the nearest unopened cage.

Ethan chuckled. "You want your own nerdly pet, don't you?"

She grinned, unabashed. "So do you. Admit it."

"I want one," he admitted. "But you go first."

Destiny opened the cage. Ethan leaned forward, eager to see her winged kitten and secretly hoping it would be even more adorable than Catalina's, if such a thing was possible. His mate deserved the cutest flying kitten of them all.

A pair of beautiful wings, as translucent blue as a morning sky, unfolded. But they didn't belong to any kind of kitten. The little blue dragon launched itself from the cage.

But it didn't go to Destiny. It flew straight to Nick. Startled, he raised his arm. It landed on his forearm and cocked its head, examining him with sapphire eyes. After the briefest hesitation, Nick extended his arm to Destiny. The little dragon didn't budge. Instead, it coiled its tail around his tattooed wrist.

"Guess it likes you, Nick," Destiny said. With a toss of her braids, she said, "No accounting for taste."

But he was too enchanted with the tiny dragon to even tease her back. "What a gorgeous little thing. Raluca will love it."

"Maybe it can sense that your mate's a dragon shifter," Ethan suggested, knowing that Destiny was disappointed even though she didn't let it show.

The blue dragon let out a trill, as if in agreement. There was an answering meow from the next cage.

"That one's yours," Catalina said to Destiny. Cradling her butterfly-winged kitten in one arm, she flipped the latch.

Another winged kitten flew out of the cage. But it too bypassed Destiny, and Catalina as well. Instead, it made a beeline for Shane. He stood perfectly still as the sleek gray tabby landed on his shoulder. Its wings were more like a moth's than a butterfly's, a soft pearly gray like the sky before dawn. The kitten folded them neatly, gave his ear an exploratory nip, and tried to climb onto his head.

"Ow." Shane gently detached the kitten and settled it back on his shoulder.

It meowed in protest, then jumped off and dove down like a hawk. The kitten landed on his shoe, grabbed his ankle with all four paws, and ferociously attacked his pants.

"All yours, Shane," Destiny said as he attempted to pry it off his leg.

Ethan turned to the cage below the ones that had already been opened, but Justin was already kneeling there. That cage was the size of the other three put together, and emitted a chorus of excited canine yelps and whines and yips.

"A litter of puppies," Justin said confidently. "Sounds like three of them. Fiona and me already have six dogs. We don't have room for nine. Ethan, Destiny, want to take the other two?"

Destiny nudged Ethan. "Think you can cope with a pair of flying puppies?"

"Oh, hell yeah." He was already grinning at the thought.

Justin opened the cage. Three little husky puppies stared up at him adoringly with three sets of ice-blue eyes, then scrambled out to jump all over him, barking ecstatically and wagging their tails...

Tail.

Wagging *its* tail.

Ethan blinked hard, but when he opened his eyes, the three-headed puppy was still there, licking Justin with three little pink tongues.

Pete's disbelieving stare moved from the puppy to Justin to Merlin. "Okay, forget what I said earlier. *That's* the weirdest yet."

Merlin gave an elaborately unconcerned shrug. "It's just a Cerberus puppy."

"Who's a good boy?" Justin asked the puppy as it rolled over to get its belly scratched.

One head panted happily, one barked, and one went on licking him.

Justin ruffled the puppy's furry heads. "You! You! You! You're a good boy!"

Roland cleared his throat. "This is all very…"

"Fucking bizarre?" Pete suggested.

Roland, apparently at a loss for words, didn't finish the sentence. Instead, he said, "Let's just put the animals in the carrying cages and keep searching the place. We can sort out who gets what later. There's still a human prisoner we need to rescue."

Everyone guiltily scrambled to unlatch the rest of the cages, Shane a little hampered by the gray kitten that was now clinging to his right arm, flapping its wings and squeaking.

As Ethan opened the nearest cage, he realized that only Ransom hadn't moved. In fact, now that he thought back, Ransom hadn't moved a muscle since they'd started opening the cages. Ethan had gotten so used to him being quiet and watchful, it hadn't registered before. But now that he was paying attention, he could see that Ransom wasn't merely still, but seemed to be frozen in place. Only his dark eyes, now locked on Ethan's, betrayed his desperation to convey some terrible warning.

Ethan reacted instantly, trusting in his gut feeling and Ransom's intuition.

"Am—" he started to shout. But before he could complete the word, the ambush happened.

"Freeze," said a quiet male voice behind him. "No shifting, no powers, no movement."

Ethan couldn't move. It was like nightmares he'd had where he was under attack and paralyzed, only in real life. He tried to struggle, but couldn't move a muscle except to breathe and blink his eyes. Everyone he could see was frozen too.

At least, the humans were. But their pets could move, and they did. Catalina's butterfly kitten arched its back, spread its wings wide, and let out a tiny hiss. Shane's gray moth kitten flew up toward the ceiling, where Ethan lost sight of it. Nick's blue dragon breathed out a tiny puff of flame. The Cerberus puppy tugged at Justin's sleeve with one head, while another whined to get his attention and the third growled at their unseen enemy.

Ethan's right hand was still on the cage latch that he'd just lifted. He felt it move as whatever creature had been inside pushed the door open.

"No!" shouted the enemy behind him. "McNeil, close that door! Don't let that beast open a portal!"

Ethan tried not to obey, but his hand moved anyway, slamming the cage door shut. But it seemed to be too late, based on the angry yell from their unseen enemy.

Though he strained to look down and around, to see what creature had emerged, he couldn't do that anymore than he could turn and see his enemy. All he could do was use the blurred edges of his peripheral vision to observe the abrupt flurry of movement from the cages that had been unlatched but not yet opened. He couldn't see what creatures were fleeing their cages or where they went. But he heard doors banging open, a chorus of squeaks and yelps and flapping wings, and saw a confusion of multicolored movement.

There was a flash of brilliant light. And then total silence. All the imprisoned beasts were gone, except for Catalina's butterfly kitten, Nick's miniature dragon, and Justin's Cerberus puppy. Ethan wasn't sure about Shane's moth kitten, but suspected that it was out of his line of sight rather than vanished through the portal. Whatever the portal was.

The unseen man spoke again. "Everyone with animals, control them. Hold them and don't let them attack. That is the only way you are permitted to move."

Catalina, Nick, and Justin pulled their pets into their arms and held them, gently but firmly. None of them spoke, but he could see the fear and fury and confusion in their eyes. Worst of all, he could see it in Destiny's, as they stood beside each other and couldn't touch, couldn't comfort each other, couldn't do anything but share the same helplessness.

Shane hadn't moved. His ice blue eyes held neither fear nor rage, but a chilly detachment coupled with a touch of ironic amusement, as if to say, *And what am I supposed to do?*

With a tinge of annoyance in his voice, the enemy behind them said, "Garrity, just capture your feline the next time it comes within your reach. Now, everyone, turn and gaze upon your master."

Ethan felt himself move without volition, as if his body was no more than a puppet controlled by another. But as horrifying as that was, he was relieved as well. At least now he'd see his enemy. There was nothing worse than being controlled by some unknown force.

The man before him had apparently stepped out of some hidden door. Or teleported. Or walked through a wall. Who the hell even knew. Ethan gave up on trying to figure out how the enemy had gotten in, and focused on who he was. The man had gray hair and a gray beard, both neatly trimmed, and wore a long white coat embroidered in black thread.

"My name is Lamorat," said the man in the white coat. "I forbid you from attacking me or leaving your places. But you may move your bodies otherwise."

Ethan couldn't help breathing a sigh of relief as he found that he could shake out his stiff muscles, look around, and take Destiny's hand. She squeezed it tight.

"And don't bother expecting a rescue," Lamorat went on. "The doors are sealed with an override lock. Mere security IDs won't open them. Yes, that includes the secret door I entered from. Only I can open them now."

Ethan had first focused on the white coat, and thought, *He's a doctor or a scientist.* Then he noticed the embroidery, and thought, to his own disbelief, *He's a wizard.*

His third inspection left him more confused than his first two. He knew some of the embroidered symbols: the two snakes twining around a stick that symbolized medicine, the skull and crossbones for poison, and, most eerily of all, an atom. But others looked distinctly magical: a pentagram in a circle, a staring eye, and a snake with its tail in its mouth. There were others that he'd never seen before.

Then he saw something he recognized all too easily: the smug sneer of the enemy who thinks he's better than you, and can't wait to make sure you know it too.

"You seemed intrigued by the symbols on my robe, McNeil," Lamorat said, and the sneer deepened. "Would you like to know what they represent?"

Here comes the monologue, Ethan thought, resigned.

Then his mood brightened. Monologues were good. Monologues should be encouraged. Ayers's monologue had led to his defeat. And this man's monologue would keep him there, doing nothing more harmful than boring them, until Fiona and Rafa and Lucas got the jump on him.

He caught Destiny's eyes, and she gave him the very subtlest of winks. Ethan relaxed. He was with his mate, who understood him perfectly. All they had to do was stall for time, and encourage the blabbermouth to keep on blabbering.

"Yes, I would like to know," Ethan said.

Lamorat cleared his throat as if he was a professor about to begin a lecture. "They represent the mystic marriage of magic and science, which enables those of us with the greatest intellect and power to rule lower beings like yourselves. I suppose you're all ignorant enough to believe that you have been captured by Apex?"

"The thought did occur to me," Justin remarked. "I can't imagine why."

Lamorat missed the sarcasm entirely. "It's because this base was built by Apex and is staffed by personnel who believe that it's an Apex facility. But the council of wizard-scientists is its true owner, and we don't answer to anything so small and petty. We're only making use of its infrastructure and techniques for our own purposes." To

Ethan's dismay, he glanced at the clock on the wall. "But, alas, time is getting on. Enough talk—"

"Hey, Lamo-rat-face," Nick interrupted. "You know what my mate is? She's a dragon. When she finds out what you're doing to me, she's gonna be fucking *pissed.*"

"Be silent, dog," said Lamorat. Nick's face turned red as he tried and failed to speak. "I am well aware of who your mate is. We have ways of dealing with mythic shifters here. Or has your puny canine brain failed to register the meaning of shiftsilver?"

Nick rolled his eyes and shrugged: *Don't know and don't care.*

"The metal on the magical animal cages." Lamorat waved his hand at the empty cages, then indicated Ransom and Roland. "And on their collars. It has no effect on ordinary shifters and animals, or even extinct shifters and animals. But it negates the inherent magic of mythical beasts, preventing their escape. And when it touches the skin of humans who can become mythical beasts, it prevents them from shifting."

Ethan kept his face carefully blank, but made a mental promise to buy Nick a beer once this was over. He'd goaded Lamorat into not only forgetting that he was wasting time, but telling them what the collars did—and that all they needed to do to let Roland and Ransom become… something… was to get their collars off.

He wondered what they turned into. Dragons, he supposed. Those were the only mythic shifters he'd heard of. It would definitely be good to have a pair of dragons on their side right now.

"And also, I have the power to control all shifters with my mind, mythic or otherwise." Lamorat's smug little sneer returned. "Anyone else feel the need to threaten me? Anyone?"

"Bueller?" Catalina called.

"Silence, feline," the wizard snapped. Her snicker cut off like he'd turned off a TV. "Now—"

"What happened to the woman who was with me?" Roland asked.

"She was of no importance," Lamorat said with a shrug. "You were the intended target. She was only taken because she refused to leave you."

"So you didn't do anything to her?"

"By no means. Since we already had her, we decided we might as well get some use out of her. She went through the Ultimate Predator process, just like the rest of you."

"And?" Roland's fists were clenched at his sides. "Where is she?"

"Dead."

The wizard's word fell on the room like a heavy stone, crushing everything in its path. Ethan's horror was echoed in the clench of Destiny's solid grip on his hand.

Roland's face went as ashen as if he'd been shot. Very softly, he said, "What was her name?"

Lamorat shrugged again. "What does it matter? The process killed her. We've improved the casualty rate a great deal, but there are always risks. You were a failure too, in fact. You were all intended to have one power in your shift form and another in your human form. But your human form has no power."

"I don't need a power." Roland didn't raise his voice, but his even tones nevertheless conveyed a sense of fury held barely in check, a fury that could burn down the world. "I don't need a weapon. I'll kill you with my bare hands."

"Silence."

"It won't work, you know," Justin said conversationally. "Sure, it's a nice trick to keep us silent and still just by telling us so. But you're not doing anything different than a common thug who ties people up and gags them."

Ethan was very interested to see that this, more than anything else, seemed to get to Lamorat. The wizard's thin face flushed with anger. "Silence!"

Justin didn't speak again, but his expression clearly conveyed that the order had only proved his point.

"Is that the best you can do?" Shane inquired. "You took him and me and Catalina. You hurt us. You changed us. But you couldn't break us, and you couldn't keep us. And you still can't."

"That wasn't me!" Lamorat snapped. "I mean us. That was Apex. We've improved on their methods. You three renegade felines found your mates, and that gave you the strength to not only break free, but stay free. Until now, of course. But these four were made by *us*." He waved his hand at Roland, Merlin, Pete, and Ransom.

"And you did something different to them?" Ethan inquired, keeping up his role as Mr. I'm Just Curious, No Need To Silence Me.

"We did indeed," Lamorat replied with immense self-satisfaction. "We destroyed their ability to recognize and bond with their mates. And as for those of you who already have mates, it's not too late to change that. We'll put you through the updated process, and sever you from your mates forever."

Despite himself, a chill went through Ethan's heart at the wizard-scientist's confident words. Was that really possible? Could anything short of death break the bond between him and Destiny?

"Love makes a mate," Destiny said, squeezing Ethan's hand. "Not the other way around. Nothing can ever stop us from loving each other. You can silence me if you like, but that just means I'll stand here silently thinking you're an idiot."

Lamorat stared at her like he couldn't believe his ears. "*What* did you just call me?"

"An idiot," Merlin said cheerfully. "A nitwit. A fool. A numbskull. A nincompoop. A ninnyhammer. A turnip-brain. A—"

Lamorat had apparently been stunned into silence himself by Merlin's stock of synonyms, but "turnip-brain" snapped him out of it. "Silence!"

For the first time, Pete spoke up. "Like Justin said. Any dumbass can make people stop talking. You're not doing anything different from slapping duct tape over our mouths. I'm not impressed."

"You... *creatures*... think *I* need to impress *you*? You're nothing! Worthless!" The wizard glared around the room, then his gaze settled back on Pete. "You, Valdez. You're a big talker when you think you're the only one in danger. But you're not. You have a daughter you'd die to protect. And I know where she lives."

Pete's entire body tensed as he tried to lunge at Lamorat, but he couldn't move from where he stood. As he opened his mouth to shout out his rage, the wizard smirked cruelly and said, "Silence."

Pete has a daughter? Ethan thought. He mentally calculated ages, realized that she couldn't be more than fifteen, and was torn between fury at a man cruel enough to threaten a young girl and bewilderment at why Pete had never even mentioned that she existed.

"And you," the wizard said, turning on Ransom. "Quiet as a snake in the grass. I silenced you first so you couldn't warn the others, but maybe I didn't need to. You're a born betrayer."

Ransom, of course, said nothing. *Could* say nothing. But

Ethan saw a flicker of some unknowable emotion in his dark eyes, and felt a chill. Was Lamorat just trying to drive a wedge between them, or did he know something they didn't?

To Merlin, he said, "Both your powers are so appropriate for a man who changes identities like other people change clothes. What will your friends think if they ever learn the truth behind your innumerable lies?"

Merlin shrugged and spread his hands in a broad gesture of unconcern, but it looked forced.

Lamorat turned to Ethan, who felt himself tense. *Sticks and stones may break my bones, but words can never hurt me,* he told himself, but the old saying rang hollow. After his childhood, the version of it that he believed was *Sticks and stones may break my bones, but words cause permanent damage.*

His tiger snorted. *Words and talk may bother humans, but fangs and claws are what kill them.*

You missed the part where it's supposed to rhyme, Ethan replied. But his tiger's remark gave him as much strength as the warm grip of Destiny's hand.

"Ethan McNeil," sneered the wizard. "Rejected by your own parents. Unloved by the very people who—"

Destiny interrupted. "And I'm a freak of nature and Catalina's a reckless woman who doesn't know females are meant to be scared and Nick's a criminal and Shane and Justin were assassins, blah, blah, blah, we all have things you can throw in our faces. And you know what? Nobody cares!"

Lamorat glared at her. "Si—"

Destiny's nails suddenly dug into his palm. Ethan didn't know her exact plan, other than the general idea of "stall and distract him," but her urgency was unmistakable. He didn't just need to distract the wizard in general, he needed to distract him *now.*

"Merlin was right," Ethan said loudly. "You *are* stupid. You think you can make us into your pet assassins? Don't make me laugh! You already tried that with Shane and Catalina and Justin, and you failed miserably!"

"I don't want you as assassins, you fool!" Lamorat snapped. "That was Apex. Little government minions with little ambitions. The wizard council and I have something much more ambitious in store for you all."

The wizard began to glance away. Once again, Destiny dug in her nails. But she didn't need to. Ethan had spotted the urgent flick of Ransom's eyes toward him, and the deceptively cool way that Shane had also glanced at him. Whatever was going on was out of Ethan's line of sight. But the others were depending on him to keep Lamorat from noticing. Ethan couldn't let them down.

"Who gives a shit?" Ethan demanded in a tone even ruder than his words. "Whatever it is, we won't do it. And you can't make us!"

"You forget," sneered the wizard, looking back at him. "It's the mate bond that gives you strength. I've already ensured that your new friends here will never form one. And as for the rest of you, I can break yours."

"Bullshit! You think anything you say can make my mate turn against me, or me turn against her? You actually think you can wave your magic wand and break our bond?" Ethan jeered. The anger in the wizard's narrow eyes was cold, not hot. For the first time, Ethan feared him. But he'd gone too far to turn back now. "Let's see you try it! Gonna sprinkle me with sparkly magic bond-breaking glitter dust? Gonna—"

"Silence!" shouted the wizard.

The silence that fell was broken by Destiny's sudden jeer of "Turnip-brain!"

"ALL OF YOU! SILENCE!"

And that was that. Ethan hoped he and Destiny had done enough. They'd definitely gotten Lamorat's full attention.

The wizard was giving him a glare chilly enough to turn Hell into a ski resort.

"You're forgetting that I control you. All of you. Utterly. Time for a demonstration of what that means. Everyone, watch and see the price of defiance." The wizard bared his teeth in a cruel parody of a smile. "Ethan McNeil. I order you to kill your mate."

CHAPTER 15

The wizard's words echoed in Destiny's ears: *"Ethan McNeil. Kill your mate."*

She'd seen that Lamorat could control them. Even now, she couldn't make herself speak. But she still couldn't believe that Ethan would ever hurt her.

And so she felt no fear of him. She saw the corded tension in his body and the set determination in his eyes, and she feared *for* him. He was fighting the wizard's order as hard as he could—as hard as it was possible for a man to fight. When an irresistible force meets an immovable object, can both survive the collision?

Destiny's own love and determination burned through her. Her tiger roared, and her woman's strength fused with her tiger's fury. It wasn't enough to break the wizard's hold. But it was enough to crack it.

"I love you," she forced out through lips that would barely move. "I'm not afraid."

And Ethan replied, though he too had been silenced. His whisper sounded like a tiger's growl. "I love you. I'd die before I'd hurt you."

"Kill her," Lamorat ordered again.

Ethan folded his arms across his chest, but otherwise didn't move. His face, which had gone red with effort, suddenly went white.

"I take back my order," Lamorat said quickly.

The instant the wizard finished speaking, Ethan collapsed at her feet.

Destiny's heart almost stopped. She wanted to drop down beside him, to check his pulse and breathing, but she couldn't move. All she could do was stand there and watch and wonder, in the worst moment of her entire life, if he *had* died so he wouldn't hurt her.

Then she saw his chest move as he inhaled, and the rush of relief almost made her collapse herself. Maybe it would have, if she wasn't already under magical orders to stand.

"I took back my order because I may still have some use for him," Lamorat said. "If I'd let it go one more minute, the strain of trying to defy me would have stopped his heart. So that's where we stand. You can obey me, or you can die."

He paused, obviously expecting a dramatic silence to fall. After all, no one was able to speak.

In that pin-drop silence, the barely audible whirr of the miniature drill that had been going the entire time they'd been distracting him was suddenly very noticeable indeed. Lamorat whipped around just in time to see dust drift down from the last of the pencil-tip sized holes that had been drilled around his hidden door.

But not in time to do anything about it. The door fell in, forcing him to jump back. It smashed down a bare inch from his feet.

Drat, Destiny thought. She'd seen Fiona pull that trick before, and she'd hoped the door would hit him over the head.

But the figure standing in the hole in the wall where the

door had been wasn't Fiona. It was a man Destiny had never seen before.

"Let them go," the stranger said.

"Silence!" Lamorat snapped.

"Nope," replied the stranger. "I like the sound of my own voice. That's the one thing you and I have in common."

Destiny's spirits rose. Whoever the man was, he was obviously on their side, and Lamorat couldn't control him. So he must not be a shifter. She wondered who he was.

Lamorat frowned in concentration. "Freeze!"

The man in the doorway gritted his teeth. With obvious effort, he took a step forward.

"I know you," Lamorat said. "You're Subject Nine. Carter Howe."

"Got it in one." Carter Howe took another step forward.

Destiny watched him with even more curiosity. She'd never met him before, but she knew who he was. He was the tech billionaire who'd been presumed dead in a plane crash. In fact, he'd been kidnapped and held by Apex until Fiona and Justin had released him. But she'd been under the impression that he was a shifter, though she didn't know what kind, so she didn't know why Lamorat's power wasn't working on him.

Lamorat edged a step backward, though unfortunately not close enough for anyone to touch him. "I read your file closely, so as not to repeat past errors. You were Apex's failure. Broken. Ruined. The fact that you can resist me at all only proves what a monstrosity you are. Still, even that *thing* inside you can't fight me for long. FREEZE."

Carter wavered, stumbled, and nearly fell. He had to grab one of the empty cages to catch himself. Then he pushed himself upright again. He and Lamorat stared at each other, locked into a silent showdown.

And Destiny, who had been fighting all along, felt the

wizard's hold on her loosen. She still couldn't budge from where she stood. But she could kneel down beside Ethan and take his hand. His eyes didn't open, but he traced the letters O and K on her palm with his nail.

Thank God, she thought. She doubted that he'd faked his collapse, but he'd obviously recovered a lot more than he was letting on.

If only they could distract Lamorat a little bit more, they might break his spell entirely. Maybe if they all shouted at once…?

Shane gave a tiny jerk of his chin in Lamorat's direction.

A gray blur dropped from the ceiling. The wizard let out a very undignified shriek as Shane's gray moth kitten wrapped itself around his head with all four legs, like the face-hugger in *Alien.*

"Go!" Catalina yelled. Her butterfly kitten flew to Lamorat, landed square in the middle of his chest, and began to enthusiastically shred his coat and everything underneath.

At the same moment, Nick let go of his little dragon and Justin released his Cerberus puppy. The next thing the beleaguered wizard knew, two puppy jaws were biting his left ankle and one was biting his right, and his pants were on fire at the crotch.

With a howl of pain and anguish, the wizard shifted.

Like a dragon, he didn't shift instantaneously. When dragons transform, the air around them begins to sparkle until they vanish within the glow; when the sparks wink out, the new form appears in the place of the old. So Destiny knew what was happening when the air around Lamorat began to thicken and seethe with flashes of light.

She tried to help Ethan to his feet, and found that she could do it, but didn't need to; he stood up easily, put his arm around her, and pulled *her* away. The spell that had held the humans in place seemed to have broken entirely; everyone was backing away from the wizard, watching him warily. The pets too were sensibly flitting or zooming or darting or bolting back to their owners.

Destiny had no idea how dangerous the wizard's shift form might be, *what* it might be, or even how big it could be. She was uneasily conscious of the size of the room, and particularly of its unnecessarily high ceiling. And also that the wizard-cloud was blocking all the exits. They were very likely about to be trapped in a room with something very, very large.

"Carter! Can you get their collars off?" Justin indicated Roland and Ransom.

Carter examined the collars, then opened his coat. Destiny was boggled to see that the interior of the expensive designer overcoat had been altered to include a high-tech mini tool belt. "Yeah. Just keep whatever that thing is off me while I do."

"Got it," said Justin. "I thought you were staying in the plane. Thanks for coming to the rescue."

Carter made a brushing-off motion with one hand while running something like a *Star Trek* tricorder over Ransom's collar. "You're welcome. Don't expect it to ever happen again."

The rest of them formed a protective circle around Carter, Ransom, and Roland. The lightning cloud around the wizard was becoming more and more active, and getting bigger and bigger, pierced with flashes of green, blue, red, white, and even black light.

The cloud vanished, leaving them staring up at a gigantic, five-headed monster.

At first Destiny couldn't even comprehend what it was. The heads resembled those of dragons, but they were attached to long, sinuous, snake-like necks. And the necks were attached to a stumpy body with four squat legs, all of it covered in extremely tough-looking plate armor. As if that wasn't bad enough, the heads were circled by octopus-like tentacles, some long and thin, some short and fat, but all covered with suckers and dripping slime.

The necks writhed, the tentacles writhed harder, and the heads made experimental-looking darts in and out. Destiny was relieved to see that they couldn't reach anyone… yet.

"Not half as cute as you," Justin muttered, patting his Cerberus pup. All three heads let out nervous whines as they stared up at the monster.

All five heads suddenly reared back. Instinctively, everyone dove aside. Destiny and Ethan clutched each other as they tucked and rolled. A wave of heat passed over her head, she heard a roar and crackle and hiss and clatter and splash, and she smelt a revolting combination of sudden stinks.

As they slammed into a set of empty cages, she looked up just in time to see the scarlet dragon head breathing out a burst of flame, the white head spraying a barrage of icicles, the green head spitting green slime that melted the walls and floor where it hit, the blue head shooting a bolt of crackling lightning, and the black head emitting a cloud of toxic-looking smoke.

"Fuckin' A," muttered Nick. *"Seriously?"*

Destiny was immensely relieved to see that no one had been badly hurt, though Roland was slapping out a fire on the sleeve of Carter's coat and Shane, plucking a needle-sharp icicle from Catalina's shoulder, had murder in his eyes. All the pets had flown or scampered free, as far as she could tell. She had a moment of alarm when she couldn't spot Shane's kitten, then decided that like its master, it preferred to lurk unseen.

"Convenient that they're color-coded," Merlin remarked.

"Just like a dungeon crawl," said Ethan encouragingly. "We've got this, nerd girl."

Destiny tapped her ear, then her mouth: *It can hear us. Don't plan aloud.*

Ethan nodded, then glanced around speculatively. They were on the same side of the room as Justin and Nick. Carter, Ransom, Roland, Shane, Merlin, and Catalina were on the other side. Destiny's eyes met Ethan's, and she knew that they were thinking the same thing. They just needed to find a way to explain it to the people they couldn't whisper to…

Then she knew how to signal at least one of them. And once he knew his job, hopefully the rest would follow.

As the dragon-thing ponderously swiveled its heads for another try, Ethan gathered her, Justin, and Nick into a tight huddle, and breathed, "The others will distract. I'll take black. Nick, green. Justin, blue. Destiny, white. Whoever finishes first takes red."

As the dragon heads reared back to attack again, Destiny yelled, "CHICKEN TIME!"

Merlin became a chicken-sized raptor and rushed the dragon-thing, leaping up and down and screeching. Destiny and the others nearest to her transformed and leaped for their targets. The monster swung its nearest head (the white one) toward Merlin, but before it could cut him to pieces with slivers of ice, Destiny was upon him.

Her claws sank in, but it was hard to keep her balance on the slithery, squirmy neck. She tried to bend her head to bite, but a slimy tentacle grabbed her around the waist and yanked hard.

A glint of silver sparkled, and the pressure released. Roland stood with one hand pressed to his side and one holding his sword high. Half a tentacle fell at his feet.

"Come back, Roland! You're next!" Carter called, as he

twisted a tiny tool. Ransom's collar dropped to the floor with a clatter.

Nick managed to get atop the green neck, but was shaken off; his wolf claws couldn't dig in the way a big cat's could. Undeterred, he leaped and snapped at the green head, dodging blasts of acidic slime. Pete ran forward, ducked under a jet of acid, and boosted Nick up. His shoulder muscles bulged with strain, but he held his position until Nick could sink his teeth into the green dragon's neck.

A tentacle whipped out and slapped Justin off the blue dragon's neck. He fell to the floor, rolling to escape a lightning bolt. The blue dragon head darted to follow him. Shane and Catalina leaped for it, their lithe black and yellow bodies moving as one, and landed on its neck. Justin hissed and clawed at it from the floor, dodging lightning bolts as his friends tried to sink their teeth in.

Beside Destiny, Ethan was trying to get a grip on the black head, biting and slashing. But a nest of tentacles pulled him off and flung him hard to the floor.

The fire-breathing red dragon head bent over him and drew in a breath. Destiny released her hold on the white dragon neck and jumped down to protect Ethan. But as she landed beside him, she realized that she was too late. She'd only share in his fiery death.

Better to die with Ethan than live without him, she thought.

But the blast of flame didn't come. Bewildered, she looked up. A beast she had never seen was ferociously attacking the red dragon head. It was a black hound the size of a pony, shaggy and fierce, wreathed in black smoke and with fiery eyes like windows into Hell.

Ethan and Destiny scrambled away. Justin stopped taunting the blue dragon head and, shielded by the giant hound, leaped on to the neck of the red dragon. He clung to it, biting and clawing, as the black hound snarled at it. The red dragon head jerked back, its tentacles cringing away, as if even that fire-breathing monster was intimidated by the hound's burning regard.

Destiny had no time to figure out what was going on, only to see what still needed to be done. No one was attacking the white dragon head. It twisted sinuously to spray everyone with dagger-sharp shards of ice. Ethan and Destiny leaped for it together. Their teeth and claws sank in as they sought to bite hard enough to kill it.

Out of the corner of her eye, Destiny saw that Catalina's butterfly kitten and Shane's moth kitten were flying at and distracting the dragon head they fought, Nick's little dragon was doing the same for his, and Justin's Cerberus puppy was leaping up and down and snapping at the tentacles that tried to drag him off.

"Everyone!" Roland shouted. "Bite NOW!"

Destiny bit down as hard as she could.

CRUNCH.

The thing that had been Lamorat collapsed with an immense thud, followed by an immense splat a split second later as all the tentacles hit the floor.

Destiny and the others scrambled off it, shifted to human form, and backed away, eyeing it warily. It was a huge heap of ugly fanged heads and tentacles, so tangled up that she couldn't trace the necks back to the body. Not that she'd want to.

"Looks like Eel Day at the Venice fish market," Justin remarked.

"I'm crossing Venice off my list of places to visit," Catalina said.

"Does anyone have any more spare clothes?" Destiny asked plaintively. Justin and Catalina might be comfortable standing around stark naked in an evil lab in front of people they barely knew, but she certainly wasn't.

With a grin, Justin ostentatiously turned his back, then bent to pick up his backpack. She was too relieved to care about him mooning her when he tossed it over his shoulder. She scrambled into the spare clothes as the rest of the non-mythic shifters did the same. When she turned back around, she saw that everyone was dressed, the fiery-eyed hound (which she had by now figured out had to be Ransom's shift form) was still a hound, and an audibly frustrated Merlin-raptor was maniacally switching between chicken and turkey sizes.

A clang of metal made Destiny jump. She whipped around, only to see that Carter had finally succeeded in getting Roland's collar off. The noise had been the metal bouncing off the floor.

She heard an unpleasant sucking sound, and swung back in the other direction.

From the midst of the enormous pile of heads and necks and suckers, a slimy tentacle as wide as her waist was blindly feeling its way out.

"Everybody back!" Roland shouted.

They instinctively obeyed his commanding voice. He stood alone, facing the mass that was once again beginning to writhe, a tall man who looked small before it, a dark silhouette in a white room.

Roland spread his arms wide. Flames blossomed along his arms, but he didn't burn. Instead, his arms *became* fire. They stretched out behind him, and for the briefest moment he was a man with wings of streaming flame. Then his entire body transformed in the blink of an eye. He hovered in midair, burning wings outstretched, a magnificent bird made entirely of fire.

Destiny had never seen anything so beautiful. She could feel the heat, as hot as a furnace fit to melt steel, but it didn't burn her. She could see the brilliance, bright as the mid-day sun, but it didn't hurt her eyes.

A phoenix, she thought, and was filled with awe. *I never knew they were real.*

The phoenix cried out in the high pure voice of a hunting hawk, and dived. He left a trail of flame in the air. A single blazing feather at the tip of one wing touched a single reaching tentacle. For a split second, the reviving monster was outlined in white-hot fire.

The light dimmed, and the bird of fire was gone. Roland staggered. Pete jumped to steady him. In the center of the room, only an immense gray heap in the shape of tentacles and dragon heads remained. And then a breath of air touched it, and it collapsed into a shapeless pile of ash.

A door slid open. Rafa, Lucas, and Fiona piled in with guns drawn.

"Humans, freeze!" Rafa yelled. "Dog-thing! Dinosaur! Lie down!"

The huge black hound turned its burning eyes toward him. Destiny could swear she saw a familiar expression of world-weary cynicism in them. And then the hound dissolved in a wisp of smoke, leaving behind only Ransom and his own sardonic gaze.

"Still want me to lie down?" he inquired.

"He's one of the good guys," Ethan said hurriedly. Waving his hand to encompass Merlin, who was now vacillating between chicken and human-sized raptors, he said, "And so's he. And these guys." He indicated Roland, Pete, and Carter.

Fiona gave Carter a cold stare, and didn't lower her gun. "I wouldn't be so sure about *him.*"

Justin put his arm around her shoulders. "He did fly us here. And he's been very helpful."

"Don't get used to it," Carter said.

"That wasn't a 'dog-thing,'" said Lucas. "That was a hellhound. But I thought they were legendary."

"So speaks the dragon," replied Rafa. "But who *are* you all?"

Ethan quickly introduced everyone, adding, "And I'll tell you the rest of the story on the way home."

Fiona looked down at the Cerberus puppy, which was panting happily at Justin's feet. "I can't wait."

"Same," said Rafa, glancing from the butterfly kitten clinging to Catalina's shoulder to the moth kitten clinging to Shane's to the blue dragon on Nick's forearm and finally and most incredulously, to the Cerberus puppy, which was now licking Fiona's hands with three small pink tongues.

"Have you finished searching the base?" Destiny asked.

Lucas nodded. "Not a stone left unturned."

"We threw everyone out," Rafa said. "Some of them piled into planes and took off, and the rest of them fled into the jungle. Either the Indian police will find them and deport them, or something in the jungle will find them and eat them."

"Hopefully the latter," said Shane, reaching up to stroke the gray kitten on his shoulder. It rubbed its head against his chin and purred.

Sounding very pleased with herself, Fiona said, "The self-destruct is ready to remote-activate as soon as we're all out."

"You didn't find any prisoners?" Roland asked, as if he couldn't help himself. But his sad eyes told Destiny that he already knew the answer.

"None," said Fiona. "Did we miss someone?"

"No." After a moment, Roland added, very quietly and more to himself than to anyone in the room, "I'll never even know her name."

Destiny, who was standing nearby, heard him. "I'm so sorry."

"I wish we could've gotten here sooner," Ethan said.

Roland shook his head. "I woke up wearing that collar. Whatever they did to me, they did right away. And she was already... gone. The only person who could've saved her was me, back in the US. If I'd convinced her to leave me... If I hadn't rolled my car in front of her, so she felt obliged to help me..."

"That was her choice," said Ransom. "It's better to die as yourself than become a person you'd despise."

"What the professor is trying to say," Pete broke in, "is it wasn't your fault. You tried to save her. She tried to save you. Sometimes things just don't work out, no matter how hard you try."

"This place—these sorts of places—break people," Carter said.

"I didn't save anyone either," Shane said softly.

"Yes, you did," Justin said to Shane. "You saved me."

"And me," Catalina added.

"Roland, you saved people too," said Merlin. "All of us. Just now. When you became a phoenix to burn the hydra—"

Suspiciously, Pete inquired, "Exactly how do you know what all these weird creatures are, anyway?"

Merlin smiled brightly. "Once I was the guest host for a quiz show in Moldava where the topic was mythology."

"Yeah, right," Pete snorted.

"Let's get out of here. We can catch up on everything later." Rafa again looked from Nick's little dragon to Justin's baby Cerberus to the winged kittens. "Grace is going to be so disappointed that I arrived too late to get her a weird little pet."

"Maybe there's more in some other room," Catalina said hopefully.

Lucas glanced up from the floor where he'd been kneeling. "I don't believe so. Fiona and Rafa and I checked the base very thoroughly. We saw some Apex workers loading sedated dinosaurs into a plane with a forklift—"

"I hope you recorded its flight path so I can avoid it when they wake up mid-flight," Carter remarked.

"—but no mythical animals. You see this?" With one long, elegant finger, Lucas indicated a patch of the floor that was very faintly shimmering. "That's the trace of a portal."

"I remember now!" Destiny exclaimed. "There was a flash of light, and Lamorat said they'd gone through a portal."

Lucas stood up and dusted off the knees of his pants. "Yes, a very few magical beasts have that ability. One of them must have been imprisoned here, and once it was freed, it created a portal to allow the rest to escape."

"But where did they go?" Destiny asked, reluctant to give up on the idea of her very own winged kitten.

"I assume back to their places of origin, where they must have been captured. There are still a few secret, hidden, protected places in the world where magical animals live." Indicating Nick's blue dragon, Lucas said, "We have dragonettes in some parts of my own country. They rarely bond with humans. You should feel very lucky, Nick."

The dragonette trilled and delicately plucked something from Nick's shoulder. Leaning closer, Destiny saw that it was a long, shining silver hair.

Lucas chuckled. "I should say, you and Raluca should feel very lucky. I believe your dragonette intends to bond with you both. Just like the Cerberus pup has chosen two pack leaders."

Justin and Fiona, who were on the floor playing with the three-headed puppy, glanced up. She said, "I want to name him."

Justin spread his hands. "All yours."

"Trio," she said. "It means trio in Italian."

"Perfecto," Justin replied, grinning.

Trio barked as if in pleased acknowledgment. Once per head.

"I'll wait for Raluca," Nick said.

"Got a name for yours?" Shane asked Catalina.

"Carol." She scritched the butterfly kitten behind the wings. Carol stretched luxuriously and purred. "For Carol Danvers. You know, Captain Marvel."

"I know." Shane smiled at his mate. His moth kitten lay draped across his shoulder, claws dug in to keep its hold, but Shane obviously didn't mind. "Mine's Shadow."

"Shadowcat? Like Kitty Pryde from the X-Men?" Catalina asked.

"Just Shadow."

"That's a good name too." Catalina noticed the look of envy that Destiny had obviously failed to suppress, and patted her on the back. "You'll get your flying kitten. When Carol and Shadow grow up, they'll have kittens and then everyone can have one!"

"That will require some patience," said Lucas. "Mythic animals have a very lengthy childhood. Those kittens will still be kittens for years to come."

"How cute!" Catalina exclaimed. "I mean, what a shame."

Rafa made a "forget about it" gesture with his big hands. "Don't worry about it. Grace and I will have our hands full with our baby pretty soon! Same with Hal and Ellie. The last thing couples with new babies need are new pets—especially a new pet that can fly or set the carpets on fire."

"I wish—" Pete broke off, then reconsidered. "Well, cat's out of the bag now." Catalina snickered. Ignoring her, he went on, "My daughter would've liked one. That's all. And that's all I'm going to say about her, so don't even think of asking."

Lucas broke the silence. "Journey and I travel too much to have pets."

"I work too much," said Roland.

Ransom said, "The last thing I need is to be responsible for another life."

"*I* wanted one," Merlin said. Then, ever hopeful, he said, "Maybe they'll turn up later."

"You heard Lucas," Pete said crushingly. "Secret hidden places. Wherever they went, it won't be any place any of us will be."

Ethan and Destiny glanced at each other. She said, "Want to make sure we don't pine away for a flying kitten?"

"New babies of our own?"

"One at a time, jarhead."

"Can't count on that," Ethan said with a smile. "Twins run in my family."

CHAPTER 16

They emerged from sterile white corridors into the heat and life of the jungle, where they were greeted by the sounds Ethan had come to know: the chatter of monkeys, the songs of birds, the chirps of crickets, the rustle of creatures in the leaves. It was the world that had shaped Destiny into the woman that she was, and now it had shaped him too.

"Want to come back some time?" Ethan asked her. "I'd love to meet Mataji and the rest of your friends. And go trekking."

"Yeah, I'd like that," she said. "We could hike as humans and hunt as tigers."

"But first, I'm buying you a new sparkly dancing dress to replace the one that got wrecked the night we met. And then I'm taking you to a club."

"Only two years late. Man, there's so much we haven't done yet."

She sounded excited and happy, not sad. Ethan too had moved past old regrets. So they'd missed out on two years: so what? They had the whole rest of their lives ahead of them, this time to spend together.

Fiona and Carter led the way to an airplane parked on the otherwise empty airfield.

"Gorgeous plane," Destiny remarked with a touch of envy. "Yours, Carter?"

"Yes, of course." Carter glanced at Trio, who had frisked up the steps and was jumping up and down at the door, barking to be let in. Carol flew from Catalina's shoulder and circled above Trio's head, making teasing dives and swoops at him. "Those beasts better be housebroken. Maybe you should lock them in the bathroom."

Everyone with pets glared at him.

"Trio's better-behaved than some humans I could name," Fiona remarked icily. "Perhaps *he's* not the one who should be locked in the bathroom for the duration of the flight."

Carter opened his mouth, then closed it. He mounted the steps without another word. Once everyone was inside, they crowded round and watched as Fiona turned on a small monitor than had feeds from inside the base. She double-checked every room and corridor to make sure no living person or being had been left inside, then hefted a small black box. Ethan recognized it immediately: a remote detonator.

"Who wants to do the honors?" Fiona asked. "Justin?"

"I'll let someone else have a go," he replied. "I've already had my shot."

Unexpectedly, Ransom spoke up. "I'd like to."

Fiona glanced around, but when no one else objected, she handed the box to him. He cupped it in his hands and closed his eyes for what felt like a long time before he pressed the button.

BOOM!

The shock wave shook the plane as the monitor feeds

went black. Outside, the moon illuminated the cloud of dust and debris that rose from the destroyed base.

Ransom handed the box back to Fiona. Without a word, his face expressionless, he got up and took a seat at the rear of the plane.

Everyone settled in. The plane was small enough that they could all talk to each other, including the pilot. As Carter taxied down the runway and took off, Ethan and Destiny put their arms around each other. They settled into each other's warmth and together watched the jungle and the ruins of the base dwindle beneath them.

Once they were on their way, they placed a call to Hal on a satellite phone.

"How's Ellie?" Ethan asked immediately. "Is she still in labor?"

Hal's rumbling voice seemed to fill the plane. "She's fine. And so are our new twins!"

"Oh." Ethan was immensely relieved, but also disappointed. He'd missed the birth, like he'd missed so many things in his sister's life. "Give her my love."

"You just did," Hal said with a chuckle. "You're on speakerphone."

Ellie's clear voice came through. "Ethan! You've got a nephew and niece. Hurry up and meet them."

"I'm flying as fast as I can," Ethan replied.

"Come straight to the house," she said. "Hal intimidated the doctor into letting us leave early. His bear was demanding that the cubs go back to the lair, where they belonged."

"I'll come as soon as we land. Hey, do our parents know yet?"

"Yeah, I called them." Ellie sighed. "Mom is on vacation in the south of France. She said, 'Congratulations. Don't you dare name the boy after your father.' Dad is busy at work. He said, 'That's nice. I hope you won't have the bad taste to name the girl after your mother.'"

"Well, for once I agree with them. Neither of them deserves namesakes."

Ethan couldn't help glancing around the plane to see how everyone else was reacting to this. Destiny squeezed his hand, and he felt as well as saw her love and lack of judgement. Lucas, who had largely been raised by a cold and hostile uncle, had sympathetic understanding in his golden eyes. But while some of the others looked angry or sad or appalled, none of it was directed at him or Ellie.

"I've made my peace with it," Ellie said, and he could hear in her voice that she really had. "Hal's parents are going to be the best grandparents ever, even if they drive Hal and me nuts doing it. And the kids are going to have the best extended family ever. They can ride on panthers and dragons and leopards and wolves—"

"And lions and tigers and bears—" Ethan put in.

"Oh my!" Ellie exclaimed, and they both chuckled. "And they'll have the best uncle in the whole wide world."

Ethan had to swallow back a lump in his throat before he spoke. "Thanks. Have you named them yet?"

"Got any ideas?"

"Sig and Sauer," Ethan suggested.

"No!" Ellie exclaimed indignantly. "Any *sensible* ideas?"

"Cloud and Tifa?"

"No! Good Lord." Ellie snorted, but Ethan was touched that she recognized the characters from his favorite video game, even though she'd never played a single one herself. "Anyway, you're too late. They're Haley Catalina and Elliot Ethan, and they're both Brennan-McNeil. I wanted there to be a McNeil family that loves and supports each other—one that's bigger than the two of us. We needed that for so long. And now we have it."

The lump in his throat returned, along with a prickling in his eyes, but Ethan no longer cared about hiding his emotions. "Love you, sis."

"Love you too." A baby's shrill wail rose over her voice. "Uh-oh. Here, I'm giving Hal the phone."

Hal took the phone back, and they gave him the report on what had happened. The one thing they left out, at Ethan and Destiny's request, was that they were mates. They'd wanted to tell him and Ellie in person.

When they were finished, Hal said, "Merlin, Roland, Pete, Ransom, Carter… Your lives have been turned upside down. You don't have to deal with everything alone. I'd like to help you. My team would like to help you—the same thing happened to some of them. Why don't you all stay in Santa Martina for a while, and we can help you sort things out?"

"Thank you for your offer," Roland said. "It's very kind, and I'd like to take you up on it. The Army's been pushing me to retire for years, and I suppose I have to now—from the military. But I'm not the retiring type. I'd like to stay a while and talk to you about running a security company. Not as competition with yours, of course. I was thinking of the east coast."

"I'd be happy to tell you everything I know," said Hal. "We have more business than we can handle, actually. I've been thinking we needed an East Coast branch, and you seem like just the man to run it. You'd need a team, of course. But maybe you've already found one…"

Roland looked over the others. "I was hoping for exactly that. What do you all think? You don't have to decide now. Take your time."

Instantly, Carter said, "Roland, Hal, I'm just here to fly this plane. *Once.* And only because I owed a favor to some people on your team. As soon as it touches down, I'm taking it and flying out of your lives. Out of *all* of your lives. For good."

Unperturbed by Carter's rudeness, Roland said, "Offer still stands, any time you want to take it up."

"I will!" Merlin said at once. "My time's up with the Marines anyway. And I'd like to grow out my hair."

Pete shot him a baleful look. "Maybe that's your other power. The wizard said you have two."

Merlin, unoffended, laughed. "Rapunzel, Rapunzel, let down your hair? Guess we'll find out."

"Welcome to the team, Merlin," Roland said, and offered Merlin his hand. They shook hands gravely. "Pete? Ransom? What do you think?"

"Marines taught me I don't play well with others," Ransom said. "Thanks, but no thanks. I'm not joining any more teams."

"I'll think about it," Pete said slowly. "East coast, huh? That's where I'm headed anyway."

"My offer stands as well," said Hal. "To all of you. But I've got a different one for Ethan. I know your time's up with the Marines. Do you want to re-enlist? Or would you rather join Protection, Inc.?"

Destiny locked her arms around his chest. "You're with me, jarhead. I've got you now, and I'm never letting you go."

Hal's deep chuckle resounded through the phone. "Oh, it's like that, is it? Congratulations!"

There was a scuffling sound, and Ellie said, "Yeah, congratulations, you pair of perfectly matched idiots. Took you two long enough to figure it out!"

A baby began to cry, and there was a bang as she apparently dropped the phone. Hal came back on. "Welcome to the team, Ethan."

"Don't I get a say?" Ethan asked, but he couldn't keep a straight face. At last, he'd officially be a member of the team he'd always secretly wished to be on. And he'd be with his mate, too! "Okay, fine. Of course I want in! And thanks."

Now two babies were crying loudly. Hal, sounding harried, said again, "Welcome! See you." There was another scuffle, a crash, and the line went dead.

"Better get there soon," Shane said. "Sounds like they could use another diaper-changer."

As everyone began to congratulate and welcome Ethan, Destiny nudged him and said, "Wait a second, you guys. Aren't you going to haze him? It's traditional."

"Yeah, I don't want to be left out," Ethan said. "Make it good."

"You could all shift and jump him," Destiny suggested.

"Or Shane could glare at me really hard," Ethan added.

"That's been done," Destiny pointed out. "Multiple times. Go on, guys. Use your imagination!"

The rest of the Protection, Inc. team looked at each other.

"Well…" said Shane.

"Perhaps…" said Lucas.

"Maybe I could…" said Catalina.

There was a long silence. Then all of them, Ethan and Destiny included, burst out laughing.

"He already got attacked by a two velociraptors, a T-Rex, a pterodactyl, a hell pig, miscellaneous monsters, and a five-headed hydra," Rafa said. "I think he's been hazed enough."

"Point," said Justin. "He hasn't been attacked by a Cerberus pup yet, though. Lick him, Trio!"

As his team once again broke into laughter, Ethan knew that though he was still flying above the middle of nowhere, he'd finally come home.

EPILOGUE

I could get used to this, Destiny thought contentedly, lying back in Ethan's arms. She was filled with delicious satisfaction after making love with Ethan the night before, and again first thing in the morning. Then, reconsidering, she thought, *I hope I never get used to it. I hope I always appreciate it like it was the first time.*

She knew that she always would.

"What're you grinning about, nerd girl?" Ethan inquired.

"Everything, nerd boy. You. Our life. The team. Our trip to India. The family we're going to have." She pointed at the wall across from their bed, where his sword and her tiger claws were hung in a place of honor. "My waghnakh."

He chuckled. "And after all your angst about accidentally stealing them."

They'd been so excited about seeing Haley and Elliot, and all the wonderful changes in their lives, that it had been weeks before they'd gotten around to unpacking their backpacks. Only then had Destiny discovered that they'd flown back to the US with priceless Indian antiques that they had no easy way to return.

She'd telephoned Mataji, who had been their point person in the plan for Indian shifters to dispose of the dinosaurs and "discover" the Golden City. As it turned out, Mataji had been about to call her to give her an update. She informed Destiny that the dinosaurs had been given a decent burial (a thousand feet deep, Destiny hoped), and that her mongoose shifter niece and her elephant shifter girlfriend had been recruited to discover the city "on a camping trip." The Indian archaeological society had been so delighted that they'd offered the finders a pair of swords from the city. As they were neither history nor weapons nerds, they'd declined with thanks.

"Considering that, you should consider the weapons yours," Mataji said. "They're going to start letting tourists visit once they reconstruct the tower they think collapsed in an earthquake. You two should come then." The old woman laughed. "Though I don't expect they'll let you sleep in the palace."

"We'll survive roughing it in a hotel," Destiny said, and ordered a pair of brackets to mount their souvenirs.

Gazing at her wagnakh, she had to admit that the joy it gave her was undeniable proof that she was the biggest history nerd ever. It was the cherry on the cake of her happiness. She had everything she'd ever wanted.

Except for a winged kitten.

But she had *almost* everything she'd ever wanted. And she could play with Carol and Shadow whenever she—

There was a scratch at their front door. She and Ethan sat bolt upright, then threw on bathrobes and went to investigate. A fluffy white furball sat on the doorstep, wagging its cotton puff of a tail. It had very pale gray-blue eyes, the color of a frozen sea, which instantly fixed on Ethan. With a joyous yelp, the puppy leaped into his arms and started licking his face.

"It likes you," Destiny said.

"I can—yecch." Ethan wiped his mouth. Holding the puppy at arm's length, he said, "I can tell."

The puppy, deprived of a face to lick, yelped indignantly. The front of Ethan's bathrobe went white with frost.

"What the—" Ethan put down the puppy and prodded his robe. The front was frozen solid. "Brr. Did the *puppy* do that?"

It thumped its tail on the floor and yelped again. A sprinkle of snowflakes, each one perfect and beautiful and unique, fell out of the air and landed on the rug.

"Guess we know where you came from," Ethan said to the puppy. To Destiny, he said, "But how in world did it get here?"

"Lucas said one of the magical animals could open portals. I guess it was this little guy."

Ethan was grinning so wide it nearly cracked his cheeks. "Hey there, Snowy. Wanna make some snowballs for us to play catch with?" Then he caught sight of Destiny's face and put his arm around her. "He's not just my dog, you know. He's ours."

"No, I think he's really yours." As if to underline her words, Snowy curled up on Ethan's bare feet and fell asleep. "It's okay, jarhead. I'll survive not having a magical pet of my very—"

A winged kitten landed on her shoulder.

Destiny jumped in surprise. It dug in its pinprick claws to keep its grip, spreading out its wings for balance. She craned her neck to get a better look at it. The kitten butted its head into her cheek and purred enthusiastically. It was smaller than Carol and Shadow, small enough to fit into the palm of her hand. Its fur was fluffy and white, like Snowy's, but its wings were feathered and blue as a jay's.

"It's beautiful," Destiny breathed.

Welcome, little sister, said her tiger.

The kitten folded her sapphire wings and purred.

"A gift for your inner eleven-year-old," said Ethan, and kissed her. The kitten arched her back and flapped her wings in alarm. "Relax, kitty. We can share her."

"I think it's just scared by your giant face."

"Hey, you love my giant face. Let's get inside and get dressed. I'm about to freeze off my other giant thing you love." He gestured at his frozen bathrobe front.

As Destiny dissolved into giggles, the kitten launched off her shoulder, seized her bathrobe cord with all four paws, and flew into the living room with the end trailing on the floor. Destiny snatched at her suddenly-open robe. Snowy woke up abruptly and pursued the cord, barking. The cord froze solid and clattered across the tiles, startling the kitten enough to drop it. Snowy began to gnaw on his prize as the kitten flew into the bedroom and perched on the brackets that held Destiny's tiger claws.

"I can tell it won't be boring around here," Ethan remarked. "Got a name for her?"

"Sky," said Destiny. As they returned to the bedroom, a thought struck her. "I thought Snowy was the animal that could open portals. But Sky's here too. Think it was really her?"

"It might not have been either of them," Ethan pointed out. "The portal creature helped all the other animals escape. It might be something we haven't even seen yet that's still out there somewhere, sending its buddies where they belong."

"Think anyone else who didn't get a pet at Apex will get one now?"

"What, you mean like Merlin?"

A little guiltily, she admitted, "No, I hadn't been thinking of those guys. I meant like Grace and Ellie and Journey. I know they wanted one... but you're right, if any animals come back for anyone else, it'll be for the people who were actually there when they got released."

"You never know," Ethan said thoughtfully, watching Sky and Snowy chase each other around the living room. "They *are* magical."

There were too many happy occasions to have separate parties for each one, so they celebrated the twins' birth, Ethan joining the team, and Ethan and Destiny's engagement all at once. Grace and Rafa, who had the biggest backyard, were the hosts.

Like all shifters who owned their own house, Rafa had made sure his backyard was enclosed in a high wall. Like the wall around Destiny's backyard when she'd been a child, where she could play outside without fear of exposure. She eyed this wall, which Grace had painted in vibrant colors, with the memory of feeling trapped, relief that it was over, and a strange kind of nostalgia. She'd had happy times in her backyard, too.

Raluca came to greet her. She wore a dress of her own design that was elegant without being formal, in a shimmering blue-gray that set off her silver dragonmarks. To Destiny's amusement, her purse and shoes matched the sapphire dragonette perched on her shoulder.

"Did you pick a name for her yet?" Destiny asked. Raluca, who like Lucas had already known about dragonettes and how unusual it was for them to bond with humans, had taken that task very seriously indeed.

"I have. Her name is Doina."

"That's pretty," Destiny said. "Does it mean something?"

"It's a very old name from my own country. And also a type of music, the kind one might hear in a remote village."

Doina trilled a musical note, making both women smile, then flew away.

"I saw you looking at the wall," Raluca said, a little hesitantly. "Does it remind you of your own?"

When Destiny had returned, she had finally told her entire team and their mates the full story of her childhood, which not all of them had known. They'd reacted much as Ethan had, with sympathy and respect. By then that didn't surprise her.

"A bit. Mine had ivy growing all over it. A wall of green, like a jungle..." For the first time, Destiny realized why the Indian jungle had never seemed alien to her. "Huh."

Lucas and Journey joined them. She was bedecked with precious jewels, as usual, with her mating gift of a golden dragon pendant in the hollow of her throat. But none of them outshone the glittering brilliance of Treasure, the diamond dragonette that had appeared and bonded with them both, and was now coiled around Lucas's forearm.

"Lucas and I had a wall that was special to us, too," Journey said. "It was part of a maze, all covered in roses."

"That sounds beautiful," said Raluca.

"It was," said Lucas.

Treasure flew up to join Doina in an aerial game with Carol and Sky. Shadow stayed on Shane's shoulder and watched.

"Lying in wait," Shane said fondly.

Another flying kitten leaped from Rafa's shoulder and landed on Grace's outstretched arm. When he did, his glossy black wings and fur, which had been the exact shade and sheen of Rafa's mane of hair, changed to match the bubblegum pink of Grace's handknit arm warmers, a gift from Rafa's mother.

Her pregnancy was starting to show, but she'd found a stylish black maternity dress, then taken a pair of scissors to the hem. It hung in artistic rags and tatters about her curvy hips, accentuating leggings the same bubblegum pink as the arm warmers.

"Show them your new trick, Leo," said Grace. "Revert fur!"

Catmeleon's wings stayed hot pink, but his fur returned to its former glossy black.

"Good kitty," said Grace, petting him. "Now we match."

None of them worried any more that their pets would be spotted by outsiders; they'd found that all the magical pets had the ability to become invisible, like mythic shifters could, and had trained them to do so in public. Snowy didn't need that training, but Ethan had to teach him not to create snow or ice in public. Justin had first trained Trio to heel, so he didn't seem to have a leash sticking out into thin air.

"I feel bad for Ellie and Hal," Catalina said. "They're the only ones who didn't get a magical pet."

"They have two beautiful babies," Rafa pointed out. "That's plenty!"

"Still…"

Then Hal and Ellie, the last to arrive, came into the backyard. Ellie was carrying Elliot, while Hal cradled Haley in one arm and something else in the other. Haley was crying, and Hal was jiggling her and crooning.

"Aww, Haley, don't cry—" Catalina began, then peered at the other thing Hal was holding, half-hidden in the folds of his overcoat so all that could be seen was some brown fur. "Hey! What's that?"

"We found it curled up at the foot of our bed this morning," Ellie said.

"A flying kitten!" exclaimed Destiny. Sky landed on her shoulder, flapping her bluebird wings to keep her balance as she too craned to get a look.

"Nope," rumbled Hal. "Thank God. I've seen the havoc

255

those things wreak. If I had twin babies *and* one of those things flapping around all day, I'd have a nervous breakdown."

"You would not," said Ellie. "All the same, I'm just as happy this little guy doesn't have wings."

"Or an excitable disposition," Hal added.

He turned his arm so everyone could see the creature he was holding. It was a fat little thing, as round as it was tall, a fuzzy brown creature like a living teddy bear with a fluffy squirrel's tail. It blinked yellow owl eyes at everyone, then clambered across Hal's chest, pulling itself along with over-sized blunt claws like a sloth, until it could cuddle up with Haley. She immediately stopped crying and began to coo.

"It's a natural babysitter," said Hal with relief.

"More like a living lovie," said Destiny. "What *is* it?"

"An owl-bear-sloth-squirrel," suggested Grace. "An owbesloque?"

"Yes, my mother told about owbesloques," Rafa said. When everyone stared at him, he began to laugh. "I'm kidding. I have no idea what it is."

"Nor have I," said Lucas.

"What's its name?" Journey asked.

"Bob," said Hal.

"Bob?" Raluca's accent made it sound like a very strange and exotic name indeed.

Ellie shrugged. "We both thought it looked like a Bob."

Hal's phone rang in his coat pocket. Elliot instantly began to cry. The owbesloque clambered over to cuddle him, whereupon Haley started wailing. The phone continued to ring.

Hal looked out at his team. "Help."

They sprang into action. Ethan scooped up Haley and held her so Bob could snuggle them both, Catalina pulled up a comfortable chair for Ellie to sit in, and Destiny fished the phone out of Hal's pocket and answered it. "Protection, Inc., how may I help you?"

"Destiny," Hal said. "That's my personal line."

She recognized the voice at the other end of the phone as Roland's. "Destiny? Is Hal there?"

Doing her best to keep a straight face, she passed the phone to Hal. "It's for you."

"Yes?" Hal, juggling the phone as he lifted Ellie's feet to prop them on a stool he'd pulled up, hit the speakerphone button.

Roland's voice came through loud and clear. "I hope the family's doing we—over there! By the lamp!"

There was a crash and cursing in the background. Ellie playfully covered Haley's ears. Nick, completely serious, glanced at her and then covered Elliot's.

"The twins and Ellie are great," Hal assured Roland. "What's going on?"

Roland raised his voice to be heard over the commotion. "Have you seen any odd little creatures like the flying kittens and so forth in the cages at Apex?"

There was another crash and more swearing, then Merlin's eager voice saying, "Whatever it is, I want it!"

Hal somehow managed to keep a straight face as he replied, "Yes, actually. Have you?"

"Possibly," Roland replied. "We just had a… creature of some sort… get into the office, which Carter says is impossible with the security system he installed."

"Carter's with you?" Hal inquired.

"Well…" Roland lowered his voice. "He said he was just going to install a security system and then leave. He's still here, though."

Carter's annoyed retort came through loud and clear. "Because I obviously need to fix it! *Then* I'm leaving!"

Roland and Hal both ignored this. Hal asked, "Well, what does the creature look like?"

"I'm not sure," Roland said. "It moves too fast to get a good look at it. Whatever it is, it's flittering around the office knocking things over."

More crashes. More swearing.

"That sounds like Pete," Hal said.

"Yes, Pete decided to join us on the condition that—"

"Roland!" Pete yelled. "Not while you're on speakerphone!"

Undisturbed, Roland said, "And of course we were very happy to have him."

In the momentary silence, Ransom's voice sounded clearly. "It seems attracted to bright lights. If we turn off the lights and hold a flashlight by a window, it might fly out."

"Ransom too?" Hal inquired.

Ransom replied himself. "On a very temporary basis."

"And we're happy to have him, too," said Roland. "On any basis. Hmm."

"What?" asked Hal.

"It's gone now," Roland replied. "Ransom's trick worked."

Merlin's irritated voice rose in the background. "I *said* I'd take it!"

"It's not like you didn't have plenty of chances to catch it," Pete retorted. "Next time bring a butterfly net to the office. Or maybe I should bring one, for you!"

Hal spoke louder, to be heard over the arguing. "Got a name for your team yet? Or do you want to be Protection, Inc: The Other Office?"

Roland chuckled. "I was thinking of Protection, Inc: Defenders."

"Good name," said Hal. To his team, he said, "Want to wish them luck?"

Everyone called out their congratulations and good luck

wishes. Catalina's voice rose above the rest. "Hope you get a flying kitten, Merlin! Hope you get two!"

Hal put his phone back in his pocket and went to put his arm around Ellie. By then Ethan was holding Elliot, who was asleep and drooling on his shirt, and Destiny was holding Haley, who watched the party with a surprisingly intent expression in her hazel eyes.

Lucas, elegant in his tailored suit and gold chains, took a hasty step back to avoid getting splashed with the bottle of barbecue sauce Nick was brandishing at Rafa, while Rafa used his longer arms to reach around Nick and douse the chicken wings with his preferred sauce. Journey and Raluca were sharing a plate of traditional Brandusan pastries that Journey had baked. As Journey gestured expansively with an apricot tart in her hand, Doina dove from the air and snatched it from her fingers.

Shane and Justin were talking quietly, with Shadow lying in wait on Shane's shoulder and Trio dozing at Justin's feet. Behind their backs, Fiona was stealthily setting up a small robot dog, though Destiny suspected that Catalina and Grace's snickers had probably given the game away.

"Take a good look, Haley," Destiny said. "It's your family."

Elliot woke up, but didn't cry. Instead, he too gazed out at them all with the same intent look in his sea-colored eyes.

"And yours," Ethan said to the baby boy. Without changing his solemn expression, Elliot blew a bubble.

"Okay, jarhead," Destiny said. "Now I want twins too. So they *better* run in the family."

"I'll do my best," Ethan promised.

Yes, purred her tiger. *We will have a fine pair of cubs nine months from now.*

Do you know something I don't? Destiny asked, excited and hopeful. They'd been trying, but she hadn't expected it to be this soon.

Ethan nudged her and whispered, "Hey, my tiger just said—"

"Mine too," Destiny whispered back. "Do you think they really do know?"

Her tiger purred, *Wait and see.*

A NOTE FROM ZOE CHANT

Thank you for reading *Top Gun Tiger!* I hope you enjoyed it. If you want to find out what happened to the new team, check out the spinoff series, *Protection, Inc: Defenders.* You can read the first book, *Defender Cave Bear*, now!

Please consider reviewing *Top Gun Tiger*, even if you only write a line or two. I appreciate all reviews.

If you enjoy *Protection, Inc,* I also write the *Werewolf Marines* series under the pen name of Lia Silver. Both series have hot romances, exciting action, emotional healing, brave heroines who stand up for their men, and strong heroes who protect their mates with their lives.

The cover of *Top Gun Tiger* was designed by Augusta Scarlett.

Did you like Destiny's story about the Indian king Shivaji and his escape in the fruit baskets? It's a true story! If you

A NOTE FROM ZOE CHANT

want to read more of his amazing adventures, like the time he captured a fort with the help of trained lizards, look up Shivaji Bhosle. (Yes, I'm a history nerd too.)

ALSO BY ZOE CHANT

Protection, Inc.

Bodyguard Bear
Defender Dragon
Protector Panther
Warrior Wolf
Leader Lion
Soldier Snow Leopard
Top Gun Tiger

Protection, Inc. Collection 1
(Contains *Bodyguard Bear, Defender Dragon,* and *Protector Panther*)

Protection, Inc. Collection 2
(Contains *Warrior Wolf, Leader Lion,* and *Soldier Snow Leopard*)

Protection, Inc: Defenders

Defender Cave Bear

Made in United States
Orlando, FL
30 August 2023